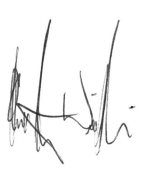

Cleo Bailey – Book 1
The Search for the Missing Muse

By Anthony Williams

Published by Brown Sparrow Publishing , Seattle WA

ISBN: 978-1-62822-002-5
Library of Congress
Control Number: 2013956114

Front Cover design by: Isaac Hannaford
Full Cover and Interior design by: Drai Bearwomyn

Printed in the United States of America on acid free paper.

BOOK 1

CLEO BAILEY

THE SEARCH FOR THE MISSING MUSE
ANTHONY WILLIAMS

For anyone who has ever found themselves lost inside of a book...

Table of Contents

CHAPTER
1

Verne's Subterranean Expedition

Cleo. Cleo. Cleo.

The single word...four familiar letters...two syllables...his own name. They stuck out like a sore thumb on the page. Cleo flipped through the pages in the book and noticed them repeated, over and over. It transcribed every move he made and every word he said.

> *This cannot be possible. If I had truly been dreaming or even hallucinating, then my name would not exist here. This can only mean one thing.*

"It was all real. Every bit of it was...real. Which means...so was she."

Cleo was leaving his small, untidy room, his gray and gloomy city, his vast yet limited planet. While the journey was not *entirely* foreign to him (for he had travelled this way once before), his destination was uncharted. For the first time he was on his way to a prehistoric world of dinosaurs, giants and underground oceans, that he and everyone else could previously only read about. He was off to a world of endless paths and near bottomless pits that should not exist. He was leaving for the wonderful creation of Jules Verne, down into the Center of the Earth.

Before he went through with taking his hiatus from the real world, Cleo did a quick walkthrough of his house. He double-checked that all of the doors were locked to guarantee that there would be no unwanted interruptions. His little brother, Linus, was on the bus on his way to school, while his father had already left for work. For the next eight hours the house was all his.

Nonetheless, he was playing hooky from school and experimenting with a power he knew virtually nothing about. He wanted to cut his risks to a minimum. After being satisfied that his home was secure of any unwelcome visitors, or residents, he retreated into his room and picked up the book.

> *How can I be sure that this will even work again? Can I really... travel into any book that I want? This is beyond crazy. This is ludicrous. What is possessing me to actually listen to that... that girl? That's assuming "she" is even real...or human. When I'm inside, will I see her again? –* Cleo thought as he vanished from atop the down comforter covering his queen size bed.

Jules Verne's *Journey to the Center of the Earth* is the story of Professor Von Hardwigg, his nephew Axel and their guide Hans Bjelke descending deep into the center of the Earth. It is the quintessential tale of ordinary people going on an extraordinary adventure. While millions of copies exist of Verne's original version, the copy that now lay open in Cleo's room was about to become a one-of-a-kind, containing a fourth adventurer, the sixteen-year-old boy, Cleo Bailey himself.

After searching for months in the Icelandic wilderness, the three men finally reached their point of no return deep within a secluded and uncharted mountain. Located at the end of a tunnel, so long that all remnants of light from the outside had been blacked out, was an enormous chasm from which they could not hope to scale back up if they chose to descend.

"Throw a flare down Hans. Let us see if the bottom is near," instructed the Professor as he inched towards the edge.

With the sunlight unable to penetrate the surrounding darkness, their only light came from their small headlamps.

"I'm glad it's warmer down here," said Axel as Hans searched his pack for the flare. "That wind felt like daggers stabbing me down to my very bones."

The guide ignored the young man and ignited the red-hot flare, suddenly illuminating their cavernous surroundings.

"God that's bright," Axel whined, squinting through the sudden glow in the otherwise dim mountain.

Hans tossed the flare down into the abyss and the three men watched as the light fell deeper and deeper until the darkness consumed it.

"Uncle, there is no bottom," Axel stated naively.

"That's preposterous dear nephew, of course there is a bottom. It is just not within sight. That is all."

They were so preoccupied with trying to calculate their height above the chasm's floor that they did not hear Cleo materialize behind them.

This is simply amazing. Unless I have completely lost my mind, which I certainly will not rule out, it actually worked. I can teleport into books. It is like magic. I wonder if everything else she said is true. – Cleo thought as he continued listening in on the men's conversation.

"Hello there," Cleo said from behind them. All three whirled around at the unexpected voice. Hans instinctively got into a feline-like fight or flight position, while Axel's skittishness caused him to stumble over a jagged rock and fall to the ground. "Sorry, I didn't mean to scare you."

"Where in the devil did you come from? How long have you been standing there?" The Professor was the first to speak up, reaching down and helping his nephew back to his feet.

"My name is Cleo. Um...I am also a traveler of sorts. I've, uh, been following you for quite a while," the teenager lied. His nervous stuttering did nothing to convince them he was telling the truth.

Cleo stood before the three travelers, a young man, barely tall enough to reach the top of a refrigerator. He had short dark chocolate brown hair. His eyes were ever-changing with the seasons: a dusky hazel in the fall and winter, and a brilliant blue in the summer and spring. He wore a purple and gold windbreaker, a pair of raggedy jeans, and a backpack with two fraying straps due to the overabundance of books he hauled around at school every day.

"No you haven't, I would have known if someone was following us." This time Hans, a professional duck hunter and an overall wilderness buff, addressed Cleo. A palpable tension began to form in the dark tunnel.

"Let's just say I'm an expert at staying hidden in the shadows when I want to."

Hans looked doubtful. His expression hardened and his eyes intensified as he studied the young man.

> *This boy is lying. One wrong move and I swear I will not hesitate to throw him into that pit.* – Hans thought to himself.

"Whoa, whoa, whoa, I'm not lying. There's no need for any talk of throwing anyone into any pit," Cleo said, moving his hands up in front of himself and taking a few steps back.

"Nobody said anything about throwing anyone into a pit," the professor said.

"Indiana Jones here just said he was going to toss me down it."

The Professor looked puzzled and turned to Hans.

"I didn't hear anyone say anything. Nonetheless, Hans, I forbid you from tossing the young man into the pit. Understand?" he said, trying to lighten up the tense situation.

> *How could he have known I thought that? There is no way he read my mind, is there? It has to be a coincidence. Although, coincidence does not explain how he appeared behind us.*
> – Hans thought.

"Hans..." the Professor repeated more sternly.

Hans hesitated for another moment before answering.

"Of course Professor. I promise. That is, as long as he doesn't give me a reason to," he added, still refusing to soften the harsh expression on his face.

> *Wait, if he didn't say anything then how did I hear it? Was I reading his mind? God, this is getting weirder and weirder.*
> – Cleo thought, even more confused than Hans as to what was happening.

"Why are you following us?" The Professor asked, changing the subject.

A bead of sweat rolled down Cleo's forehead.

> *That is a good question. Why am I here? I'm not even entirely convinced where here is.*

"He asked you a question. Why are you following us?" Hans persisted.

"Oh, well I wasn't exactly following you. I'm actually looking for someone, a woman. Maybe you've seen her?" Cleo asked hopeful.

"What makes you think we would know anything?" Hans asked. His hand was brushing back and forth on the handle of the axe that was dangling from his belt.

"She had been travelling in this area. I did not *expect* you to know something. I was simply hoping you would." Cleo defended, hoping the blade stayed attached to Hans's belt, and not his hand.

"Who told you she was travelling in this area? Uncle, are we not the only three people alive that know this place even exists?" Axel asked, turning to his uncle.

"As far as I knew, yes," he responded, flustered by the prospect of this discovery being widespread knowledge.

"Are you sure that's the only reason you are here, conveniently at the exact same time as us?" Hans passively accused.

"I promise my only reason for being here is to find this woman." Cleo reassured them. "She is in her early thirties, not much taller than I am." Cleo stopped, trying to remember what she had looked like the last time he saw her. "She looks young for her age. People sometimes even mistake her for a teenager. Listen, can you just tell me if you have seen her? Please." Cleo asked, continuing to divert the conversation away from his sudden arrival and back to his reason for being there in the first place.

Hans continued to give Cleo a death stare, while the Professor rubbed the small stubble of hair that had grown on his chin over their months of travelling.

> *I knew I should not have come here. I know hardly anything about this...this abnormality of mine. It's probably going to get me killed. And for what?! Who knows if she was even real?*
> *– Cleo worried.*

"I know I sound shady, or crazy, or both, but please, trust me," he pleaded.

"There was a woman that we came across a few weeks ago in the mountains," the Professor finally spoke up. "I don't know if she's who you are looking for. She does, however, match your description of a short, young woman. Excuse me for my rudeness," he added.

"You did?" Cleo asked, surprised at the prospect of finding some useful information. "Did she seem out of place? Like she didn't belong where she was. Did she look healthy? Real?"

"Well, she wasn't a ghost if that is what you are implying," Hans answered curtly.

"She appeared to be backpacking through the country. We made small talk. She asked how our travels were going. Then we went our separate ways. We only spoke briefly. I only remember it at all, because I thought it was odd for a woman so young to be traveling all alone," the Professor stepped in. "I am sorry, I do not know any more than that."

>*It may be a small trace, but it is a trace nonetheless.*
>– Cleo thought.

"No that's plenty. Thank you," said Cleo.

"What exactly is your plan young man? You are clearly not from around here. Your accent sounds American. What are you doing chasing some girl halfway across the world in such a dangerous environment by yourself? You are just a kid. Shouldn't your father be doing this?" It was in Hans's nature to be mistrusting of those around him. It was one way that he had become such an adept survivalist, but something about Cleo was especially rubbing him the wrong way.

"I appreciate the concern, but that's my business. Besides, if what I believe is true, I am probably better prepared to deal with what lies ahead than the three of you," Cleo said cryptically.

Hans cackled aloud, sending an echo through the cavernous walls.

"What lies ahead? I suppose you know all about that. Don't think for one second boy, that you're coming down there with us. We don't have the supplies, nor the patience to let you tag along." There was a slight amount of contempt in Hans's voice.

"No, of course not. I would not burden you with my company. I will find my own way. Now if you don't mind I'm just going to take a break and figure out my next move while you lower yourselves into that hole over there." Cleo walked close to the edge of the abyss and took a seat on the rocky floor.

Hans, Axel and the Professor clearly had no idea what to make of the young man sitting before them, but they decided that they simply could not waste any more time trying to figure him out. They had a long and arduous journey ahead of them that required their full attention if they were to survive it.

"Very well Cleo. Good luck on all your future endeavors. Wherever they may lead you." The Professor reached out and shook Cleo's hand before urging Hans and Axel to the cliff's edge.

Cleo sat on the edge of death, mere inches from plummeting into the unknown abyss. His childhood fear began to show as his hands started tremoring. From the time he was a young boy, he was never overly fond of heights. He disliked going into the Empire State Building with his parents as a kid, and there he could at least see the bottom.

> *I don't know why I'm shaking so much. I'm fairly certain that if I were to fall, I could leave the book before I hit the ground... wherever that may be. Plus, even if I weren't able to, wouldn't it be just like a dream? The second I become a Cleo-pancake, I wake up and everything is exactly how it was before?* – He thought in an attempt at instilling himself with false bravery. The fearlessness was only momentary as he backed up a few feet.

It proved to be nearly impossible for the three of men to traverse the narrow and rocky shaft. As a result, the men's progress proceeded at a sloth's pace. The lack of decent sized platforms combined with the sheer steepness of the shaft greatly hindered their descent. Their journey seemed destined to fail before it had even truly begun. Thankfully, the Professor's brilliant mind came up with an ingenious way to lower each of them down the enormous hole.

"We'll fold the rope in half, tie it down on this side, and lasso it down onto the next platform. Then we'll use it as a sort of zip line and slide on down, one after another," he outlined to his two companions. They slowly and steadily repeated this process, maneuvering their way down the shaft. Occasionally it proved to be quite tricky to fit three full-grown men onto a platform so small that it would have trouble fitting an eight-year-old.

> *That's quite an impressive technique, I must say. I don't think I ever would have thought of that.*

As awed as Cleo was by the method of their descent, he was more so by the magnificent qualities of the indiscernibly deep wormhole in the mountain. It was nothing like his world of highways, skyscrapers and suburbs. It was an enormous cylindrical tube, at least 300 feet in circumference. The walls all lined with jagged obsidian and cooled lava rocks. Oddly enough, there was not a single living creature in the entire shaft, not even a cockroach or a bat. It wasn't that the overall appearance was overly spectacular, but the sheer depth and existence of it made it an incredible sight.

> *The darkness reminds me of when mom and I were on the trampoline. I must have been about the same age as Linus is now* – Cleo thought of his little brother who was at home, safe.

The memory was from over ten years ago, when Cleo was but six years old. It was a cool, summer night and he and his mother lay on their trampoline in the backyard, staring up into the night sky. All they could see was complete and utter darkness. No stars, satellites, planes, nothing could shine through. Cleo remembered being scared and gripping his mother's hand as a gentle breeze softly moved the surface of the trampoline up and down.

"Where are the stars at mom?" Cleo asked her.

"They are up there, they just cannot be seen. The clouds cover everything up, son," she answered.

"It feels like we are floating in space."

"Hahaha, yeah I guess you're right."

> *The darkness here is just as impenetrable as back then. Except this time, she's not here to comfort me.* – He thought, peeling his attention away from his now solemn memory.

Cleo sat there for nearly an hour, until the three men were no more than a faint dot of light in the distance. Cleo figured he probably could have convinced them to let him tag along, but their long, tumultuous journey took over three months to finish. The shaft alone took over a day to descend. He did not have that kind of time to devote. Especially, when he still did not know exactly how much time would pass in the real world.

Cleo stood up and backed away from the cliff.

Ok, let's hope I can make this work on purpose this time. – Cleo thought, closing his eyes. He concentrated intensely on the subsequent scenes in the book. *I do not want to be in this shaft anymore. I want to be at the bottom. Wait, no! I also don't want them to see me. I want to be at the bottom, but somewhere in the shadows.*

He visualized himself hiding in the background while the three adventurers were resting. At first, nothing happened.

What if that was a fluke? What if that only works in some books? What if I'm stuck here? I can't make it to the bottom by myself.

He refocused his thoughts away from being trapped in an Icelandic mountain, and back on skipping ahead in the book. He suddenly felt a gust of wind and a million goose bumps form all over his body. His stomach dropped, as if he were in a death-defying roller coaster coming out of a barrel roll. All the breath in his lungs was snatched away, leaving him with the terrible feeling that he was going to suffocate. His whole body went numb. He no longer felt the rough stone beneath his boots. The world around him began to spin and he felt like he was being dragged from it. He was afraid to open his eyes. Although, he highly doubted that he would have been able to open them even if he wanted to. The few seconds it took for all of this to unfold felt like a small eternity.

Ugh, I am NOT a fan of travelling like this! I think I might vomit. – He thought as he regained the sensation back in his extremities. He fell hard to the ground, scraping his elbow and bumping his head on the rocks. *Well, on the bright side I'm now at the bottom.*

He rubbed the knot forming on the top of his head. He opened his eyes and waited a few moments for his surroundings to come back into focus. He was now inside a dark tunnel, with a faint light coming from around the corner. He silently tiptoed his way to see what the origin of the light was. He peeked around the corner like a kid trying to spy on his parents. Hans and company were resting at the bottom of the mountain's hole. They had built a small campfire and were replenishing their spent energy.

I feel a little guilty. Look at how hard it was for them to get to the bottom. It cost them blood, sweat, tears and many hours to get down here. All it cost me was a few seconds, a scraped elbow and a wave of nausea.

Cleo decided not to dillydally around, and proceeded down the tunnel alone as they continued to rest after their epic descent. Before completely falling out of sight of the shaft, he looked towards the top. A cold shiver crept up his back at the thought of never seeing the light of day again.

This is all still so unbelievable. I am inside of a book. I am like a dab of ink systematically placed on a piece of paper.

Cleo knew from his previous *normal* readings of the book, that the world's longest rappel was only the beginning of what would be one of the most epic adventures ever written. The underground explorers' next task was moving through the daunting lava tunnels that followed. Like its abyssal prelude, the actual appearance of the tunnel was not what was so awe-inspiring. Its appearance was in fact nearly identical to the shaft. The floor, ceiling and walls were all rough and jagged with black obsidian, razor sharp and jutting out from all angles. The idea that this phenomenon merely existed was the truly incredibly nature of the tunnel. It was large enough to drive a full-sized truck through, and its endpoint was the very heart of the planet.

I would totally ace that Geology test now. Mrs. Stilnick thinks she knows a lot about this kind of stuff. I guarantee she has not seen anything like this, even in her books. – Cleo thought bitterly.

Mrs. Stilnick was his Geology teacher that had failed him on his midterm earlier that year. The test covered a variety of topics including different rock types, volcanoes and the Earth's crust. It was the only *F* he had gotten on a test in his entire High School career to date.

Cleo sifted through the granola bars, bottles of water and Band-Aids in his bag until he came across a small flashlight. He pulled it out and turned it on. It was a cheap one he purchased from the local dollar store and only lit up ten feet or so in front of him.

I guess it's better than nothing. – He thought, as he began to move more quickly through the tunnels.

He wanted to create as much distance between himself and the others as he could. The last thing he needed was to have to explain to them how he managed to descend the giant pit before them, without any gear and without them ever seeing him. While Hans specialized in hunting fowl, Cleo assumed those skills could easily be transferred onto a human if he desired. He would rather not have to get into a physical altercation with the man.

Despite possessing the ability to return home at any time, (or at least he hoped) Cleo was still nervous and a little skittish as he dove deeper and deeper into the Earth. He had a lot of experience hiking in the woods and mountains back home, but this was in a league of its own. One misstep and he would end up with a broken ankle, or a piece of rock protruding through his body.

I think I'm far enough away that they won't hear the echo if I yell, but how should I even refer to her? I don't even know what her age will be. It is more than possible that she will have no idea that I even exist. I think I will play it safe for now.

"CALLIOPE! CALI! Are you anywhere down here? Can you hear me?! CALLIOPE!" He hollered at the top of his lungs.

The only response he heard was the repetition of his own voice off the rock walls. Once the echoing stopped, there was again a bitter silence. Cleo had not expected a response, given the small probability that she would be hanging out at this particular part of the story. Nevertheless, he was disappointed by hearing only his own voice seeming to mock him.

"Well a lot of good that did," he said aloud. Over the last several years, he had developed a tendency to talk to himself. He could have entire conversations with only a mirror. It prevented him from becoming too caught up in his own mind.

Fine, I'll try another part of the story.

Cleo took a deep breath and closed his eyes.

I don't even know where I'm trying to go. I barely remember this story. I just hope I end up somewhere useful. – He pictured himself deeper in the unknown tunnel. Once again, it took a few minutes before anything happened. Eventually the uneasy feelings of queasiness, detachment and fear suddenly passed through him. *I really hate this part.*

When he fully came to, he found himself only a handful of pages further along in the tale. He also appeared much closer to the group of travelers than he intended.

I need to remember that next time!

There were only a few yards between Cleo and the travelers. Luckily, they seemed to be focusing all their attention on simply staying alive. They had no awareness of anything else around them.

"I'm so thirsty uncle. When are we going to find water?" Axel's voice was raspy and dry.

"Soon my boy, soon," the Professor tried to reassure his nephew.

Cleo did not know how many miles or days they had walked, but in that time, their supplies had dwindled to a dangerously low amount. It was a testament to Hans' survival skills that they even lasted this long.

"Here, there's enough for one more drink," Hans said, handing his nearly empty canteen to the young man.

Axel did not bother refusing the offer. He took the last drink of water, which proved to be just a few droplets, barely enough to even wet his tongue.

I fear that it will only slightly delay the inevitable, if we do not find water soon. – Hans thought.

Wait, there it is again! That definitely came from Hans, but his mouth did not move. I must have read his thoughts! – Cleo had to rein in his excitement so to not accidentally reveal himself to the men.

With their water supply officially gone, they walked along in complete silence. Cleo took care to follow along from a safe distance to observe their downward spiral.

They had long lost track of the duration of time they had been walking. Was it a day, a week, a month? They didn't have the faintest clue. It was nearly impossible for them to have any accurate account of the passing of time while underground. On average, the human body can last between two and four days without water, but the immense amount of energy they were expending spelunking through the Earth was rapidly diminishing that timeframe. Axel was sucking at the air like a fish out of water, the Professor's brittle old body was moving at a snail's pace, and even Hans was beginning to lose hope.

Cleo knew what their collective fates were, but that did not make watching them suffer any easier. He also constantly had the same worrying "what if" thoughts nagging him from the back of his mind.

> *What if I have triggered a butterfly effect? What if my simply being here has changed what will happen? What if their saving grace is no longer just around the corner like it should be? What if my mere presence has somehow doomed them? Should I step in and save them? What can I even do?*

Thankfully, before Cleo's overactive mind forced him into an action he would likely regret, their fortunes changed.

"Vatten!" Hans yelled.

"Water? Water!" Axel translated the Danish word.

Beneath them, they could hear the faint sound of water rushing through the Earth.

"Follow me," Hans instructed, quickly leading them along the narrow tunnel.

They trailed their guide, periodically stopping so he could feel the wall, shake his head and continue trudging along. Cleo followed along only close enough to see their lights shining ahead. He did not see any accidental run-ins at this point.

After a few minutes, Hans came across a spot on the wall that he liked.

"Here, it's right here. I know it is." Without any explanation as to why this was *the* spot, he pulled a pickaxe and a crowbar from his pack and began to thrash wildly at the wall.

After a while of sending the jagged rock flying in all directions, Hans finally broke through the thick wall of stone that had been shielding them from their life source. The moment a hole was pierced into the rock barrier, a stream of water shot out like a cannon. Axel was so thrilled he immediately plunged his hands into the jet stream.

"AHHHH!!!" His cry echoed off the walls. "It's boiling hot!" Cleo shook his head at Axel's impulsive act.

> *That's something I would do.* – He thought, guiltily taking a sip of ice cold water from the bottle out of his backpack.

The next ten minutes felt like a lifetime to the men as they waited for the water to cool off. They would have drooled like dogs, had there been any fluids left in their mouths to salivate.

> *It's as bad as watching Linus eat chocolate, or looking at what Santa put under the tree on Christmas morning. Look how happy he is.* – Cleo thought as he watched Axel jubilantly take his first drink. Even miles away from any hint of sunlight, the cavern appeared to brighten as the men filled their bodies and packs with water.

The desire to return to the surface had escaped all of them, Axel in particular. Only hours before, he knew for certain that this tunnel would be his tomb. Now, he once again viewed it as a path to incredible discoveries.

> *This really is incredible. I no longer can imagine simply reading about a scene such as this. No amount of words could possibly do it the justice it deserves.* – Cleo thought as he looked on.

While life flowed back into each of their bodies, Cleo remembered why he was there, and it was not to see what the lack of hydration does to the body and mind.

If she is here at all, it's obviously not in this section of the book. I need to move on. – He tried to focus his mind on a key chapter that he vaguely recalled.

"We'll call this Hansbach Stream, after our friend here," was the last thing Cleo heard the Professor say, before he vanished from their presence without a sound.

This time when he reappeared, he could not see a thing, not even his own hand directly in front of his face. To say it was pitch black would be a gross understatement. It may as well have been in the middle of a black hole. There was not a microcosm of light in the tunnels.

This is definitely not what I had in mind. – Cleo thought, frustrated.

"SOMEBODY HELP ME! PROFESSOR! HANS!" Axel boomed throughout the tunnel. The sudden cry out startled Cleo so much he nearly let out a shriek.

Axel's cry for help reminded Cleo what part of the story he was now in.

This must be the part where Axel manages to get himself separated from the others. His lantern ran out of fuel and to top it off, he was almost out of all his food and water.

Cleo silently listened from the shadows of behind Axel as his emotions quickly took a turn for the worse. What started out as Axel being mostly calm and composed quickly migrated into panic, despair, and finally into hopelessness.

I already had to watch him physically wither away. I would really prefer not to have to watch his mental state deteriorate as well. Hans and the Professor at least have each other. What does Axel have? A few more sips of water and an empty lantern.

"Oh God, please help me. God...please," Axel whimpered. Axel's breathing was becoming more rapid and labored by the moment.

He needs to calm down. If he doesn't do it soon, he is going to hyperventilate and pass out. – Thought Cleo.

Cleo noticed he too was beginning to breathe faster. It brought back memories of his childhood that he would rather forget altogether.

As a young boy, Cleo hated the dark almost as much as he hated heights. He slept with a night light until he was almost ten years old. It didn't help matters that while growing up, his older cousin, Davy, would feed off this fear. On many occasions when the two of them got together, Davy would lock him inside of a closet or even stuff him into a hope chest for hours at a time, just to scare him and listen to him scream.

This isn't even close though. Those closets may as well have been the beach in the middle of July compared to this nightmarish blackness.

Recalling the childhood memory was not doing Cleo any good. It was only making his own anxiety rise that much faster.

This is ridiculous, I'm about to have a full-scale panic attack, yet I'm the one with the capability to simply leave. Axel is the one trapped with no hope for survival. He must be on the brink of falling into a catatonic state. – He thought, trying anything he could think of to calm himself down.

Cleo could not handle standing by while Axel suffered any longer. He was already in a fragile state of mind after the last near-death experience. Cleo doubted that Axel could take much more before he cracked beyond repair. He decided that he had to try to help Axel out of his hopeless predicament.

"Axel," he said from behind him.

Axel had been calling out to the Professor and Hans for some time, imploring them to help him.

"Uncle? Is that you?" This time, Cleo could hear the cracking of Axel's voice on every word.

Could that really be my uncle? How is this possible? Did they really hear my cries and are now answering my pleas, or have I finally lost my mind? – Axel thought, waiting for an answer.

Cleo's telepathy again surfaced with no warning. Although frankly, in the sheer darkness, Cleo could not be certain that Axel was not indeed speaking aloud.

"No Axel it is not, but do not worry. You are going to be all right. Trust me I have seen it. You will find your Uncle again. Do not despair any longer. Continue to call out among these walls and I swear to you, your voice will reach your friends." Cleo tried to calm him down.

"Who speaks to me from the shadows? Are my ears playing tricks on me? Are you just a figment of my delirious mind?" Cleo could feel Axel moving slowly towards him. His voice was closer and more confident.

Cleo was hesitant to intervene too much, for he did not know what the consequences would be. He was afraid that his interactions with the characters would have drastic results.

It could be just like all of those time travel tales. The theory of the butterfly effect. The mere fact I spoke to the characters could mean their eventual doom. – Cleo thought as he spoke no further and shrunk back further into the shadows, narrowly avoiding Axel's outstretched arm.

"If there is indeed someone there, please speak up. Please, I beg you. You have to help me!"

Axel continued to aimlessly inch along the darkness, feeling the walls around him, hoping to contact whoever or whatever was speaking to him. Cleo backed up until he could feel the unforgiving chill of the wall on his spine.

Uh oh, I think it's time to get out of here. – He closed his eyes and tried to focus on another scene of the book. Axel's warm breath upon his face disrupted his concentration and thus halted his departure from his self-made predicament.

"Axel my boy, is that you?" A voice softly echoed through the tunnel.

"Uncle Hardwigg?" Axel turned away suddenly and he retreated a few steps.

A few minutes passed in total silence. Suddenly the two of them heard a response.

"Axel, that is you! Where are you?" The nearly inaudible voice of Axel's Uncle bounced off the walls around them.

"The sound must come along the gallery itself. This place must possess some peculiar acoustic properties," Axel rationalized aloud to himself, forgetting all about the mysterious voice that had guided him to a calmer state of mind just moments before.

Axel and his Uncle bantered back and forth this way for at least an hour while Cleo stayed as silent as possible in the background. The sounds of their voices, ever growing louder, slowly guided the Professor and Hans in Axel's direction. It took far longer than it should have to bridge the gap as Axel's pace was as slow as a sloth, for he had to do so entirely by feel, rather than by sight. Cleo frequently heard Axel tumble to the ground, cursing as he got up.

Cleo's desire not to draw any unwanted attention proved much more difficult than he envisioned. Considering he could only go on the sounds that Axel made as they walked through the darkness, there were intervals of time that Cleo blindly continued, hoping he would not run into the young man.

Just as they saw a light beginning to shine through up ahead, Cleo tripped and went crashing to the floor.

Ahhh!! My knee! – Cleo screamed in his mind, clenching his jaw. It took everything he had not to shout out in agony and alert everybody of his presence.

Luckily for him, Axel's tunnel vision for finding his friends, and the sudden light in front of them distracted him from any noise Cleo made.

At least I have Band-Aids in my bag. I wish I could see in here though. My knee is probably bleeding everywhere. – Cleo thought, placing his hands over his injured leg and feeling a warm, moistness starting to slowly flow down his shin. Cleo looked up and saw the light begin to shine brighter and brighter. He could make out the silhouette of Axel running towards it.

"Is that you Uncle? Hans!" Axel shouted.

"Axel? Axel my boy, we're coming!" cried the Professor.

The rustling of their equipment banged up against the walls as they hurriedly made their way in his direction. As Axel reached the bend he, quite literally, ran into his companions. The collision nearly knocked over their normally sure-footed guide.

"Oh Uncle, I thought I'd never see you again. I didn't think I'd ever see *anyone* again!" He said, crying into his Uncle's shoulder as they embraced.

Cleo fumbled around in his bag, searching for the bandages he normally kept inside.

> *Must be nice to find someone you miss so dearly. I wonder if I will ever get to experience that again. It's not going to happen just sitting here though, is it?*

He pulled himself up from the rocky floor and wiped his hands clean on his pants. He then closed his eyes.

> *Time to try another place. If I remember right, the next part they travel over a massive underground ocean. Unless she is miraculously a stowaway on their small, haphazard dingy, I think it's safe to say I can skip to the other side. Moreover, I certainly will not miss sailing in dangerous and unpredictable waters.* – Cleo thought.

Cleo was not overly fond of the water. Like his misfortunes with the dark, as a boy he suffered through a traumatic experience. At the ripe old age of seven, he went white water rafting with his mother and father. They were going down the Triton River with an amateur guide.

Everything was going perfect until it wasn't. The guide misjudged one of the rapids and Cleo was tossed overboard. Thankfully, his mother dove in after him and managed to drag him to the riverbank before their family trip took a tragic turn.

His father always seemed to remember the incident a little differently. He claimed that Cleo was only in the water for a moment and was never in any danger.

"How do you know what happened? You weren't the one gasping for air, or swimming frantically to get out of the water. You were the one that stayed in the raft," which was, as of the past few years, one of Cleo's typical responses.

These kinds of comments generally ended any discussion of the incident. Cleo always thought his father denied the truth of the events, because he was ashamed for not jumping in, and for leaving his mother to take charge and rescue him.

> *I'll admit though, it will be a shame missing the fight between the Ichthyosaurus and the Plesiosaurus.* – Cleo thought, bringing his focus back to the present. Picturing Verne's scene of the carnivorous dolphin-like creature waging an epic battle against the ocean's version of a Brachiosaurus almost was enough to make Cleo reconsider. *Not even that would be worth getting in that boat. I think I will attempt to skip ahead to when they dock.*

Without giving his decision another thought, he concentrated intensely, and eventually whisked himself away from the heart-warming reunion between Nephew and Uncle, and further into Verne's tale.

When Cleo opened his eyes, he was lying square on his back, in the middle of a sandy beach.

"There's got to be an easier way to do this," he commented, his backside now soaking wet from being halfway submerged in water. He stood up and could not believe what his eyes were seeing.

> *I can accept straw men that walk and talk. I can even believe*

that there is a whole world beneath the surface of our own. But this...

Roaming around a petrified forest filled with trees that would rival the redwoods of California and mushrooms the size of Great Danes, were ancient Mastodons. They dwarfed the African Elephants Cleo had seen at the zoo.

"These have been extinct for thousands and thousands of years. This... should not be possible. To see these firsthand is, quite frankly, nothing short of a miracle," he spoke aloud to himself.

He looked around and noticed the three familiar adventurers standing a little ways down the beach observing the same magnificent wonder. While Hans and Axel were gaping at the mammoth creatures, the Professor's attention was on another larger than life creature. Lumbering through the old forest was a giant man, at least twelve feet tall.

> *Who's that supposed to be, Paul Bunyan? He looks like some sort of prehistoric sheepherder, with these mastodons as his flock. That is, if the sheep were the size of trucks and the herder was a large tanker. He is not exactly who I was looking for. Unless of course Calliope has **really** changed* – The thought made him chuckle. Well, it looks like that girl was wrong about this one. Maybe she's in a different book.

Cleo was about to return home when through the petrified timber, no more than a stone's throw away, he saw a pair of blue eyes staring at him. Cleo peered through the old forest to see them coming from a young woman. Shivering due to his drenched body, he slowly moved closer to get a better look at her when she suddenly stepped out from her hiding place.

"I was afraid I'd see you here one day," she said, causing Cleo to stop dead in his tracks.

Cleo was speechless. He had so many questions he did not know where to begin. He could not organize his thoughts into an intelligible sentence.

"How old are you?" She asked, stepping over the vegetation towards him.

"Uhh...I'm...I'm 16, as of yesterday actually," he stuttered.

"Is that right? Well Happy Birthday!" She said simply, giving him a loving smile.

"Wait, are you real? Is it really you...Calliope?"

"We're on a first name basis now are we?" She laughed. "I think mom will suffice in here." She reached over and grabbed Cleo, pulling him close to her. "You're so much bigger than the last time I saw you. You're not a kid anymore. You're becoming a little man. I guess I shouldn't be entirely shocked. Ten years is a long time."

> *Ten years? She remembers me when I was six. That was... what, five maybe even six years before it happened?* – Cleo thought, resting his head on her shoulder.

She pushed his head away so she could get a better look at his face.

"Five or six years before what happened? Cleo, why are you in here alone? I can't imagine I'd be so irresponsible to let you come in here by yourself. Especially the day after getting your ability."

"Because you're dead," Cleo blurted out suddenly. It was the first time he had ever uttered those three heartbreaking words. Cleo felt like he had been punched in the stomach. He struggled to catch his breath and his equilibrium was completely thrown off.

"I'm what?" The smile faded from his mother's face.

"You...died..." He could not bring himself to say anymore.

Her face became as white as glue.

"How did it happen?" The tone in her voice suggested that she was more concerned with the impact it has had on Cleo and Linus than her real world self.

"Plane crash," Cleo answered flatly.

Calliope took a few moments to process everything before she spoke again.

"So you don't know anything about what you can do, do you?" She asked, turning the topic from her fate back onto Cleo.

"No, not really. I am still not entirely convinced any of this is real. I ran into you, or what I guess was a teenage you, yesterday." Cleo's mind was on autopilot. He was barely aware of what he was saying. He was trying to memorize every detail of his mother's face; the face that he had not seen in almost half a decade.

I didn't realize just how much I had forgotten about what you looked like. Even if none of this is real, and this is simply the most lifelike dream ever, at least I was able to see you again. – He told himself.

"You're not dreaming Cleo. Every bit of this is real," she again responded to his thoughts.

"Did you just read my thoughts? How did you do that?"

"Yes, but that's not what's important right now. Listen very carefully son." Her smile had vanished and her face hardened. Her voice also changed, becoming reminiscent of when Cleo was younger. Any time she was warning him about doing something stupid, she would lower her voice and speak slowly, emphasizing every single word.

"Never stick your fork, or anything else in the light socket. Do you understand?"

"You must always look both ways before crossing the street. Do you understand?"

"Cleo Bailey, don't you dare jump off that roof, do you hear me?" That last one, was always one of his favorite memories. He could only imagine what his mother thought of a nine-year-old standing on the roof of their house attempting to jump onto a trampoline.

Her voice now possessed the same dire tone.

"When you leave here I need you to find a man named Ramiel. He owns a bookstore in town called Twice Told Tales. I need you to go to him and introduce yourself. He will tell you everything you need to know. Do you understand?"

"Not really, no. What's all this about?" Cleo asked, now thoroughly confused.

"Just trust me. Find Ramiel, he will tell you everything. I promise." She pulled him in for one final hug. "Do you know how to exit?"

"Yeah, the...um...other *you* showed me how." Cleo said, unsure of how to refer to her.

"Good, then waste no more time. It is far too dangerous for you to be here without knowing what you can do."

Cleo intended to listen to what the woman claiming to be his mother said. However, he felt that he needed to take one final detour first.

> *If there were ever a time for this to work correctly, please let that moment be this one.*

After briefly focusing on the specific, final scene in Jules Verne's epic adventure, he vanished before his mother's eyes. Almost instantly, a small, makeshift raft resting in a vast geyser replaced the prehistoric timberland. The geyser was at the bottom of a volcanic chimney with no end in sight. Hans, Axel and the Professor were sitting nervously on the raft as water and magma filled the space around them.

"Make sure to hang on tight. This next part is quite intense," he said as he appeared before them. His sudden arrival startled the men so much they nearly tumbled off the raft to what surely would have been a grim fate.

> *That would have been disastrous. I need to rethink my idea of popping in on people.* – Cleo thought, grimacing at the idea of accidentally killing the trio.

"Good Lord child, where did you come from?! Wait, you're that young boy we met when we first arrived here aren't you?" The Professor hollered, as he attempted to gather his bearings.

Hans was perhaps the most surprised of the three. He sat with a gaping mouth and stared incredulously at the teenager before him.

"Yes I am. I just wanted to let you know I found who I was looking for. I also wanted to thank you for letting me tag-along on this incredible journey of yours. I shall never forget it. Goodbye," and before a single word escaped their wide-open mouths, the rising magma reached the underbelly of their raft, thrusting them blindly into a dark unknown. The rapid upward propulsion of the raft came quicker than Cleo anticipated and interrupted his departure from the imagined world.

I need to focus now, otherwise I will lose consciousness and who knows what will happen then. - He thought, struggling against the increasing G-Force against his body. No...I'm starting to slip away. I...have...to fight it...

"AHHHHHH!!!!!" Cleo suddenly let out a blood-curdling scream as a pain unlike anything he had ever experienced surged through his body. He opened his eyes and found himself no longer sitting on the raft, but lying down on his bed. He looked down and saw a ball of fire the size of a softball burning away his charcoal gray, long-sleeved shirt.

"Oh GOD!" He yelled, ripping the shirt from his body. He threw it to the carpet and stomped out the fire with his worn-down boots. "I'm lucky I didn't burn the whole house down," he said, trying to look at the bright side of things.

He turned his attention to the burned area on his arm. It was bright red, the same pigment as the tomatoes in his fridge and excruciating to the touch. Cleo held his arm in the air and ran out of his bedroom and straight to the bathroom.

The house was empty, so nobody heard his screams as he ran his arm underneath the bathtub faucet. Once the initial sting wore off from the chilly water streaming onto his seared flesh a great sense of relief fell over Cleo. He stood in a pained silence as he replayed the last few moments in the story repeatedly in his head.

So I can get hurt inside of a story. Does this mean I can die as well?

After a few minutes of constantly streaming water onto his arm, he finally wrapped it in a clean bandage from the medicine cabinet and returned to his room. Lying in shambles on his floor was his charred shirt, now just a prize for the dumpster.

He picked up the dog-eared copy of *Journey to the Center of the Earth*, and collapsed onto his bed in exhaustion. He rested his head on his soft, feather-filled pillow and stared at the cover of the book. He reached across his body and gently touched his bandaged arm, wincing as a jolt of pain traveled up it.

"Does this mean that she's alive?"

He placed the book onto his nightstand and rolled onto his good arm.

"Whoever this Ramiel is, I need to find him. He could be the only way I'll ever know the truth."

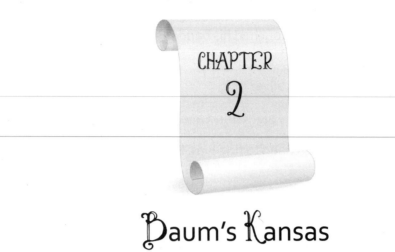

CHAPTER 2

Daum's Kansas

Cleo sat up in his bed, his brow and back drenched in sweat. He strained to see through the hazy layer that was still present over his eyes. He reached up and wiped away the eye-boogers and cloudy film that had been hindering his sight.

"Ouch!" He winced as he lifted up his arm. He looked down and saw the stained bandage wrapping his forearm.

So much for it all just being a dream.

The seared flesh was a reminder that his life would likely never be the same. As did the copy of *Journey to the Center of the Earth,* that lay safely on his nightstand. He flipped through its pages to confirm his suspicions and fears.

"I'm everywhere," he said. Identical to the first time he entered the literary world, his name was scribed everywhere throughout its pages. He walked over to his desk and vigorously thrust it into the drawer, trying to confine whatever magic the pages contained. The force sent a single piece of paper falling off the shelf above, floating like a feather in the wind and coming to rest on his chair. He picked it up off the oak seat.

"Wow, I forgot all about this. It's been ages since I've even thought about it," he said.

The singular white piece of lined paper was once a treasured piece of his past.

Terra Somniorum – The Land of Dreams

It was the title page of a story that his mother had written just for him. It was all that was left of a story that he had heard countless times. She read it to him nearly every night before bed. Its enchanting and mystifying world made it almost impossible to fall sleep and provided Cleo with the most wonderful dreams.

> *I miss those days so much. Back when my life was normal.*
> – He thought. Feels like forever ago. Although, based on the
> contents of that book, I think I would take my life from even
> two days ago.

Two days ago, he had to endure, quite literally, the longest day of his life. Two days ago, his entire world turned on its head. Two days before, he was a somewhat normal teenager (albeit a teenager that had to deal with more tragedy than any child should ever have to). Like everyone else, any escape from what had become his life would only come through his imagination. He could only envision what the lands of *Narnia* or *Middle-Earth* looked, felt and even smelt like. Words embossed on the pages of books were just that, words. Now, for Cleo, as every picture was worth a thousand words, every word was worth an infinite amount of possibilities.

Too bad they don't have a show called My Extremely Boring and Predictable Sixteenth Birthday. – Cleo thought as he turned the channel from My Super Sweet Sixteen.

"Two hundred channels and there isn't anything to watch on a single one of them." He turned off the T.V. and carelessly tossed the remote onto the couch.

He got up from the worn down chocolate brown microfiber couch and walked through the eerily silent house and back to his bedroom. He could not remember the last time he cleaned his room and as a result, it was a disaster. Clothes littered the floors, dishes were stacked in corners and there was a disturbing odor emanating from his trash can. He pulled the blinds of his window open, letting in the unfamiliar light from the outside world.

"Surprise, surprise, another rainy birthday. When it rains it pours huh Knuckles?" Cleo rolled his eyes at the wet weather occurring outside, and spoke to his pet hedgehog that was playfully rolling about in his cage. "I can't believe it's been almost five years since I got you, and to think, I tried to convince dad to let me have a dog." He reached in and apprehensively pet Knuckles' back, knowing the slightest agitation would result in at least a few needles sticking out from his hand.

Cleo looked down at a picture of his mother resting on his desk, familiar in its antique brass frame.

"Mom..." he whispered, running his hand across the metal frame. "I wish you could be here."

The accident was over five years ago, and Cleo could still recall it as if it were yesterday. He was eleven years old, in the 6th grade at the time. He was sitting in his advanced math class doing a geometry test when he was beckoned to his teacher's desk. That was never a good sign.

"Cleo, you need to go to the office now. You should bring your stuff with you, Cleo," said his teacher, Mr. Baker.

"Is there something wrong Mr. Baker? You look really sick," Cleo said jokingly to his teacher. Mr. Baker was usually an abnormally chipper man at all times of the day. Now however, he looked full of despair. His only response was a forced smile and an awkward silence.

As he made his way to the office, Cleo felt increasingly uneasy. His stomach began to hurt and he could feel himself tensing up. He hung his head low as he walked and started to hyperventilate, the same way as when his mom or dad would three-name him after he broke a rule.

"CLEO MAXIMUS BAILEY! We have told you a dozen times not to throw balls in the house!"

"I wasn't throwing it. I was tossing it."

Growing up he legitimately thought there was a difference and that difference should provide him a reprieve from punishment.

He was wrong. Every. Single. Time.

The distance to the main office was no more than a few hundred feet away, but it may as well have been to the moon and back. Scenario after scenario kept running through his mind.

Am I in trouble for something? I don't think I did anything wrong.

Did something happen to Bryce or Penny? That might be it. Everyone knows how close we are. I imagine that I would be the first one that they would tell.

What about Linus? Did he get hurt somehow? He's not exactly a daredevil though.

Do they call you to the office if a grandparent, aunt or uncle dies? I don't remember anyone in the family being sick.

What about mom or dad? Could it have to do with them? Where are they supposed to be today?

Before he could rack his brain for their whereabouts, he walked through the front doors of the office.

"Just head into Mr. Martin's office sweetie," said Miss Debbie, the head secretary. Cleo could tell she was trying to avoid eye contact with him.

The office was mostly empty, except for a few staff members grabbing supplies or making copies. Cleo walked down the short hallway and turned the corner to his principal's office. He reached for the doorknob when he noticed a familiar face inside. His father was sitting in front of Principal Martin's desk, his back to the door. Principle Martin was sitting in silence behind the desk, his hands folded under his chin.

Cleo slowly turned the handle and entered the room, trying to prepare himself for whatever he was about to hear. He poked his head into the room. When his father turned around his appearance made Cleo's stomach drop even further. Cleo had never seen his father in such a ragged state. His eyes were swollen and red. His face hung low. His hands were shaking. Dried tears stained his tan cheeks. The look of utter defeat robbed Cleo of his voice.

"Sit down son," the words almost indistinguishable from one another as they rolled out hoarsely.

Principle Martin stepped out of his office, placing a hand on Cleo's shoulder but remaining silent as he walked out and closed the door.

"Where's Linus?" Cleo asked, noticing the absence of his two-year-old brother.

"Our neighbors, the Farthings, are watching him." His father, Michael, stared out the window of the room. The view was quite unspectacular, a stubby tree that was reminiscent of Charlie Brown's sad excuse for a Christmas tree, and an obscured view of the staff parking lot. The partially sunny skies above were just barely visible. He turned to Cleo and opened his mouth to say something. Nothing but a gasp of air escaped. He stood up, pushing his chair towards the door, and walked to the window.

"Dad, you're scaring me. What's wrong?" Cleo could feel himself losing control over his emotions. He was terrified at what his father was about to say.

Michael dropped his face into his cupped hands and began to sob.

"It's your mother Cleo. She's gone."

The word may as well have been four random letters strung into an incomprehensible sound to Cleo. He couldn't understand what his father was saying. He refused to understand.

"Gone? What do you mean gone? Gone as in gone for the week? Gone like she ran away gone?" Tears were gushing down Cleo's face.

"She was flying back from your grandma's. She was bringing back some of her things. The weather was worse than she thought. Her plane...it hit the side of a mountain."

Cleo felt like he was on the world's worst roller coaster ride. His heart stopped and his stomach turned inside out. His hands and feet became numb, his mouth dried up, and what little strength his scrawny body possessed seemed to disappear.

"No. No. That's...that's not possible. She flies all the time. She's always going around the country for book signings and readings. She's a great pilot. There has to be some mistake dad. You just heard them wrong. You are always misunderstanding what people say. You're WRONG!" Cleo shouted, not caring who could hear him.

His dad reached over and pulled Cleo's head into his chest.

"I'm so sorry son, I'm so sorry."

Cleo reverted into the same three-year-old boy that cried hysterically when he had to flush his lifeless goldfish down the toilet. The same boy that had to be consoled when his finger was accidentally slammed in the car door as a toddler. He buried his face in his father's jacket and cried until he did not have the strength to shed another tear.

The following weeks crawled by at an agonizingly slow pace. The authorities investigating the crash never found the body, but presumed her dead.

"Maybe she's alive then. Maybe she somehow escaped the crash and is simply lost in the woods." He would tell his father, friends, counselors, anyone who would listen.

"Cleo, I'm sorry, but she's not coming back. It has been three weeks. Even if she survived the crash, there is nothing simple about surviving that long in the wilderness with no supplies. You have to accept what has happened," his school counselor once responded, desperately trying to reason with him.

When compared to *death* in the mangled wreckage of a plane, everything is simple.

Nothing could dissuade Cleo's hope. They issued a death certificate, but to Cleo it was merely a piece of paper. A memorial was set up on the corner of the street by Cleo's house. Cleo never once looked at the flowers, lit candles, or kind words the people of the community wrote about her. Even at the funeral, he refused to say goodbye to the most important person in his life.

"This is pointless. There is no body. We should not be having this," he said.

Cleo sat at his desk and stared at the picture frame on it. Remembering the saddest moment of his life was something he did on a daily basis.

"I'm sorry I never said goodbye that day mom. I don't know how I'm ever going to be able to say it," he said pushing the painful memories as far back into his brain as they would go.

His mood now mirrored the dark and gloomy weather that was occurring outside. He took the picture frame and placed it face down, gently, on his desk.

No, today is my birthday. I will not dwell on the past. Today is about whom I can spend this time with. Not about whom I cannot. I will have fun. Never mind the fact that it will be spent, yet again, just watching a movie with Bryce and Penny.

Ever since his mother's accident, his father had skimped on both his and his brother Linus's birthdays. In fact, he had generally forgotten about them entirely. If Cleo wanted any semblance of a celebration, he knew he would have to plan it himself.

Why is it even bothering me so much? It's just another birthday. Sixteenth or not, they're all the same. Besides, I hate parties. They are just an excuse to get gifts from acquaintances I talk to once a month. It will be better with my two best friends. That is all I need.

He left the picture on his desk and walked through his house and out the front door to the front porch. He took in a deep breath of the clear mountain air. He reached up and massaged his temples while listening to the rain symphonically pound onto the ground. The serenity surrounding him brought a smile to his face. That was his favorite thing about the town he lived in and one of the biggest reasons he was content with staying there. The blaring and dizzying noises of the big city were absent. The natural sounds of nature were his orchestra.

The small-secluded town was named, North Bend. It was located a little under 45 minutes east of Seattle, and rested at the base of a series of towering mountains. Cleo had a love/hate relationship with the town. On one hand, it wasn't exactly close to anything of any relevance. It was going to be nearly a 30-minute drive for him and his two friends to get to the theater. On the other hand though, he could never imagine giving up the close proximity of some of the gorgeous views nature had to offer.

The splashing of the rain onto the pavement, the sound of it dripping down the gutters of his house, it was all so soothing to Cleo. There were still a couple of hours before his friends would arrive though, and he needed to find something else to kill the time.

> *I don't want to watch T.V. and I don't feel like surfing the internet. I have the house all to myself. What should I do?* – He mentally ran over his usual activities.

You would think that with living in a place where it was always raining, everyone who lived there would have a surplus of indoor activities to do, but that was never the case. Cleo found himself spending most of his free time, pondering what to do with his free time.

> *I guess there is always homework.*

He begrudgingly marched back into his bedroom and pulled out his copy of *The Wonderful Wizard of Oz.* He had a book report that was due the following day and he still had not even finished reading the book.

Although the book was a few grades below what he was capable of reading, he was grateful that his teacher, Mr. Castorina, assigned it to his class. While he had never read it, his mother constantly talked about it being one of her favorites as a child. That small connection to her meant a lot to Cleo, for they had begun to dwindle over time.

"After reading The Wonderful Wizard of Oz, write a two-three page paper that analyzes the world of Oz, its inhabitants, and compare it to the current state of the United States." Cleo read aloud his assignment.

"Because it makes total sense to try and find the similarities between a make-believe world written nearly 100 years ago and 21st century America," he complained to Knuckles, fast asleep in his cage. He glanced at the clock and saw that it read 2:30 pm. "I have at least three to four hours of work to do and barely two hours to accomplish it. Whatever, I'm sure I can wing the majority of the paper."

This kind of attitude towards his schoolwork had become increasingly more common since his mother died. His grades and homework were consistently placed on the backburner, and he was becoming increasingly more cynical towards school. His father frequently was forced to come in for Parent-Teacher conferences about either his grades, behavior or both.

"Cleo is a very smart child, he is just very lazy."

"He seems to have stopped caring about everything that's school related."

"What can we do to help?"

"Does your home provide a nurturing and encouraging environment for your son?"

The worst one came the year before, when he was a sophomore. Cleo had a particular English teacher, Mr. Olsen, whom he loathed. Mr. Olsen was on the older side and the majority of the student body thought he should have retired long ago. On more than one occasion, Cleo let Mr. Olsen know of his opinion on the matter. After another afternoon of making wisecrack comments, Mr. Olsen had enough.

"Cleo, this needs to stop. To begin with, you are not even pretending to try. Except when it comes to disrupting my class," Mr. Olsen said to him while holding him after class.

"Actually I don't need to *try* to accomplish that," Cleo said with a smirk that further irritated his teacher.

"Secondly," he continued, ignoring the comment. "You're lazy. You are more than capable of earning a respectable grade in this class if you wanted to. Instead, you choose not to do your homework, write uninspired and lackadaisical essays, and you rarely read the books I assign. Soon enough you will realize you can't lazily stroll through your entire life."

If it were anyone else questioning Cleo's character he would have blown him or her off. He simply would shrug his shoulders and continue to live with giving the comments little to no weight. However, since it was his archrival, Mr. Olsen, there was no way he was going to let it go.

"Of course, because whether or not I complete your pointless homework assignments determines if I'm lazy or not. I forgot that getting good grades in your meaningless class is what is important in life. It's not about your family or friends. I guess it's easy to judge others when you don't have any of your own. Isn't it Mr. Olsen?" The moment

Cleo said it, he regretted it. Cleo knew that the old man had lost his wife to cancer a few years back and that the comment would strike him deep.

"I'm sorry, I shouldn't have said that," he immediately apologized, but it was too late.

"Get out of my class. Now." Mr. Olsen's face turned beet red and his stare was piercing.

The little outburst earned him a meeting with his teacher, the principal and his father. After more than an hour discussing his issues, disappointing his father, and apologizing to Mr. Olsen, Cleo narrowly avoided being suspended. Instead, the four of them agreed to a plan that Cleo was forced to adhere to, or else. Any more problems, behavior or academic, would result in suspension.

Although it was now a new school year with a new teacher, the plan stayed in effect. As such, it was Cleo's desire to avoid punishment that truly propelled him into doing homework on his birthday.

He opened the book up to the page he had bookmarked and noticed he had no less than 100 pages left. After a brief scan of the page, he found the passage in which he left off and began reading.

> *They walked along listening to the singing of the brightly colored birds and looking at the lovely flowers, which now became so thick that the entire ground was carpeted with them*, he read in his head.

He tried picturing the scene in his head. It was only one sentence but he could imagine exactly what was happening. It felt as if he could hear the birds chirping and the warmth of the sun beating down on him. His room around him began to shudder as if he were caught in a terrible windstorm. He put the book down and surveyed his room. Nothing had moved even a millimeter. The books were all still perfectly alphabetized on his shelf and Knuckles was still fast asleep in his cage.

> *I must be more tired than I thought.* – He was thinking while rubbing his eyes. *I have to keep reading. Mr. Castorina is not going to buy the excuse, "My eyes felt funny," for why I did not complete the assignment.*

He shook off the weird feeling and continued reading.

There were big yellow, white, blue, and purple blossoms, beside great clusters of scarlet poppies, which were so brilliant in color they almost dazzled Dorothy's eyes.

This time the feeling was far more intense. Along with the room again shaking, he felt his own body change.

What the hell is going on? It's like I'm floating away. My hands, my feet, I can't move them! I can't move anything! – He tried to push the book away from his body, but his limbs would not respond. It was too late. He no longer had any control over what was about to happen.

Wait, is that me? Why am I floating above my body? – He thought as his spirit hovered over his body while it appeared to be stuck in some sort of catatonic state.

Oh my God! What's happening to it? Why is it breaking... Whoooaaa – He tried to yell out, but could not. The last thing he saw was his body fracturing into a billion little particles, like dust swirling around in the morning light. Everywhere around, his bedroom began to do the same, dissolving like salt in a pot of hot water. Suddenly, he jerked forward, swirling into the very pages of the book lying open on his desk.

As suddenly as it started, his out-of-body experience ended equally abruptly.

"Ugh...what was that?" He said, feeling dizzy and nauseous, as he was finally able to open his eyes.

"Where's my room? And why am I outside?" Cleo spoke aloud, clutching his stomach with one hand, and his forehead with his other. He was no longer lying on his bed, but instead was sitting on his backside in a field of grass. It took a few moments for Cleo's vision to fully clear. When it finally did, he could not believe what he was seeing.

It was as if he stepped into the last undisturbed sanctuary on Earth (although technically he no longer *was* on Earth). Not a trace of pollution littered the skies. It was clearer than the waters of The Maldives and bluer than any ocean, blueberry, or forget-me-not flowers he had ever seen. Transposed on the day sky were countless kinds of birds soaring about and the bright sun, incandescently lighting up the world around him.

I wish I knew I was going to lose my mind. I would at least have worn sunglasses first – He thought, blocking its brightness from his eyes with his hand.

He tried to get his bearings. He looked around to survey his surroundings. Behind him rushed a raging narrow river. Fish leaping through the air as they struggle to make their way up against its rapid current. On the opposite bank was an ominous forest, encompassed in a dark and intimidating aura.

In front of him was a wild and unkempt field. It had clearly never felt the blades of a mower before, as it rose no less than three feet from the ground and swayed back and forth in the gentle breeze. Alongside the long grass were flowers of every color imaginable. Amongst the typical blue, red and yellow stood ones colored turquoise, fuchsia and crimson.

Wherever this may be, it is unspeakably beautiful.

Rising far above the field, set against the horizon, were towering snow-capped mountains.

"I'm definitely not anywhere close to home. Those are way taller than any of my mountains back home." He mumbled to himself, looking across the field. "What is that out there?" He squinted his eyes to try and get a better look at the object that caught his attention.

"Aren't they beautiful?" The voice of a young girl startled Cleo out of his enchantment, intruding upon his perceived solitude in this haven of Mother Nature. He spun around and saw four beings slowly entering the field to his left. He narrowed his eyes and noticed a girl, dressed in a blue and white gingham dress, and carrying a small picnic basket. On either side of her were three strange looking creatures.

There was a man standing over six feet tall, dressed entirely in metal and carrying an axe. Goofily prancing about on his left appeared to be another man, this one was covered head-to-toe in straw. At the end of their line was a lion. At least, based on appearance, what Cleo *thought* was a lion.

> *That can't be an actual lion. He's not on all fours like a real one. He is walking upright like a human.*

The young girl bent over and pulled a handful of flowers out of the ground. She brought them to her nose and inhaled their aroma.

"I suppose so. When I have brains, I shall probably like them better," answered the man that looked oddly like a scarecrow.

"If I only had a heart, I should love them," added the metal man.

"I always did like flowers," said the Lion. "They seem so helpless and frail."

> *Did that lion just talk? Is this...Oz?*

Cleo could not believe what he was seeing or hearing. Here, standing before him were four...beings...that inexplicably resembled the ones he had just been reading.

> *There is no way this is possible. I either have fallen asleep at my desk and this is some strange dream, or I am sick and this is all a delusion of my mind.*

"Your name wouldn't happen to be Dorothy, would it?" asked Cleo taking a few steps closer to the group.

The man of metal wheeled around, raising his axe at the young man who was approaching from their flank.

"Stop where you are! If you've come to harm Dorothy I shall lop off your head where you stand!" he threatened.

"No, I mean you no harm. There doesn't need to be any head lopping." Cleo slowly backed away, letting out a nervous laugh.

"Yes, I am Dorothy. How do you know my name?" Dorothy spoke up, taking refuge behind her protector.

"Um...lucky guess."

The lion and straw man both stepped forward, clearly not buying the answer, and further shielded Dorothy from him.

"My name is Cleo, and quite frankly I have no idea how I got here, or where here even is for that matter. I just remember reading..." he stopped.

> *What do I say to them? "Hey, so by the way, you guys are all fake and characters in a book. I was reading about you, and then POOF, here I am talking to you. Sound crazy? Well that's because it is.*

"And passing out," he continued. "When I woke up I was here," he lied, attempting to put the three threatening beasts before him at ease.

"Well I can answer at least one of your questions. *Here* is the land of Oz."

> *So that solves it, I have officially gone crazy.* – Cleo thought, nodding his head incredulously.

"Does that mean you are stuck here as well?" Dorothy asked, stepping out from behind the tin man.

"Umm," he pinched his arm as hard as he could in hopes of waking up. All he received in return was an indent in his skin, not a return to the world of the conscious.

> *Of course, why should it be as simple as that?*

"I guess it appears that way."

Dorothy turned to Baum's other three characters and spoke too low for Cleo to hear.

"I don't think that's a good idea," Cleo heard the Lion speak up.

"I must agree with him Ma'am," the Tin Woodman chimed in.

"No, I've decided," she said, ignoring their insistence. She turned back towards Cleo. "Why don't you come with us? Perhaps the Wizard can help you return home."

I somehow doubt the Wizard can cure whatever ailment is preventing me from waking up. Then again, what do I have to lose?

"Sure, why not," he agreed.

Suddenly a little dog popped its head out of her picnic basket.

"This is..."

"Toto," Cleo finished instinctively.

"Another *lucky guess?*" the Tin Woodman chided disbelievingly.

"No, I heard her talk about him when you entered the field," Cleo lied again. In the real world, Cleo was as honest a child as you would ever meet. He found it somewhat discomforting that he was able to be so quick on his feet with lies.

"I think I remember her saying that," said Scarecrow, scratching his hollow straw head.

The Tin Woodman did not look so easily convinced. Dorothy on the other hand just smiled it off.

"You see that city out there on the horizon?"

Cleo looked across the field at the object that captured his attention a few moments ago.

"So that is a city?" Cleo could just make out the top of a building. Its tip obscured by a green veil.

"That's what I've been told. I've never actually been there myself," admitted Dorothy.

This caused Cleo to laugh.

"So you're travelling across a mysterious land that you've never been to, with three men, none of which are human, to see a Wizard who may or not be able to help you?"

"I'm offended by that comment. I am still human. I was just cursed." The Tin Woodman said, shifting the axe to his shoulder.

"No offense intended. We just don't exactly have men made of soda cans back home," Cleo said.

"Yes, the answer is yes. That pretty much sums it up," she answered before the Tin Woodman could respond.

"Ok, whatever works. I just wanted to make sure we were all on the same page. But on one condition," Cleo said standing up nice and straight. "No singing while we walk. Deal?"

Dorothy looked a little confused why this would be a deal breaker to Cleo, but she shrugged her shoulders and nodded.

"I don't have any plans to burst into song, so that shouldn't be a problem."

As they hiked through the fields, Cleo made sure to stay by Dorothy more often than not. He knew that the Tin Woodman trusted him as far as he could throw him, so he wanted to avoid confrontation as much as possible. They kept mostly quiet for the initial part of their trek, which Cleo enjoyed as it gave him time to consider what was happening to him.

I have never had a dream that seemed so real before. The grass feels and smells like real grass. I'm sweating what appears to be real sweat. The birds sound and look like real birds. If I look past the fact that three make-believe storybook characters are walking and talking beside me, I would think this is all 100% genuine. – Cleo began to get lost in thought as they made their way through the sky-reaching meadow. *So if this is not a dream, what are my options? I know I'm not dead. I mean, homework is boring and all, but it doesn't literally kill you. Unless I'm the first person in history to get food poisoning from my cereal, I don't think I could be having a hallucination. What does that leave me? It all being real? Say it is. What then? I can't shake this nagging feeling that I somehow belong here. Like I'm more a part of this...world, than my own.*

With Cleo focusing all his attention on how and why he was there, he did not notice the drowsiness that had set upon him or his new companions. All five of them had stopped conversing with one another, and were stumbling frequently. It took the Scarecrow nearly knocking him over to realize what was happening.

"Is anyone else feeling really tired all of a sudden?" Cleo asked, helping Scarecrow regain what little balance he possessed. He noticed that not only were their movements slower, time itself seemed to come to an agonizingly slow crawl.

"Yes, I feel like we've been walking forever," the Lion answered, tripping over his own tail.

"It's so pretty here. It smells simply wonderful. Why don't we take a break and sleep amongst these poppies?" Dorothy suggested.

The group had been so fixated on their path to Oz that they became oblivious to what they were walking through. The luscious green fields had long given way to a massive poppy patch. However, this was not just any poppy patch. In addition to being visually captivating, the velvety red petals also discharged sleep-inducing opium. Opium that would result in a sleep so deep that one may never wake up.

"Dorothy, we need to keep moving. We cannot stop here. It is far too dangerous," the Tin Woodman, impervious to its effects, warned.

Dorothy nodded in agreement but immediately succumbed to nature's Nyquil and collapsed to the ground.

"What shall we do?" asked the Tin Woodman, his voice cracking in fear.

"If we leave her here she will surely die," said the Lion. "The smell of the flowers is killing us all. We will fall asleep, and we will never wake up. I myself can scarcely keep my eyes open and the dog is out already," motioning to Toto sleeping in Dorothy's basket.

> *What will happen if I fall asleep? If this is a dream or a coma of some sort, will it wake me up? - Cleo thought as he slowly began to drop to his knees. Will I stay asleep in this field forever? I guess sleeping in such a perfect place would not be the worst way to spend eternity.*

"Cleo...not you too...don't..." the Lion's shout may as well have been a whisper as Cleo closed his eyes, unsure if he would ever open them again.

I can't see anything. I can't hear anything. It's just darkness. I hate the dark. This dream is even worse than the last one. No, this is not a dream. This is a nightmare. I need to wake up. NOW! – Cleo began to panic.

Am I dead? Is this what death looks like? Did those damn flowers kill me? That's going to look so embarrassing on my tombstone. Here lies Cleo, loving son, loving brother, killed by a flower. Oh, God please don't let this be real. I can't stay here forever. Take me back to Oz. Please. Anything but here.

After a painstakingly long time the darkness began to subside. He opened his eyes and squinted, unsure of what he would see. He hoped it was the ceiling of his bedroom or the inside of his book stuck to his forehead. Instead, the sun shone brightly down onto his face.

"You've got to be kidding me. I'm never getting out of here," he said, shielding his eyes. "I did say send me back to Oz. At least it's not the dark."

He sat up and found that he was not back in his home as he hoped. He was in the same field he fell asleep in, only with two major differences. The first was the absence of the poppy flowers upon which he had collapsed. Bushes filled with raspberries and mulberries had replaced them, along with Russian Sage covered in honeybees.

Knowing my luck, those are killer bees and poisonous berries.
– He thought grumpily.

The other variance in his surroundings was a swarm of little mice that surrounded his four newfound friends. Scarecrow and the Tin Woodman were standing next to a wooden wheelbarrow, containing Lion and Dorothy with Toto curled into a ball in her arms. Tin Woodman was conversing with one mouse in particular.

"If ever you need us again, come out into the field and call, and we shall hear you and come to your assistance. Good-bye!" cried the little mouse. Then just like that, the horde of mice sprinted off through the field.

"Uh…guys, were you just talking to a mouse?" Cleo said groggily.

"Good to see you finally came around," said the Tin Woodman. "That wasn't just any mouse. That was the queen of the mice. Her and her family, all ten thousand of them, saved you, Dorothy and Lion."

"Don't forget Toto as well!" Scarecrow cried out.

> *Did they really save my life? Who knows, maybe that's the only way for me to leave this world. I need to die first.* – Cleo pondered.

"Thanks," Cleo said, rising to his feet.

"So you still don't know why or how you got here?" The Tin Woodman asked.

"No I don't. Do you still not believe me?" Cleo asked, annoyed.

Just as Tin Woodman opened his metallic jaw to respond, Dorothy began to stir awake.

"Oh my, what a splendidly odd dream I was having," she said, stretching out her arms and yawning. "What happened? Why are we in this wagon?"

The Tin Woodman sent a piercing stare towards Cleo. Cleo took it to mean *I will never trust you. Watch your back.* Then again, the man was made of tin, so his facial expressions were limited. It was just as likely that the stare meant, *Hey, you over there. Grab that oil can and lube up my jaw for me please.*

Regardless of what the look meant, he turned to Dorothy and informed her of the events that had unfolded.

"Here we are worried about the Wicked Witch and we're almost done in by some flowers. We really aren't in Kansas anymore," said Dorothy innocently.

"Look how close the city is now. The sun is getting lower. Let us wake the Lion and get moving. I know I don't want to be out here in the dark, and I'm sure Lion would feel the same," the Scarecrow spoke up.

"I wish we could let him sleep longer. He's so content," Dorothy said while the Lion purred loudly from the wheelbarrow.

Tin Woodman gently nudged Lion with the butt of his axe. Since he was no longer bedding in the poppies, he woke up instantly.

"You should have left me there," he said, extending his claws and letting out a growl that came across as nothing more than a harmless grumble. "I was having such a nice dream."

With the sun quickly dropping closer and closer to the horizon, they gathered their things and set off again towards their destination. This time they managed to travel at a steady pace, sparingly taking breaks to oil their metal friend or stuff straw that had gone astray back into Scarecrow's body.

"It seems like the more we walk the more magical this land becomes," Cleo said to Dorothy. "This doesn't feel like any old field back home. Everything out here, the sky, the grass, the air, it all seems... otherworldly."

"It reminds me of back home. There are fields like this everywhere," she said, her eyes drifting towards her feet at the thought of her home.

> That's right, her character is from over a hundred years ago. Not to mention she's from Kansas. It probably did, and maybe still does, look like this everywhere over there – Cleo thought. He had slowly begun to accept the fact that he may very well be inside of Baum's creation, and not just trapped in his own mind.

> How else could I know all of these details? I have never read this story before. There really is no other explanation.

As they grew closer and closer to the city, Cleo started to notice that it wasn't only the prairie around them that shone green. The flowers all started to possess green petals. The sun's rays had changed from their predictable yellow into a pear green. Even their clothes started to contain traces of green.

"That is the most magnificent thing I have ever seen," stated Dorothy as they finally approached the entrance to the city. Standing between them and the magical city of Oz was a gate, large enough for even Paul Bunyan himself to walk through, and made entirely of priceless, perfectly cut emeralds. Imprinted on every gemstone was an intricate design depicting an old man wearing a long robe. Standing guard in front of the gate was a man armed with a spear and wearing some of the strangest sunglasses Cleo had ever seen.

"I am the Guardian of the Gates, what is your business here?" He asked as they approached.

"We need to see the Great Oz immediately," answered Dorothy.

"What is your business?"

"We have come to ask him for his help."

"As do many." The guard's attempt at appearing intimidating was completely undone by his goofy looking glasses. The only emotion Cleo felt standing in front of him was the desire to burst into laughter.

"I cannot promise you will gain his audience, but I will take you to his palace. But first you must each put on these spectacles," he spoke handing them each a pair of shades that looked like they came straight out of the 1970s. They had huge circular plastic frames with lenses nearly an inch thick.

"Why?" asked Cleo.

"Because, otherwise you shall be blinded by the brightness and glory of the Emerald City. Even those who live in the City must wear them at all times," answered the guard.

The five travelers placed the glasses on their faces.

"You look pretty ridiculous," Cleo said to Dorothy.

"You're one to talk," they both laughed at their Elton Johnian appearance.

They walked through the gates and entered the city. The city was more splendid and glorious than any city Cleo had ever seen in person. He had grown up near Seattle, Earth's Emerald City, but it paled in comparison. The streets in Oz were not pavement, but rather made purely from emeralds.

> *Reminds me of the cobblestone streets we saw in San Francisco* – Cleo thought of the time he went with his mother on one of her business trips the year before she died.

There were shops of all varieties and sizes set up around the city. They all seemed to struggle to stand out amongst their same-hued neighbors. The jewelry shop was a small glossy jade building, while next to it a malachite green brick building was home to a store devoted strictly to hats. On the corners were fruit and vegetable stands, interchanging from lime to olive greens. The setting sun cast shadows on the alleyways, making them appear to be dark forest green tunnels snaking their way through the city.

The people that were wandering about were just as intriguing as the city itself. Many of them camouflaged in with their surroundings. The men wore suspenders and top hats, while the women wore silly looking bonnets and homely dresses. There were more shades of green than at a Leprechaun convention. Despite the lack of individuality, there was a bright-eyed smile on every single face in the city. Even the fact that five strangers were walking through their city added only to their curiosity, not their fear.

At the very center of the city was a tower that looked quite similar to Seattle's Space Needle. The spire palace made Seattle's iconic structure look closer to an Elementary School art project.

"That tower there is the Wizard's palace. That is where I will take you," the guard said, noticing them gawk at the tower.

> *I'm not a carpenter or anything, but I'm pretty sure that entire thing is made of emeralds* – He thought reveling at the sight. Looking at the tower made him feel homesick.

> *I need to start looking for a way out of this…experience. Maybe*

*there is something of importance here in the city. It'll probably
be a lot easier if I look around by myself.*

"You guys move on ahead, I want to look around a little bit," Cleo said
to the other four.

The Tin Woodman gave Cleo a look of skepticism.

"But we are about to meet the Wizard. You can't leave now," reminded Dorothy.

"I will be fine. You talk to him first, tell me what he says. I've never
seen anything like this place and I'm not quite ready to leave," he
said facetiously.

Dorothy clearly did not share that same sentiment.

"I am ready to go home Cleo. Please be quick, I would hate to have to
leave without you," she said earnestly.

"Don't worry, I'll catch up with you," he hoped he would be gone before
he would have to.

He turned around and walked down an adjacent street. The street was
mostly deserted. There were far fewer people wandering the rocky
roads than many of the ones they had walked by.

> *There isn't anybody selling anything. None of these buildings
> appears to be their shops. They must be their homes –* Cleo
> thought. *Home...I wonder if this will work?*

"There's no place like home. There's no place like home," he said, while
foolishly tapping his heels together.

A handful of citizens in the area looked at him with questioning looks,
as if he were a crazy person.

"What are you looking at? It was worth a try."

He looked over his shoulder and noticed Dorothy and her companions
were outside of the emerald needle briefly talking to the guard before
proceeding inside.

I really need to figure out how to get out of here – He thought. *Who knows how long I've been here? Penny and Bryce probably already found me. I'm sure Bryce tried to wake me up with a solid slap to the face. Penny would have taken the tender route and called an ambulance. I bet I'm now lying on a hospital bed as the doctors figure out why I fell into a coma and how to get me out of it.*

The thought of Penny waiting by his hospital bedside brought a smile to his face.

What if the doctor can't wake me up? What if I need to do it myself? Could there be a door of sorts that I need to step through in order to wake up? – He worried.

He began looking around for a door or window that he could retreat into that would spit him back out into consciousness. He searched the ground, the horizon and even the skies for some sort of hint as to where he was supposed to go.

I sure hope it is not up there – He thought, looking up towards the heavens.

Nothing seemed out of the ordinary or at least as far as ordinary in Oz goes.

"You, you don't belong here," a voice suddenly called out from a nearby alleyway. He spun around fearfully.

"I won't argue with you there," he answered, seeing that the voice came from a girl not much older than him. She looked far different from every other person he had seen in Oz so far.

She's straight out of the 80's. – Cleo thought as he judged her.

She was slightly shorter than he was, had big curly brown hair and enormous golden hoop earrings. She had olive skin, nearly the exact same pigment as he had. She wore a jean jacket covered in sparkles, a poofy pink skirt and a pair of old school leg warmers.

"My name is Cleo," he said, trying not to laugh at her outdated appearance. "I'm actually trying to find my way out of here."

"You're not a part of this story," she said flatly.

"How do you know that? And what makes you think this is a story?" he said anxiously.

"Because, *I* am not a part of this story. Are you a story hitcher too?" She continued to move slowly towards him fearlessly. For every step she took, he followed suit by taking one backwards.

"A what?"

"It's my term for it. I think I need to trademark it soon. It's like we're hitching a ride in all the various books, and then hopping out when we're finished with them."

Cleo didn't know why she wasn't intimidated or frightened by him in the slightest, but it unnerved him.

"What makes you think I don't belong in this story?"

"How else could a human get into the imaginary world of Oz?" Cleo expected the girl to add a "duh!!" at the end with an eye-roll, but it never came.

"Right, so you're saying we're literary hitchhikers?" Cleo said skeptically as his slow retreat backed him into the wall of a building.

"Basically, I'm still pretty new to all of it. I just learned how a few months ago. You should look for me in some of my other books. I bet I am in loads more. I plan on going into *Tarzan, War of the Worlds, Journey to the Center of the Earth.* Basically, anything I can find after this one. I might be able to be more help to you in those."

Cleo stood dumbfounded and speechless in front of the girl.

> *This girl is psycho; she is even crazier than I am. Either that or I'm in a world of trouble.* – Cleo thought.

"Based on that look on your face, I'd say it's about time that you left. Do you know how to get out of here?" she asked, sensing that Cleo was not ready for any of this.

"Not in the slightest. Else I would have been gone just as soon as I got here."

"Alright, then listen up. It's at least one thing I can teach you. Focus your mind on where you came from. Try to picture every inch of it. Before you know it, you'll be back," she instructed.

"Right," he said disbelievingly.

What do I have to lose?

"By the way, what's your name?" he asked.

"Calliope, nice to meet you Cleo."

"Say that again," Cleo knew for sure he misheard her.

"Calliope."

Cleo's mind went blank.

> *That's impossible. That can't be her name. Calliope. That's the same as my mother. This can't be her. If this is a dream my subconscious is cruel to play such an evil trick on me. If it's not...I...I...*

"So are you ready to go?"

> *She even sounds like her. If I look past her clothes, she even kind of looks like her.*

"Is anyone home? Or did I lose you?" her voice brought him out of the crevices of his mind.

"Yes, sorry. Thank you...Calliope." Saying the name aloud created a lump in his throat.

> *Alright, if this is going to work I need to worry about that later. I can only focus on my bedroom, nothing else –* He thought, trying to steer his focus onto the task of returning home.

> *There is my bookshelf. On it are all sorts of different books. There's*

1984, Animal Farm, The Giver, Picture of Dorian Gray, Watership Down, – He recalled with almost photographic memory.

Wow, I'm surprised I can remember so many of them. In fact, I can remember all of them. Half of them I haven't even read in years. What else is in the room? There is my bed, which isn't made. The covers are hanging halfway off, the pillows are stuffed down into the crack between the bed and the wall. There are seven socks thrown around. Wait, seven? That means I'm missing one. Seriously? Grr, now I'll have yet another useless, matchless sock.

"Nothing's happening," he complained to the young girl, eyes still shut.

"It takes a little bit of time. Especially on your first time. We can't just pop in and out. Give it around 30 seconds or so. If it still hasn't worked, then something is wrong," she said nonchalantly.

Cleo sighed and continued to picture his bedroom. Hanging on his wall were two M.C. Escher prints, *Drawing Hands* and *Relativity*, both of which were crooked. Knuckles was fast asleep in his cage. Knuckle's cage was a lot like Cleo's room, desperately needing to be cleaned. Before any further details of his untidy room could flood his mind, he was overcome with the same feeling of detachment from his body that he had initially gotten upon entering Oz. He squeezed his eyes intensely to keep them shut.

I'd prefer not to see myself split into a million pieces again.

Just as abruptly and mysteriously as he entered the one hundred year old novel, his familiar bedroom replaced the magical world around him. He arrived once again sitting at his desk, fully put back together with, what he hoped, not a single cell missing from his body. He looked around his room and saw that everything was exactly as he had remembered.

"I don't believe it, it worked. That crazy girl was the key to getting out of there."

He immediately got up and ran out of his room.

"Dad! Linus!" He yelled, moving in and out of each room, expecting to find someone frantically waiting for him. "Penny? Bryce? Is anyone here?"

Each room he went into was empty.

He walked into the living room and checked the answering machine, expecting any number of messages from concerned family and friends. All he saw was a **0** under "new messages". He was shocked and hurt by the fact nobody seemed to care.

> *I was gone for at least a day and no one noticed? On my birthday nonetheless? I wasn't expecting everyone and their uncle to be waiting by my side, but...nobody?*

He hung his head and walked back to his room. He sat at his desk and picked up his cell phone to see if there were at least any text messages on it. He punched in his passcode and looked at the home screen. There weren't any new voicemails or notifications, but there was something else that was quite startling to Cleo.

The time read: **March 14th, 2012. 3:55 pm.**

> *3:55 pm? On March 14th? That means only an hour and ten minutes have passed. I know without a shadow of a doubt, that I was out of it for longer than an hour. None of this makes a lick of sense.*

Cleo didn't know what to believe or how to figure out what was happening to him. He frustratingly ran his hands through his hair. He looked up at a picture of his mom hanging on the wall over their fireplace.

> *Who was that woman? She could not have been you. Aside from the obvious facts that she was about 17 years old and you are dead. She had to have been a figment of my imagination, or a memory from my subconscious.–* He tried to rationalize.

"But...have I ever even seen a picture of you that young?" he said.

> *I need to ask dad when he gets home for one. It's the only way I'll know for sure.*

He suddenly felt like calling his friends and telling them not to come over, despite it being his birthday. Unfortunately, by the time this idea kicked in, he heard a knock on the front door. He walked swiftly over to the living room. He peered out the door's peephole and saw his two friends, Bryce and Penny, standing on his doorstep. He opened the door and tried to redirect his focus away from the strange and unexplainable occurrence.

"Hey Cleo! Happy birthday!!!" yelled Penny.

Penny was just barely shorter than Cleo. In fact it was so close that if she wore any sort of heels she surpassed him. She had long, auburn hair that was curled at the tips. Her eyes were sapphire blue and seemed to sparkle in the sun.

"Happy birthday man," said his other friend, Bryce, in a dull monotone.

Bryce could not look any more different from Cleo. Bryce was what you would consider tall, dark and handsome. He was a shade over six feet tall, black hair that always contained far more hair product than it should , and wore designer everything. He had acquired his expensive taste from his parents, and rarely wore anything that was not imported.

"Hey guys, thanks." He did his best to force a somewhat believable smile.

"You ready for your birthday surprise?" Penny asked giddily, moving up to Cleo and giving him a big hug.

This time he didn't have to fake the smile that came across his face.

"Yeah, let's go. I need to get out of this place."

> *I have no idea what is going on, but I do know I need to keep it to myself. Whatever is going on in my mind, I need to **keep** it in my mind.*

As he walked out of his home, he felt a little better, realizing that the paper he needed to write was going to be a breeze. Now that he saw firsthand what Oz was like, he could easily write a political comparison between Oz and the real world.

> *There will not be a parent-teacher conference this time*
> *– He thought.*

When they reached Bryce's car, Cleo let Penny have shotgun.

What if it was all real? What if I wasn't just hallucinating or having the most intense daydream ever? I know that it should not be possible...but what if?

"Dude, are you listening?" Bryce said, as Cleo was slipping into the back of his car.

"Sorry, I was thinking about...something. What'd you say?" Cleo asked, trying to stop his racing mind.

"I said let me back into your place real quick. I need to use the bathroom before we go," Bryce repeated, annoyed.

"Oh yeah," Cleo said, getting back out of Bryce's car. "You should have said something while we were still at the door though man."

Bryce just shrugged his shoulders. They walked back up to the doorstep. Cleo reached into his jean pocket and pulled out his keys.

"Stop, I don't actually have to go," Bryce said, putting his hand against the door.

"What?"

"I don't need your bathroom. I just didn't want to say this in front of her." Bryce said. Bryce was quite a bit bigger than Cleo was, so their close proximity made him feel like Bryce was towering over him.

"Say what?" Cleo said confused.

"I know what you're hiding dude."

"What are you talking about Bryce?"

Bryce leaned in a little closer.

"I know your secret. In fact, I think I've known it for longer than you have."

CHAPTER 3

Cleo's Comedy of Errors

How could he know what I can do? I don't even know what I can do!

"You're wrong Bryce. I'm not hiding anything," Cleo said.

"Come on man, I'm your best friend. You really think I wouldn't realize what's going on?" Bryce prodded.

"Uh...umm..." Cleo stuttered.

Cleo stood on his doorstep, nervous and not knowing what to say. It was eerily similar to the day he and Bryce first met. It was 8 years ago in the very same spot.

Eight Years Ago

Cleo was only eight years old when he first moved to the town of North Bend. His parents were tired of the big city, and moved them from the heart of downtown Seattle, to the boondocks of the small mountain town. Cleo was in his room unpacking his toys and books when his mother called his name from the living room.

"Cleo! Come to the front door, there's someone here who would like to meet you!"

> *Who would want to meet me?* – He remembered thinking as he apprehensively listened to his mother.

"Hello, my name is Bryce. I live just across the street," a young boy introduced himself from the front door. The boy was Cleo's age, yet looked like he could be at least ten.

"H...Hi. My name is Cleo. I live here," Cleo stammered out shyly. He stayed behind his mother while she stood by the door quietly.

"Haha! Yeah I assumed that you didn't actually live next door," Bryce said laughing enthusiastically. "Well I saw the moving truck outside and figured you were just moving into the area."

"Yeah, we are."

Cleo still hadn't moved from his spot, halfway in the living room.

"Well, you seem like a pretty cool kid. You should come over sometime and play. It was nice to meet you. You too Miss..."

"Bailey. Calliope Bailey." His mother answered, shaking the young Bryce's hand. "Bye Cleo," Bryce waved courteously.

Cleo waved awkwardly to Bryce as he jumped off the steps of the deck and skipped merrily back to his house.

"Look at that. Barely here an hour and you've already made a friend sweetie."

"Yeah, I guess he seems really nice," he said before returning to organizing his bedroom.

Present Day

That would be quite ironic if my friendship with Bryce ends in the same place as it began. If he really knows the truth about me, how could he possibly want to stay my friend? – Thought Cleo.

"I really don't know what secret it is that you think I am hiding," Cleo said as his pulse raced.

"Dude, you're in love with Penny. You have been for a long time. It's obvious," Bryce said, jabbing Cleo in the stomach with his finger.

"I'm not in love with Penny," Cleo said, relieved at Bryce's theory. "We're just friends. Nothing more."

"I'm sure," Bryce said, rolling his eyes.

"Come on man, we're gonna be late. Let's get out of here." Cleo walked back down the steps to lead Bryce back to his car.

"Seatbelts boys," Penny said, mothering them as Cleo hopped in through the rear passenger door.

"So where you guys taking me anyways?" Cleo asked Penny and Bryce as they pulled out of Cleo's driveway and headed towards the interstate.

"It's a surprise, you'll just have to wait and see. You're lucky I didn't blindfold you," Penny answered coyly.

"Frugal's," Bryce blurted out.

Penny rolled her eyes at Bryce and gave him a dirty look before smiling back at Cleo.

"Surprise," Penny said, visibly annoyed.

Frugal's Burgers and Shakes was Cleo's all-time favorite place to eat. They had the juiciest and thickest burgers in the state and their BLT's had a half-pound of bacon piled on top of them, to go along with a succulent homemade BBQ sauce. It was located on the outer rim of Seattle, about 30 minutes from Cleo's driveway.

"I can't remember the last time I went there. It has to have been a least a couple of years," Cleo's mouth watered at the thought of their food.

"I would have gone to *Rosita's* or *La Verde*," Bryce added in his two cents on their destination.

"Well Cleo doesn't need $30 dinner to have a good birthday," Penny responded in a snarky way, still annoyed by Bryce ruining the surprise.

> *I thought I was the only one that noticed his flashy taste.*
> – Cleo thought looking at Penny in admiration.

Bryce came from a wealthy family, and he had no qualms about displaying that wealth. While he couldn't help his house being the biggest in the town, he didn't make any effort to hide his family's money in other aspects of his life. He always dressed in something imported from Italy, France or some other European country. His watch alone cost more than everything Cleo owned...*combined.*

Ten minutes in, their trip hit an unexpected snag. While they drove down the soggy highway, a loud boom suddenly came from underneath the car.

"Ahhh!" Penny screamed as the car jerked to the right on the rainy highway.

"What the hell is going on?" Bryce exclaimed as he struggled to keep the car on the road. "And don't scream in the car Penny! Are you trying to get us into an accident?"

A thumping sound beat repeatedly from under the right side of the car.

"Did you run over something?" Cleo asked from the backseat.

"No I didn't run over anything. Don't try and tell me how to drive Cleo," Bryce snapped back.

"I wasn't *telling* you anything. Why don't you just chill out and drive?" Cleo answered as Bryce glared at him in the rearview mirror.

After a few tense moments of guiding the gimped car through speeding traffic, Bryce managed to steer them safely off to the side of the interstate.

"Penny, I heard the noise come from that side of the car. Get out and tell me if you see anything wrong," Bryce ordered.

"What? I don't know anything about cars. And it's pouring down rain Bryce, check yourself," Penny said incredulously.

"I can't, because I'm next to the road. It's safer if you do it. Do you want me to be killed out there? Besides, I don't know anything about cars either. Just see if anything looks wrong."

"I'll do it," Cleo said before Penny could click the buckle on her seatbelt. He looked and saw Penny mouth "thank you" in her side mirror as he slid out of the dry, warm car and into the miserable, wet weather.

Cleo took one look at the side of the car and immediately figured out what the problem was. While moonlighting as a mechanic was certainly not one of his after-school activities, he didn't need to be, to notice the glaring problem.

Great! Flat tire.

He hopped back inside the car.

"So what's the verdict?" Bryce asked without as much as a hint of gratitude.

"It seems your car is suffering from the same problem as a $200 junker could," Cleo said, looking at Bryce through the rearview mirror. Bryce raised his eyebrows, waiting for Cleo's response. "Flat tire. Before you even ask, no I have no idea how to change one."

"Whatever. I wouldn't trust you to fix it anyways. Your talents are usually more destructive, not mending. I'll just call AAA, it's nothing they can't fix." Bryce pulled out his cell phone to try to remedy their predicament.

"Well, this hasn't quite turned out how I planned for you. I'm sorry Cleo," Penny apologized, turning around to face Cleo while Bryce mumbled into his phone.

"It's not your fault," Cleo responded. "Thanks for getting me out of the house. I was starting to go stir crazy in there."

Penny smiled back at him.

"Alright, so here's the deal," said Bryce, closing his phone shut. "They are a little backed up today. I guess there was some pileup that they have to deal with first," Bryce said annoyed. "So it'll be about two hours before they can get here."

"Would your dad be able to help Bryce? Or yours Cleo? I'm sure one of them could fix this. It would be a lot faster than waiting two hours for someone to come bring us a new tire," Penny offered.

"My parents are both out of the country," answered Bryce.

"My dad's at work. I doubt he would know the first thing about changing a tire," Cleo said.

"Well, same here. My parents would serve little help. My dad's an accountant. If it doesn't have to do with numbers, he doesn't have the answer," Penny laughed. "We could always walk up to the next exit. Find something to do for the next couple of hours," suggested Penny.

"There's no way I'm leaving my car here. There is also no way that I am walking that far in this monsoon. You guys are more than welcome to, but I'm staying put," Bryce whined.

A cloud of tension thicker than the storm system overhead was forming in the car.

"It's fine Penny, we can just stay here," Cleo said in an effort to keep the peace. "I'm gonna take a nap while we wait. I'm exhausted."

Cleo was physically and mentally depleted from his recent excursion into Oz. It also didn't help matters that he had no desire to sit and try to make small talk for two hours with Bryce in such a cantankerous mood.

He leaned his head up against the window and closed his eyes. Even with the sounds of the cars whizzing past in the background, it did not take long for him to pass out.

No sooner than his eyes were closed, Cleo found himself inexplicably back in Oz. Except this time, he was no longer a sixteen-year-old boy.

This time he was covered from head to toe in long blades of straw. He tried to move but couldn't, for he was nailed to a wooden cross in a hayfield. He tried to speak but found that he no longer possessed a mouth. He tried to think, but no thoughts could be conjured. All he could do was stare straight ahead at the horror approaching.

All around, the field was ripped from the ground and sent soaring into the sky by a mile-wide tornado. The twister scattered about an immeasurable amount of dust and debris. Soon he could feel the pieces of his immobilized body being torn asunder. First, his legs were detached from the post, then his arms. Just as the last of his broken body was lifted into the air, everything went dark.

When he came to, the swirling winds had vanished, but the sensation of lifting into the air persisted.

"I don't want to be straw anymore. No more tornados," he babbled, opening his eyes. "What's going on?" He said, sounding slightly more frantic than he intended.

"Straw and tornados? Must have been some dream," Penny said, facing Cleo from the front seat. "We were wondering if you'd ever wake up. AAA is here, they're fixing the tire."

Cleo looked down at his phone for the time. True to their word, AAA's roadside service arrived two hours on the dot after Bryce's phone call. The car was released from its jack and their savior tapped on the window. Penny rolled it down slightly to keep as much rain out as possible.

"There you guys go, is there anything else I can help you with?" the mechanic asked.

"We had to wait two hours for something that took you ten minutes to fix? If it was that easy, you could have come sooner. Whatever *giant* accident you had to attend to would have still been there," Bryce complained over Penny's shoulder.

"Ungrateful kids on mommy and daddy's dime," the robust man responded, shaking his head in disgust and walking back to his truck.

"What did he just say? What's your name?" Bryce shouted out his window towards the man. The man ignored Bryce's immature outburst, got into his car and drove off down the road.

"Just forget it man, we've been sitting here long enough. Let's get out of here," Cleo said after letting out an exasperated sigh at his friend.

Bryce scowled in his rearview mirror before starting up his car and driving off towards their destination.

The final fifteen minutes of their drive was much less eventful than the first 130. They arrived at the restaurant without any other incidents occurring. Despite the place being more crowded than usual, they were able to get a small table relatively quickly.

"Hello, my name is Autumn and I'll be your server today. How is your day going so far?" The young woman asked as she showed them to their seats.

Cleo and Penny exchanged looks of amusement.

"Simply splendid," Penny answered, holding back a laugh.

Autumn was oblivious to it all and walked away with a ditzy smile on her face. They briefly looked over the menu, but needed little time to make their decisions. The menu was simple, yet contained endless possibilities. There wasn't pasta or salad. Rice, mashed potatoes and macaroni salad were not an option. The choices were sandwiches and burgers. That was it. However, Cleo could choose nearly any ingredient he could think of, as long as it fit between two slices of bread or a bun.

"I'm going with chicken and pineapple. What about you Pen?" Cleo asked, folding up his menu.

"Tofu and veggies, what else would you expect?"

"Gross," Bryce pretended to choke in disgust. "I don't see why neither of you just go the sweet and simple route, beef with a whole pig of bacon."

After a few moments Autumn the waitress returned and took their orders. She looked extremely stressed out when she arrived. Strands of her hair were sticking out of her ponytail in all directions. Her notepad that she took their orders on seemed to be in complete disarray. She acted like a frightened squirrel, turning her head at the slightest of sounds. After scribbling down their respective mealtime desires, she retreated to the kitchen.

"She sure is an eccentric one isn't she?" Bryce commented, taking a drink of his water.

Strangely enough, their orders arrived only a few minutes later. Cleo's stomach was growling loudly, so he didn't give the quick response a second thought as she approached their table, three plates in hand.

"Alright guys. Sorry for the delay. It's a pretty busy night as you can tell," she snorted nervously, looking very flustered. "So here is the BLT, minus the T. This one is the Chicken Club with tater tots, and last but not least the French Dip," she said, passing out the dishes before smiling and walking away.

The three of them all looked at each other confused.

"We didn't order any of this, did we?" Penny asked under her breath to Cleo.

"I don't think so," Cleo said, contemplating eating the meal in front of him anyways. "Though quite frankly, I don't think I care. I may just have to eat these tots."

"No, this isn't even close," Bryce said, turning back to Autumn as she was walking away. "HEY!" he yelled at her. "This isn't what we ordered, could you try getting it right this time?"

She stopped dead in her tracks and turned around. Patrons at nearby tables all turned towards Bryce.

"Wait, none of this is yours?" Her face was turned beet red and she quickly walked back to their table.

"Not in the slightest," Bryce answered rudely.

"I'm so sorry. Let me figure out what happened." She hastily removed the plates from the table and hurried off.

Cleo and Penny exchanged looks of horror.

"Dude, would it kill you to be a little nicer? You can tell that she is having a rough night. Give her a break," Cleo said.

"What do you care?" Bryce snarled.

"It's called being decent, try it sometime."

Bryce ignored Cleo's retort and went back to fiddling with his phone.

"Those tater tots did look quite tasty, maybe we should get an order of them when she comes back," Penny said, again trying to play peacekeeper.

"Sure, let's get a *small* order," Cleo said, widening his eyes.

As in just enough for the two of us – He thought.

Penny got the idea and smiled, but remained silent.

After a brief wait, Autumn showed up again, this time with their correct orders in hand.

"I'm really sorry for the wait. Looks like the kitchen mixed up a few of the tables," she apologized, sending a clearly forced smile in Bryce's direction.

"Don't worry about it. It looks like it's been a pretty crazy night. Thank you," Cleo smiled at the young woman, hoping she only spit in Bryce's food and not all of theirs. She smiled back and quickly walked away before Bryce could make another uncalled-for comment.

"And of course it's cold. I don't know why we bothered coming here. This place always has terrible service." Bryce further complained, sticking his finger into the middle of the burger.

"We came here because it's *Cleo's* favorite place to eat, and seeing how it is *Cleo's* birthday I thought it would be appropriate," Penny said, jumping to the defense of her decision. "Besides, my food tastes perfect."

"Oh yeah, it's *Cleo's* day, how could I forget?" Bryce muttered under his breath.

"Funny, mine is warm, juicy, and tender. I can't imagine why yours would be any different," Cleo said sarcastically, taking another bite of his dinner.

Penny was starting to become visibly frustrated with Cleo and Bryce's bickering. She was not going to play their games or choose sides, so she kept quiet the remainder of the meal. With her peppiness and mediator skills now absent from their dinner, Cleo and Bryce both sensed her change in mood and stopped volleying snide remarks at one another. The three of them ate the rest of their food without any more chatter.

Their meal went by much faster once everyone focused solely on eating and not conversing. They all managed to polish off their plates in a matter of minutes.

"How was your dinner?" asked Autumn, looking much less frazzled when she returned to clear their dishes.

"It was great, thank you," Cleo responded politely.

"Would you like any dessert?"

Penny looked at the birthday boy for a decision on his wishes.

"I think we're good," Cleo answered, rubbing his puffed out stomach.

"Alright, well here's your check, you can pay whenever you want," she said removing the empty dishware from their table.

Penny reached out and grabbed the check the moment it left Autumn's hand. Bryce sat still, pretending not to notice its arrival.

"Alright, so your half is $15 before tip, Bryce," she said, ignoring Cleo's outstretched hand.

"What do I owe?" Cleo asked.

Bryce shuffled through his wallet and pulled out a ten and a five.

"I said before tip," her tone sharper, as she continued to pretend that she did not hear Cleo.

"Service like that doesn't deserve a tip. She's lucky I'm paying for it at all," he said, standing up from the table.

Penny thought about arguing, but she had heard enough of it for one day. She took $20 out of her purse and placed it on the table next to Bryce's money.

"Let me see the bill, I need to know how much to leave," Cleo said, again reaching for the paper in Penny's hand.

"We got it, don't worry. It's your birthday present," she said, standing up and putting on her jacket.

He didn't like them paying for him, but he greatly appreciated the gesture. As they walked from the table, he lagged behind and tossed a few bucks of his own onto Bryce's payment. Penny noticed out of the corner of her eye and shook her head, a slight grin spreading across her face.

The theater was located just across the street from the restaurant. Cleo looked down at his watch as they approached the ticket booth.

8:30.

> *We're four hours in and we haven't even gotten to the movie. I'd almost rather just go to sleep* – He thought.

"What are we going to watch?" Cleo asked Penny.

"*The Bar Mitzvah.* You said you wanted to see it that day we saw the trailer a few months ago."

Cleo remembered the premise sounding funny. It was essentially about a Jewish boy's bar mitzvah gone wrong in every way.

"Awesome, I didn't even know it was out yet," Cleo said as Penny bought their tickets.

"Stop paying for everything Penny. You already got dinner. I'll at least get the popcorn and candy, deal?" Cleo offered as Penny handed him his ticket.

"No. No deal. You don't buy your own stuff on your birthday. It's a rule. Bryce will buy the snacks," said Penny.

Bryce opened his mouth to protest, but decided it was best to roll his eyes and stay silent instead.

After a brief wait in the concession line, they finally entered the movie with their buckets of buttery goodness and half-filled boxes of sugary treats in hand. The movie was playing in a small and mostly full theatre.

"So much for finding decent seats," Bryce whined as the lights dimmed and the previews started to play.

"It looks like we'll have to sit at the very top or very bottom. I don't see three seats together anywhere else," Cleo whispered, standing on the steps and scanning the room.

"I'd rather be in the back than front," Penny whispered back.

"Keep looking, I want to be in the middle," Bryce said with no effort to conceal the volume of his voice.

"Shh," Penny said, putting her finger to her lips and walking up towards the back of the theater.

Bryce begrudgingly followed in tow. After half a dozen excuse-me's, sorry's, and pardon me's, they sat down in the very back row, a few seats in from the aisle.

"At least 100 people in this place and I get to be next to the sick one," Bryce groaned as the man sitting on his left sneezed into his coat sleeve.

The dark theater concealed the giant grin across Cleo's face, as he was able to sit next to Penny, and not Bryce nor the sickly man. After a handful of previews, the feature presentation began.

Penny sat in the middle, holding the popcorn within reach of both of the boys. Bryce pouted and refused to eat a single kernel. Cleo reached across in the dark for the buttery snack, and brushed up against Penny's hand on accident. Suddenly his stomach squirmed with nervous butterflies.

> There is nothing going on here. This is all Bryce's fault. If he hadn't said anything I wouldn't have even noticed how soft her hand was. — He thought, withdrawing his hand from the bucket, holding more grease and butter than popcorn.

Before Cleo had even finished his small handful of popcorn, he was roaring with laughter. The opening scene of the film had the entire crowd in hysterics. Cleo was in such fits that he choked on his soda. Penny gave him a firm swat on the back to try to help.

"Thanks," the words were lost in the noise of the theater.

Just as the title screen started to roll, a horrible scratching sound like fingernails on a chalkboard came over the speakers, followed by complete silence.

"I don't think that's part of the movie," Cleo whispered.

The mouths of the characters on the screen were moving, but nothing was coming out. Then the picture started to flicker before going dark altogether.

"Come on, what the hell man," Bryce shouted.

Other annoyed viewers throughout the theater mimicked his cry.

"Just as the movie was getting good too," Penny said, taking another bite of popcorn.

They sat for about ten minutes, the crowd quickly becoming louder and more boisterous, before the lights came on and an usher walked to the front.

"Excuse me everyone, can I have your attention please?"

He was a scrawny kid, not much older than Cleo and his friends. He wore thin-framed glasses with short black hair, slicked down and parted in the middle. He was clearly nervous at the prospect of talking to a packed theater full of angry movie-watchers.

"I am very sorry, but there has been a malfunction with the system and the movie will not be able to continue. We will be giving you all free ticket vouchers, as well as you will be allowed to go next door and see the new *Groundhog Day Massacre* for free if you'd like. If any of you would prefer, you can also wait for the next showing in an hour and watch that one instead. Again, I'm deeply sorry for the inconvenience."

There was a collective groan from most of the audience, many of them swearing and marching down the stairs.

"Screw this, let's head home," Bryce said, standing up to leave.

"No, let's go next door and watch *Groundhog Day Massacre 8*. We came all the way out here. I want to be able to watch something for Cleo's birthday," Penny was disappointed with how none of her plans were turning out how she intended.

Cleo was beat and quite tempted to go along with Bryce and head home. He could also see how much it meant to Penny that they stay.

"Hey, it's not your fault. This day is going perfectly. Let's go watch it. It'll be even better than the other movie," Cleo said, going along with her suggestion. Cleo could see Bryce rolling his eyes from over her shoulder.

The theater was mostly empty, and those that were present were mostly teenagers even younger than the three of them.

"We seriously have to sit through this crap? It's like the 8th sequel, none of which are any good. To make matters worse, it's the only PG-13 film of the entire series. Even the death scenes are going to be total crap," Bryce continued his crabby, childlike behavior.

"It'll be fine. We'll see a bunch of moronic twenty something's thinking they can outsmart a ruthless killer. They'll go into the dark foreboding basement, or ominous looking forest despite their clear-minded friend saying to turn around," Cleo said, giving his play-by-play of the impending movie. He did this partially because he thought the outplayed storylines were so ridiculous they were actually funny, and partially because he knew it would annoy Bryce. "Then, even as each of their friends dies, one by one, their morbid curiosity will propel them to look behind the curtain that sways softly back and forth, earning them a free pass to a gruesome death. Finally, and against all common sense, the brainless main character somehow succeeds in defeating the mass murderer who happens to be his own father's secret twin."

Cleo and Penny were both laughing hysterically at his rendition of the movie.

"But wait!" Penny yelled, deciding to jump into the fun. "Just before the credits roll the evil twin rises from the dead and lunges at the screen!"

"SHHH!!!" Someone shouted from a few rows behind them as the lights dimmed.

Penny and Cleo's cackling grew louder.

"If you guys don't shut up I'm leaving you here," Bryce said, glaring at the two of them.

Neither of them had any desire to walk 30 miles in the rain, so they did their best to control their glee, exchanging some not-so-serious looks as their second feature presentation of the hour started. The movie was accompanied by more laughter than ever should be with multiple homicides and buckets of incredibly fake looking blood. 98 minutes after the film started, 142 minutes after they arrived to the theater, and nearly 360 after they left Cleo's driveway, the movie was finally over.

"We almost nailed that entire movie. The killer ended up being the mother, not the father's twin, and I'm a little disappointed they never went into a forest. But all in all, we were almost spot on," Cleo said as they got back into the car to head home.

Penny snorted loudly, trying not to lose them their car riding privileges with more laughter.

"That was the biggest waste of an hour and a half of my life," Bryce said, pulling the car back onto the dark and now foggy road.

"Even more than the two hours we spent waiting for a new tire?" Cleo said, trying to make his friend crack even a hint of a smile.

"Yes, even more than that," Bryce refused to let go of his grumpy frown.

Their return trip was much closer to the 30-minute mark that it should have been. No flat tires or traffic accidents delayed them this time.

They first stopped by Penny's home to drop her off. The rain showers had turned into nothing more than a misty sprinkle, and the fog was barely visible by the time they pulled up to her house.

"So did your birthday live up to your expectations?" she asked as she and Cleo stepped out of the car.

"Seeing as how I didn't have any, they far exceeded them," Cleo said, moving towards her door to hop into the front seat. "But seriously, even with all the little missteps it was great. Thank you."

"You are more than welcome," she said giving him a hug.

"See you at school on Monday Penny," he said hopping back into the car.

Bryce did not echo Cleo's goodbye. Almost before Cleo's door was shut all the way, he pulled back onto the road.

"Nothing at all going on huh?" Bryce said, tilting his head the way a parent does when they know their child is lying.

"What are you talking about?"

"Forget it," Bryce shook his head.

Nothing was said between them for the last few blocks as they pulled up to Bryce's home.

"Thanks for tonight man," Cleo said as he turned to walk next door to his own home.

"Yup, no problem. Later," Bryce said, walking up to his house without so much as a *Happy Birthday*.

With the hourglass-stopping celebration with his friends finally finished, Cleo dragged himself through the front door, hoping to lie in bed and attempt to process what he had gone through that morning. However, when he walked through the living room he realized any rendezvous with the sandman would have to be placed on hold.

"Cleo, you're home. Happy Birthday," his father spoke groggily from the couch. "How was the game? Did we win?" he asked, clearly not aware of where Cleo had been for the entire day.

"We went to a movie, not the game. It was ok I guess. We didn't get to see the movie we wanted. We had to settle for this really cheesy horror movie." He glanced at the dining room table and saw a birthday cake adorned with sixteen candles. It had the words **Happy Birthday Clio** scrawled across the top, surrounded by frosting balloons.

> *What a sad excuse for a birthday cake, even for a store-bought, and Clio...really?*

"Oh well, at least you had fun with your friends. I got that for you. Sorry about your name. I didn't notice that they spelled it wrong until I got home. Would you like me to cut you a slice?" his father asked, noticing him looking at the cake.

> *Not particularly, but considering you actually remembered this year, I guess I have to, don't I?*

"Sure, thanks," he said, moving to sit at the table.

"I wasn't sure if you were going to have dinner or not, so I also made you your favorite. Macaroni and Bleu cheese, sprinkled with pieces of chicken and bacon. I have it in the oven. Do you want any?" Michael cut Cleo a big slice of the cake, getting as much of a sugary balloon that he could.

"Yeah, that sounds great. I'll take a little bit. Thanks," Cleo said, his stomach aching from the mere thought of stuffing any more food into it.

> *I wouldn't be surprised if I throw it up later, but I can't let such a rare occurrence go to waste.*

His father walked into the kitchen and returned with a generous portion of his delectable macaroni and cheese.

"You remember when we used to have bouncy castles, clowns and paintball battles for my birthdays," Cleo said to his father wistfully.

"Yeah, I was worried you'd never grow out of such extravagant birthdays. It's so much easier to plan these days," Michael said, returning to the table with Cleo's second dinner.

> *Must have taken a whole ten minutes to plan this one, huh dad?* – Cleo thought bitterly.

"Would you be terribly upset if I didn't sing you Happy Birthday? Your brother is finally asleep and I don't want to wake him up, and to be honest I'm really not up for singing."

> *That's unlikely, he won't be asleep for at least another hour or two.* – Cleo doubted, taking a bite of his birthday dessert.

Linus was only six-years-old, yet he already suffered from insomnia. The simple task of a normal 8 o'clock bedtime routinely turned into at least an hour or two of tossing and turning for the young boy. Cleo was the only one who knew anything about his brother's restless nights. Linus rarely made any noise, and their father never bothered checking on either of them after they went to bed. It was not only at bedtime that Linus didn't speak. Linus was an abnormally quiet 1st grader. He almost never spoke unless he was asked a direct question.

His teacher mentioned to their father the possibility that Linus was autistic. Michael immediately dismissed the idea.

"He's just a recluse. There's nothing wrong with him," he responded defensively.

> *I'm sure dad is right. God knows what he will already have to deal with.* – Cleo thought as he took a bite of his favorite meal. *Mom's dead, Dad is never around. He's already going to be made fun of for his name. Last thing he needs is for mean kids to ridicule him for being autistic. I still can't believe they did that. Who names their kids Linus and Cleo?*

Cleo's mom, a history buff her whole life, had a borderline unhealthy fascination with Greek and Roman mythology. She was named after the muse of poetry and she wanted to continue the family tradition with her children. Cleo's moniker was after another muse, the muse of history.

"So I *am* named after a girl?" Cleo once asked his mother to confirm what some of his peers had alleged.

"Technically, but her name was spelled with an I. Yours is with an E. So now it's a boy's name," she tried to justify.

"Where did Linus's name come from? It doesn't sound like a girl's at all," he asked.

"Linus was the name of the son of Calliope," she responded after a slight hesitation.

"Wait, you mean to tell me you named me, the first born, after a girl. But Linus, the younger *boy* after the "real"," he motioned air-quotes with his fingers, "Calliope's son? Are you kidding me?"

"Well, to be honest son, I was hoping our second kid would be a girl. So then, I could have both of my children named after muses. We were going to stop at two, so I never planned...we never planned," she said catching herself, "on naming any of our kids Linus. Don't worry, Cleo and Linus both are beautiful names. Don't let anyone tell you differently," she said.

> *I can't believe I was so mad over something so petty.* – He thought, forcing another bite of cake into his mouth. Hanging from the wall on the far side of the room was a family portrait, the only one containing both of his parents, Linus and himself. It was taken two months before her disappearance.

"Dad, how'd you and mom meet again?" He asked his father. Cleo remembered exactly how they met; he just wanted to talk about something to break the uncomfortable silence in the room.

His parents had told him the story many times before. It was back when they were both in college. Calliope submitted an article to the school's paper where Michael was one of the editors. He was so moved by the content, he knew he had to meet its author. He wrote her back, requesting they meet for coffee.

Cleo's father is self-admittedly a hopeless romantic, and he always said that the moment she walked into the café it was love at first sight. Calliope on the other hand always joshed him, saying it took her many more than one sight to fall for Michael.

Their romance blossomed quickly and they were married a month before Cleo's birth. When Cleo asked them if they married because of him his father answered, "Of course not. It may have expedited the process, but we would have gotten married whether you were in the picture or not," followed by a hearty laugh.

On this night however, his father did not relay the tale back to Cleo. His response was curt and dry.

"We've told you many times before. I don't want to rehash it again. Why do you even want to hear it again?" He sounded hurt by the question and avoided eye contact with his son, as if rekindling the memory would be too painful to bear.

"I've just been thinking about her a lot today. I feel like I'm beginning to forget things about her. I'm not even sure I remember the sound of her voice."

> *Whoever that girl was doesn't count. She didn't sound anything like her. I know it.*

His dad looked at him for a moment without moving or saying a word.

"Stay here," he abruptly got up from the table and left the room.

"I..." Cleo started to say.

> *I didn't mean to upset him so much.*

After a few moments his father returned, with an old-fashioned tape recorder in his hands.

"What is that?" Cleo asked, while his father placed it on the table.

His dad did not answer but simply pushed the play button.

"Hey you, I must have just missed you. I'm getting ready to fly out of here. Tell the boys I love them and I'll see them soon. Goodbye sweetie, I love you," the sound of his mother's voice played over the antiquated answering machine.

His dad stopped the tape.

"I've listened to this message almost every day since she died. They are the last words I'll ever hear your mother say. You're not alone son." He looked up at the portrait and a tear fell down his cheek. "I have that same fear. Every single moment of every single day."

The sudden burst of emotion took Cleo by surprise. Even after his mother died, his father rarely wept in front of him.

I...I don't know what to say.

"I'm sorry."

He reached over and put his hand on his father's shoulder.

For the remainder of the meal there was an awkward silence. His father's face was red with embarrassment. He felt weak from crying in front of his son, on his birthday no less. Neither knew how to break the thick ice that was present between them.

Cleo and his father never had effective communication with one another. Cleo always had a much deeper connection with his mother. It was so strong that after her death Cleo silently wished that his father could have switched places with her. It was one thing he and his father had in common.

Cleo hurried through the last bites of his food.

"Thanks. Sorry I'm not hungry enough to have seconds. We had kind of a big dinner. I'm really tired, I'm going to bed now. Good night dad," he said, cleaning his plate.

"Good night son. Happy Birthday," his father said, his hollow voice proof that birthdays were no longer the gleeful celebrations that they used to be.

Cleo gave his father a weak embrace before retiring to bed, defeated by complete and utter exhaustion and a stomach stretched to its very limits.

Present Day

Cleo took the page of his mother's book and placed it gently into his desk drawer, on top of the now altered copy of Verne's *Journey*.

> *That settles it then. If this is indeed all real, then I need to find whoever this Ramiel is.*

Cleo was awake at 8am on a Saturday, an event that virtually never occurred. He had only slept for about eight hours and still felt weary from his trip into the heart of the planet. On the upside, the weekend had finally arrived so he had plenty of time to research the claim of the woman bearing an unnerving resemblance to his deceased mother. However, he also had to contend with the fear of what he may discover.

> *What's wrong with me? Who am I? What am I? –* He wondered as he lay in bed.

He got up typed *Twice Told Tales* into the search engine of his computer. Aside from a shop in Ashland, Ohio and another in Synecdoche, New York, there was nothing listed anywhere near the west coast.

"Alright, let's try the old fashioned route." He went into the living room and grabbed the North Bend phone book, which was barely thicker than an issue of Sports Illustrated. Listed under the bookstores heading were only two companies. Fortunately, one of them was the shop he was looking for.

"It can't be a coincidence this place is only four miles away," he said, writing down the address.

Due to a lack of a driver's license, and a car, he resigned himself to pull his bike out of the garage and pedal the four miles. The weather had cleared up since the previous day. The rain was absent, and all he had to contend with was a manageable sheet of fog blanketing the city. That being said, it would not have made much of a difference to Cleo. He was so lost in thought that he did not remember a single foot of the trip. It could have been 20 degrees outside, hailing and trembling with periodic earthquakes and he still would not have been roused from his thoughts. He barely flinched at a truck slamming on his breaks and honking furiously as Cleo rode through an intersection without bothering to slow down.

What am I doing? Who is this Ramiel?

Was that really my mother?

What am I?

Could she really be alive?

Questions devoid of answers flooded his mind.

Though his consciousness focused on seemingly unanswerable questions, his subconscious somehow knew the destination. He instinctively turned down roads he was barely aware even existed. The neighborhood consisted mainly of small townhouse residences with a few ma-and-pa shops interspersed. As he rode past *The Tortoise and the Hair Salon,* he came to a building veiled by eight-foot tall emerald green arborvitae trees. Its only evidence of being a business was an old dingy wooden sign hanging from a short rusted metal rod standing in a narrow opening in the trees. The sign was barely legible and read **Twice Told Tales.**

No wonder I've never seen it before. It's almost invisible unless you're standing on the front doorstep.

Cleo walked down a stone path leading to a small brick building. The shop looked like it had been there longer than the town itself. The quaint building had vines weaving in and out of its faded brick façade, creating a life-sized checkerboard pattern. Seasons of greenery snaked down from the roof towards the dirt below. The windows were all stained glass and refused to reveal what lay inside. Just above the front door was a miniaturized sphinx head attached to the outside wall. At the foot of the door was a doormat that read, **Warning – Adventures Abound Lay Within.**

> *I feel as if I've been here before. But that's not possible. I didn't even know it existed until last night.* – Cleo thought, hanging his helmet from the handlebars of his bicycle. Despite reservations about the sudden déjà vu, he leaned his bike up against the building and walked inside.

The interior of the shop was much like the outside, covered in years of age and deterioration. Cobwebs strung about in every corner while layers of dust covered nearly every shelf, counter and book in the shop. Its diminutive appearance from the street proved to be deceiving. The store was narrow but long, resembling a bowling alley that stretched on forever. Piles and piles of books occupied nearly every inch of real estate.

Cleo walked towards the counter, it being manned by an elderly gentleman. Across from him was a woman who looked almost as old as he did.

He took a glance at Cleo over the woman's shoulder. "Welcome to Twice Told Tales," he said, giving Cleo the sincerest of smiles.

> *I get the feeling that he rarely gets multiple customers in here at the same time.* – Cleo thought, giving the man a customary nod of his head in acknowledgment.

"I'm looking for that old classic book. It's the one that is really popular. I was hoping you would have a copy?" The woman asked the old man. Such a ridiculous question would have annoyed most anyone else, but he simply smiled and began running through various titles and storylines that it could be.

> *Who knows how long that's going to take. I may as well look around until he is done with her.* – He supposed.

The shop contained such an astonishing amount of titles that Cleo did not know where to begin to look. There didn't seem to be a method to the organizational madness, save for it being *very* loosely alphabetized.

The age of the books made the shop seem more like a museum than a bookstore. Leather bindings bore decades of wear, cracking up and down their spines. Covers and dust jackets more wrinkled than the face of the librarian at Cleo's school. The shop's smell was akin to an old tanner's workshop.

"I thought I read a lot, but I haven't heard of the majority of these titles."

Cleo looked around at the books on the shelves in his immediate vicinity. The order in which they were organized was clearly something only the shop's employees themselves understood. *Moby Dick, Dracula, The Iliad, Fahrenheit 451,* all shelved cover to cover, regardless of genre, author or era in which they were written.

After perusing through shelf after shelf, he noticed a hallway at the back of the shop, almost entirely obscured by the shelves of books. Cleo looked around to see if anyone was nearby.

The old man must be working alone.

Realizing that he was alone, he walked back towards the hallway.

It turned out to be more of an extended doorway leading into a closet. The closet was like the rest of the shop, packed with various books of varying centuries. The big difference was that none of them were caked in the ages of dust, like the ones on the sales floor.

These all look like they are handled on a regular basis.

Cleo skimmed through the titles until he found one that rested on his own bookshelf at home.

"Watership Down. One of my favorites that mom used to read to me as a kid," he said, picking the tale about a group of rabbits looking for a new home up off the shelf. He flipped open the book and began skimming the tattered pages. He stopped on one word that he did not remember ever seeing before. **Ramiel.**

"I've read this book more times than I can count. I know for an absolute certainty that there is no character with that name. There is no way this is a coincidence," he muttered under his breath.

That can only mean one thing.

He set the book down and frantically began searching the shelves for one title in particular that he knew very well. As fate would have it, the precise title was on the next shelf down. *The Wonderful Wizard of Oz.* The same Oz in which he had gone traipsing through just two days earlier.

He quickly skimmed the pages until he noticed the same name popping up on multiple pages.

I am certain that the Great Wizard of Oz did not have a name.
Yet here he is, referred to as Ramiel, the Great Wizard of Oz.

Cleo continued to scan the book's pages. Printed on nearly every single one were details that should not exist, unless one simple fact was true.

He can do it too.

Cleo flipped through them until he came to a stop on an especially altered scene.

Dorothy, Tin Man, Lion and Scarecrow stood before Ramiel, the Great Wizard. With the horrid witch finally dispatched, they desperately were hoping he would live up to his end of the deal.

"Scarecrow, come forward," the Wizard calls out as the straw man wobbly walks in front. "I bestow upon you a flame-resistant racing suit to protect you from your greatest weakness."

Scarecrow retreats to his friends, as Tin Man is the next to come forward.

"Tin Man, I give you one of my greatest inventions. A can of WD-40, so you may never suffer from stiff joints again."

As Tin Man backs up the Lion takes a step forward.

"Lion, this here is the best kind of courage. It is a bottle of liquid courage."

Lastly, Dorothy stands and walks up to the Great Wizard, Ramiel.

"Please Great Wizard, return me home to Kansas. That's all I ask for."

"Your path home goes through the Witch of the South, Glinda. Go there and she will return you to your family."

"Thank you," Dorothy says, grateful for the final directions to go home.

"Before you leave, take this one final gift from me," Ramiel says handing her a postcard. On it is a picture of Dorothy's farm in Kansas. Across the bottom is the simple phrase, "There's No Place Like Home."

"Um...thank you," Dorothy says unsure of what it is supposed to mean.

Cleo closed the book and stared at its cover.

"Is Ramiel the man behind the counter?" Cleo questioned aloud. "Is it possible that he can also do what I'm capable of?"

Suddenly a gravelly voice spoke from behind him.

"And just what do you think we are capable of doing?"

The low, rough tone caused a chill to rush up Cleo's spine. His fingers released the book they were gripping. The crashing of the book to the floor was white noise to the loud thumping of Cleo's heart in his chest.

CHAPTER
4

Homer's Homeward Bound

Cleo slowly turned around to see the face that accompanied the deep voice. Standing above him was the old man behind the counter. He clearly had lost the youth in his body decades ago, but his eyes appeared to have aged for many more centuries. The length of his light gray beard appeared not to have been trimmed in Cleo's lifetime. It hung far below his chin, extending to the top of his sternum.

Cleo's fear over what the old man's intentions could be robbed him of his ability to speak.

> *This isn't good. This is not at all how I wanted this to go down. What do I say now? I don't know anything about this man, save for what a woman, that may or may not actually exist, told me. What if he's dangerous? Just because he looks like Father Time doesn't mean I can trust him. He could want to kill me or study me.*

"So what is this talent that you believe we have in common?" pressed the man. He stared intensely at Cleo, studying him as if he were some sort of rare and unique specimen.

Do I lie and play dumb? I did come here to find answers. It would be ridiculous of me to make something up. What if this was all a mistake?

"*Wonderful Wizard of Oz*, huh? It is a marvelous book, an absolute classic. That version is probably a little different than the one you're used to though, isn't it?" The man continued talking over Cleo's silence. "Now I'll ask again, what do you believe it is that *we* can do?" The look on his face was a warning to Cleo that he had better say something soon.

"I...I met a woman in a story. It was Jules Verne's *Journey to the Center of the Earth*, to be exact. She told me to find this shop and more specifically, to find you. She said that you would be able to help me."

"You met a woman *in a story?* Exactly what do you mean by *in* a story?"

Cleo picked up the book lying on the ground beside him. He flipped open to a page containing Ramiel's name.

"I think you know exactly what I mean," he said showing Ramiel's name to him. "I know you're him. You're Ramiel," he said matter-of-factly, yet seeking confirmation of the idea he already believed to be fact.

Ramiel narrowed his gaze at the young man.

"Yes, I am. But what, may I ask, makes you think that the preposterous idea that I can somehow travel into a book, is truth?"

"Because I can do it too," Cleo's confidence rising with the truth now out in the open.

"Very curious...What may I ask, is your name?" Ramiel said, unflinching at Cleo's revelation.

"Cleo," he answered without hesitation.

"Cleo," Ramiel repeated. The name seemed to spark a hint of recognition in the old man. He folded his hands together beneath his chin and took one long, deliberate blink.

"I won't try to deceive you any longer. What you perceive to be truth... is. I am the same as you," he finally admitted.

"Ramiel, what exactly is this? Why can I do it? Why can we do this? Is there something wrong with us? Am I even...human?"

"Know this Cleo; there is nothing *wrong* with you or with us. We are as human as anyone else around us. We are simply gifted," Ramiel spoke sternly. "I've often thought of people like us as magi, shamans, superheroes, perhaps even a sort of lesser God."

Cleo started to picture what Ramiel would look like as a superhero, dressed in spandex with his beard hanging out of the mask. He chuckled to himself at the thought, but decided not to say anything.

"Cleo you are a very unique individual. Never think of yourself as anything but."

Cleo had not thought of himself as unique over the last few days. Freak, weird, delusional, psychologically unstable; these were the types of words that Cleo had begun to associate with himself. However, unique had a much more positive connotation to it, a word he much preferred over considering himself as an alien oddity.

"How long ago did your ability show itself?" he asked Cleo.

"Two days, on my 16th birthday."

"Your 16th birthday, huh? Not surprising, that seems to the most common time in which it emerges. Happy belated birthday I might add."

"Thank you."

Ramiel walked around Cleo to one of the shelves behind him.

"No, not this one. Not this one either," he mumbled to himself as he rifled through the books.

"What are you looking for?" Cleo asked.

"Aha!" He cried jubilantly, pulling a particularly ancient text off the dusty shelf.

"How about, as my birthday present to you, I show you how to use this newfound gift of yours? And I'll do so in one of my all-time favorite tales, *The Odyssey*."

"You can bring people with you?"

"Of course I can. You can also, you know."

Cleo's face lit up at the prospect of bringing Penny, Linus, or even burying the hatchet with Bryce by carrying him along into a magical world.

"Alright Miyagi, I'll be your Daniel-san," Cleo said with a playful bow.

Ramiel looked confused, clearly not understanding the cultural reference.

"Yeah, you can go ahead and teach me. Thanks," Cleo said sheepishly.

"Great! Well, first things first. You need to know *how* to bring others along with you. Wait here a second," he briefly walked out of his hidden backroom, before returning with two chairs.

"Alright, please sit down and listen carefully," he said, placing the two chairs side by side.

"Before I show you *how* to bring someone else in, you need to know a few extremely important things. Our ability is far more dangerous than you realize. While it enables us to escape to countless paradises, it also exposes us to perils that originate from the most creative minds in history. This risk increases exponentially when we bring someone along with us, especially when they do not possess our gift. You must stick close to them, at all times, for their escape from whatever piece of literature you enter relies solely on you taking them out. Without you, they will be stuck forever. Do you understand?"

"Yes," Cleo was quick to agree.

> *This doesn't seem all that dangerous. Especially considering we can leave whenever we want. Just get to the good part already!* – He thought, not overly concerned with Ramiel's dire warning.

"Good, now I'm going to place my hand on your shoulder while I read. Be still, we must stay in contact the entire time if I am to bring you inside," he warned Cleo to prevent or quell any jitters that he may have been feeling. Ramiel flipped through the pages of his book until he came to one he liked. He held the book with his free hand and began reading aloud.

"And we came to the land of the Cyclopes, a fierce, lawless people who never lift a hand to plant or plough but just leave everything to the immortal gods."

Cleo first began to feel his consciousness slip away. Then he felt a slight tug on his arm.

"All the crops they require spring up unsown and untilled..."

The words trailed off as the two men, at different ends of their respective lifelines, were swept into the very pages before them.

Cleo realized he was unintentionally squeezing his eyes shut with every muscle in his face. When the tingling sensation that permeated through his body stopped, he reopened them, revealing an ancient Greek ship docked off the beach of a tropic island.

"Welcome to the Island of the Cyclops, Cleo. Located in Homer's nearly three thousand year old epic poem, *The Odyssey*," exclaimed Ramiel in his best tour guide voice.

Odysseus' ship was one of a baker's dozen anchored in the seas off the island's coast. Cleo and Ramiel stood on the mostly vacant ship deck as Odysseus and his men made their way onto the island to investigate. There were only two men staying on board to look after the ship. Cleo and Ramiel walked to the edge to get a better look at the island. The island was a remarkable sight.

"You see up there at the top, where those mountainous caverns are?" Ramiel asked, pointing to the apex of the island.

"I'd barely call this a mountain, but yes I see it."

"That is where the Cyclops themselves dwell. They are merciless man-eating giants with one-eye and a hatred for everyone and everything."

The mountain was not particularly large in stature. It dominated the majority of the island but was much smaller than the ones where Cleo lived. The ship docked at the eastern edge of the island, which enabled Cleo to see the majority of it without leaving the ship. There were countless numbers of wild goat grazing in a pasture at the northern base of the mountain. On the southern side was a beautiful meadow that seemed entirely undisturbed by men and beast alike.

"It's gorgeous."

"Yes, it truly is. Although we'll see if you still believe that when we meet its inhabitants."

"If this place is so dangerous, I don't understand why you would bring me here?" questioned Cleo.

"There are multiple reasons. First off, it is a great way to see a sample of the horrors you may someday face. At the same time, it is also a tale where it is not overly difficult to avoid said horrors. It also happens to be one of my favorite mythological tales in existence."

"What's so great about it?"

"It's the ultimate tale of persistence, faith and overcoming overwhelming odds. With his cunning, resourcefulness and patience, Odysseus is one of the greatest characters ever written. Tell me, have you ever heard of the great Captain Nemo from *20,000 Leagues under the Sea*?"

"I vaguely remember him. I read that book a few years ago, although I couldn't tell you much of the plot."

"Well his name is largely derived from this story. You'll see why later on." He beckoned Cleo to follow him. "See down there. That is Odysseus and his men. He has been on a voyage trying to get home after the infamous Trojan War. He is the epitome of the will to find your way home. To find where you belong," Ramiel said pensively.

"How long have you been able to enter stories?" Cleo asked, changing the subject.

Ramiel looked away from Cleo towards the men climbing the mountain.

"Too long..."

"Do you still enter them?"

"Occasionally, but not as much anymore given my age and frailty. And... there are other reasons too," he said, looking down at his delicate limbs.

Cleo wanted to ask what those other reasons were but he felt it wasn't his place to do so.

"There also hasn't been anyone to mentor in quite a long time."

"So there are others like us then, other people that can go inside of stories?" Cleo said, intrigued at the thought of others with his uniqueness.

"There used to be many more of us that could. Over the years, it has become rarer and rarer to be born with this gift. You are the first person I have met with this ability in quite some time. It's been almost 20 years since anyone else has come along with it."

Cleo was about to ask who that other person was, when Ramiel put his hand on the young man's shoulder again.

"Alright, enough chatter. It is time for your next lesson. I want you to clear your mind of everything. Think of nothing but the book in which you entered."

Cleo had so many different thoughts circulating his mind that it was not the easiest of tasks to focus on only *The Odyssey*.

"Concentrate on the very pages of the book. Their smell, their feel, the ink itself printed on them. Even if you have never read it before, the entire story will become...an open book," Ramiel said with a smile, taking pleasure in his self-perceived cleverness.

Cleo tried to picture what Ramiel was telling him but he struggled mightily. The minutes passed with no success. Whenever he felt like something was to take place, his mind wandered. It wandered to his mother's doppelganger in Oz, or the world Verne created. It imagined all the places he could take Penny. It worried of the unpredictable reaction that was likely to come from Bryce.

"Unfortunately Cleo, this is not something I can show you. You must learn it yourself. It will take practice, but it is paramount that you do so. For now, I will take us to where we need to go. Before I do, it is imperative that we keep as quiet as possible from here on Cleo. Our presence must be unknown at all times."

"Why are you so worried of some make believe giants? If it gets too hairy you can just take us out of there in an instant."

"It's not as easy and quick as you think. Particularly when there is a twenty-foot tall monster baring down on you with teeth the size of your arm and an appetite that is particular for anything with flesh and bones. You will see that what has always been myth, fantasy or pure imagination to you, now becomes real."

"How are we supposed to talk to each other then?"

"Easy. Have you noticed yet that you can read people's thoughts when you're inside a story?" he asked.

Cleo remembered the few times before that he accidentally peered into the minds of some of the characters around him.

"Umm...yeah, but I have no idea how it happened. One minute they were talking to me, the next I could hear what they were thinking. I don't know how to work it."

"It's actually quite simple. Do not hear with your ears. Listen with your mind. Project your words not with your mouth, but with this," Ramiel said pointing to his head.

"Oh ok, that sounds super simple," Cleo said sarcastically.

"You go first. Project a thought into my head. Then listen to my response."

You kind of smell like burnt toast. - Cleo thought in an attempt to test Ramiel's skill.

I resent that statement. – The voice popped into Cleo's mind as easy as if it were spoken aloud.

"Whoa, it worked," Cleo said, shocked that he was able to get it on his first try.

"It'll be more difficult when you're trying with a normal character, and not me. Nonetheless, that was good work. Now let us get going. Remember, silence is definitely a virtue today."

"Isn't the saying '*patience* is a virtue'?" Cleo remarked sarcastically.

"There are many virtues, and today silence is the golden one. Now come so we can get a closer look."

Cleo's palms were clammy as he gripped the old man's brittle hands. Moments later Ramiel temporarily shifted them out of the plane of existence.

One tingly, cool breeze later and the odd couple instantaneously found themselves crouching behind an enormous boulder mere feet outside of the cave at the apex of the mountain. The boulder was adjacent to a trail that led up to the peak, yet was large enough that it still obscured them from the view of the company of soldiers walking towards them.

Why are they even coming up here Ramiel? Even I can tell that this is clearly a bad idea. – Cleo asked telepathically, hoping he was using his ability of mind-speak correctly.

Because Cleo, they are in dire need of food and water. If they do not find some soon, then there is a good chance that everyone on those ships will die. Odysseus will risk almost anything to protect his men. – He answered, motioning for Cleo to back up slightly further out of their view. *He may not be the most renowned mythological hero, but in my humble opinion, he is the greatest of them all.*

The enormity of the cave was simply breathtaking. The entrance was no less than 12 feet tall by 10 feet wide. Cleo could have driven a semi-truck inside with room to spare on all sides. The rising sun lit up the inside of the cave. It was full with baskets the size of hatchback cars, all containing cheese, bread and fruit. Next to those were bowls of milk that could be family size swimming pools. Near the back were pens ballooning with sheep, double the size of any on Earth, all baaing to one another synchronically. The sight of all of this potential nourishment caused the starving sailors to salivate and foolishly run into the unknown cave.

"Sir, permit us to take the cheeses and drive the sheep out down to our ships. We could immediately set sail out of this forsaken land." One of the soldiers pleaded with Odysseus.

"Not yet," Odysseus spoke. The next thing Cleo heard did not come from Odysseus's mouth. *I must see what kind of creature is the owner of this cave.*

> *His curiosity is going to cost him dearly, isn't it Ramiel?* – Cleo asked to no answer.

"Let us sit and eat first. If whoever dwells here does not return by the time we are finished, then we will proceed to the ships." Odysseus resumed speaking his thoughts aloud.

He didn't need to wait very long to have his curiosity satisfied, for immediately after they made their offering to the gods, a giant one-eyed creature of gargantuan size and strength casually strolled toward the cave.

Every bone in Cleo's body wanted to get up and sprint down the mountain at full speed.

> *Holy...*

> *Shhh, stay still Cleo. He doesn't even know we are here. This is Polyphemus. He is the greatest of the Cyclopes and a son of Poseidon.* – Ramiel thought, firmly gripping the back of Cleo's coat to keep him in place, in case his breaking nerves caused him to flee.

The lumbering giant walked past Cleo and Ramiel without the slightest inkling that they were even there. He walked into the cave where Odysseus and his men were huddled together near the back.

Look at how much firewood he's carrying. I've seen logging trucks with smaller payloads. – Cleo thought as Polyphemus tossed the giant bundle of wood to the side without as much as a grunt of exertion. He quickly lit some of the timber, creating a bonfire in the cave. As the flames danced towards the ceiling, Polyphemus finally noticed his uninvited guests.

"Who are these adventurers who come to my cave? Be they friends or pirates?" The Cyclops asked calmly, without a hint of fear or surprise in his voice.

Odysseus's response was inaudible to Cleo and Ramiel and they dared not move any closer to hear any better. Whatever the response was, it could not have amused the one-eyed monster for he immediately seized two of Odysseus's men and devoured them whole.

Cleo stared in horror into the cave. Just then, Odysseus looked up and saw Cleo. The two of them held eye contact for only a second, but Cleo saw clearly the fear now present in his eyes. Still savoring the taste of the two soldiers, Polyphemus grabbed a huge boulder from inside the cave and blocked the entrance. The last thing Cleo saw or heard was Odysseus reaching out to him and crying out in horror, "HELP US!"

"Oh God he's eating everyone in there isn't he?" Cleo whispered, forgetting their golden rule and suddenly on the brink of vomiting.

"Not yet. Two full grown men is quite a meal, even for a Cyclops," Ramiel responded, no longer fearing someone or something overhearing his voice.

"Why don't the men kill him? There are so many of them, surely they could overpower him."

"Even if they succeeded, you saw how large that boulder was. It would take a hundred men to move it. Polyphemus's death would secure their fates. They would be entombed with no hope of escape."

"Do they really have much more hope with that monster still breathing?" Cleo asked.

"You'll find out soon enough. There is nothing more to see here. Let us go just a little further," Ramiel said, putting his hand on Cleo's shoulder.

They immediately became a billion little specks of dust, blown away in the swirling wind. For a brief moment all that was left of their existence were their footprints, implanted in the dirt behind the rock where they hid.

As quickly as they disappeared, they reformed back together in almost exactly the same spot, only inches from their prints, still visible in the dirt. The sun was no longer present in the sky. A galaxy of stars sprinkled amongst the full moon had replaced it.

"The night sky is beautiful here isn't it Cleo?" Ramiel said, gazing into the pale moonlight.

Before Cleo could answer, their nighttime serenity was disturbed by the most horrific howl Cleo had ever heard. It shook the entire mountain as if the Earth itself was trembling.

"What was that!?" Cleo cried out to Ramiel, shrinking back tightly against the rock.

"That was Polyphemus shouting out in pain for Odysseus and his men stabbed him square in his single eye, forever blinding him."

> *Do not speak now Cleo, just watch.* – Ramiel spoke into Cleo's mind.

The ground began to shake again as suddenly a squad of Cyclopes, all smaller than Polyphemus, but still gargantuan in size, barreled up the mountain to the cave's entrance. Cleo gasped loudly.

> *Stay silent! Back against the rock Cleo!* –Cleo could hear the urgency even in Ramiel's thoughts.

Cleo could not help his childish curiosity and snuck a peek around the corner of the rock. One of the smaller Cyclopes had heard Cleo's gasp and was lumbering towards their hiding spot.

> *Ramiel, one is coming this way!* – Cleo panicked.

Cleo could smell the monster's stench as it was merely feet from them.

> *Give me your hand! It is no longer safe. We are leaving.*
> – Ramiel thought reaching for Cleo.

Suddenly, the other Cyclops spoke up, stopping the small one that was making his way toward them in his tracks.

> *Wait, he's turning back around.* – He thought, still foolishly looking at the incoming beast.

"What hurts thee, Polyphemus? Does a mortal in this unguarded hour of night oppress thee, by fraud or power?"

"Friends! Nobody hurts me!" Polyphemus yelled, clutching his bloody eye.

"If nobody hurts thee, then it is done by the Gods. Pray to Zeus or your father Neptune."

The Cyclopes returned the boulder to the opening of the cave, walling off whatever curse befell upon Polyphemus. Ignoring their leader's cries, they one-by-one left the area. With his companions retreating from Polyphemus's cave, the small Cyclops lost interest in the noise from behind the rock and strolled back with the rest of his brethren.

> *That was too close Cleo. You MUST be more careful.* – Ramiel silently scolded him.

> *I'm sorry. I will, I promise. I have a question though. Why did the Cyclopes not attack Odysseus? Why did they believe the Gods stabbed him?* – Cleo asked confounded by what just occurred.

> *Because of a previous act of brilliance by Odysseus. Earlier in the day, Odysseus told the giant that his name was Nobody, or Nemo in Latin. Therefore, when he cried to his friends "nobody stabbed him" they took him at his word. They assumed that it had to have been the Gods.* – He answered.

Cleo was actually quite impressed at Odysseus's cleverness.

So the name of Verne's character means Captain Nobody?
— Cleo thought randomly, suddenly connecting the dots.

Yes it does. I'll let you figure out why he named him that on your own. For now, there is one more scene for you to see. This time I want you to move us forward.

I can't promise it'll be very accurate. — Cleo warned.

You will be just fine. Close your eyes and picture the book itself. Think of the story as if it were laid out in front of you, page by page. That if you wanted, you could simply reach out and choose which page to enter. Whether or not you have ever read the book will not matter. It will come to you. — He instructed. *I want you to take us to the morning. Don't forget to keep physical contact with me at all times. I would greatly prefer to be intact when we arrive.*

Cleo had no idea whether or not the old man was joking, but considering his previous lack of a sense of humor he did not want to find out. He gripped Ramiel's shirt very tightly and closed his eyes. One nausea-inducing tug later and they dissolved into thin air. When they reappeared, the moon hadn't moved at all in the night sky.

"At least we're both in one piece," Ramiel said encouragingly. "Try again."

Once again, after some struggle, Cleo removed them from the plane of existence and returned them a fraction of time later.

"Focus on the very words themselves Cleo," Ramiel ordered. "You are straining too hard. You are trying to move us forward to *a page*. I want you to *choose* which page we will go to. Relax, pull the pages from the crevices of your mind, and take us there. Again."

Cleo closed his eyes, took a deep breath and imagined the pages of Ramiel's book sprawled in front of him. Time slowed as its words began to appear before him. He had no awareness of the world around him. All that existed was an endless string of characters at his disposal. It felt as if he were walking through space with each individual letter acting as a star upon which he could stand.

"There," he said aloud, finding the exact sentence he wished to use.

When he opened his eyes, the orange and violet lights accompanying the morning sunrise replaced the silver of the moon resting on the black tapestry of the night sky.

"It worked didn't it! How close are we?"

"You can answer that. Peer into the storyline, tell me where we are."

Cleo closed his eyes and concentrated on pinpointing their location. Gazing into the storyline took him more than a few minutes, but finally he was able to see the precise page where they were located.

"It is the next day. It's exactly where I was aiming," he said to Ramiel, opening his eyes.

"That is correct. It came faster to you this time too," Ramiel said, although Cleo thought for sure the exact opposite was true.

"What have we missed? Are any of them still alive?" Cleo whispered, keeping a worried stare on the cave.

"Some of them, but not all. A few more of Odysseus's men were lost to the stomach of Polyphemus. Now, let us sit here in silence. Odysseus's daring plan is about to come full circle," Ramiel said in admiration of what was about to unfold.

There were no sounds coming from the hilltop. The large rock was still blocking the entrance to Polyphemus's domain, and his fellow Cyclopes were nowhere in sight.

>   Ramiel, why do they think they need some wily plan in the first place? With him blinded, can't they just make a run for it? There is no way he would be able to catch them. – Cleo thought to Ramiel.

>   You have clearly not seen a Cyclops in action. – Ramiel responded psychically.

>   Unfortunately, I missed them the last time they were in town. – Cleo thought sarcastically.

That brought a smile to the generally stiff-faced old man.

Well, you would be surprised at how quick Polyphemus and Cyclopes in general are. Regardless, even if they managed to make it passed him, he could crush them all with a single throw of any of the massive rocks on this mountainside. Moreover, if they somehow managed to dodge the flying boulders and made it to their ships, he would sink every one of their ships before they left the shores.

A loud gurgling growl came from the cave. Cleo tensed up and focused his full attention on the cave. Cleo's hands began unconsciously shaking. Not even the vultures circling overhead could deter his attention from the massive boulder as it slowly moved away from the entrance.

We are in no danger, just be still and watch what happens.
– Ramiel thought to Cleo, trying to reassure his safety.

The now blind giant stumbled to block any potential escape. One by one, the sheep exited his abode. He repeatedly reached down and ran his hands along their backs. Cleo looked more carefully and noticed that the men had tied themselves to the animals' underbellies and were leaving the cave with Polyphemus none the wiser.

Odysseus assumed that Polyphemus would check the backs of the sheep, but not underneath. He assumed correctly. Now all the men are escaping their captivity with Polyphemus not suspecting a thing. – Ramiel preemptively answered Cleo's impending question.

As Polyphemus replaced the boulder to block the entrance, Odysseus and his men cut themselves from the underbellies of the critters and sprinted down the trail towards their ships. Before they were out of earshot Odysseus stopped his retreat, turned towards the mountain and yelled back at the blind giant.

"Cyclops! So he was not such a weakling after all, the man whose friends you meant to overpower and eat in your hollow cave!"

This enraged Polyphemus so much that he hurled giant boulders in the direction of Odysseus's voice, nearly crushing him.

"I am not Nobody: I am Odysseus, son of Laertes, King of Ithaca!"

This last act of hubris will cost Odysseus. Later on, Poseidon, Polyphemus' father, destroys Odysseus's ships, killing all of his men. There is much to learn from Odysseus's triumphs and from his mistakes. – Thought Ramiel to Cleo.

"RAWRRRRR!!" Polyphemus was so angry he grabbed a nearby tree and used his titanic strength to rip it from the ground, roots and all. He swung it around like an oversized tennis racket, sending it crashing into the giant boulder that Ramiel and Cleo had taken shelter behind. The force sent the boulder rolling down the side, nearly crushing both of them.

A loud "UMPF!" came from Ramiel as a dangling branch struck him and sent him hard to the ground just off the side of the path leading down the mountain. Cleo rolled out of the way and ran to the cave's entrance, taking refuge against its stone door.

"Ugh...Ramiel, are you alright?" he called out, forgetting his surroundings.

Polyphemus turned toward Cleo's voice.

"Who is there? Are you one of Odysseus's men, here to fall upon me a lethal strike from the shadows? SHOW YOURSELF!"

Cleo realized in the nick of time that the giant could not see where he was, and scampered off to the side of the cave. Splinters of wood showered over Cleo as Polyphemus hurled the twenty-foot tree in his hand against the cave's entrance.

Ramiel? Are you alright? Can you hear me? – Cleo telepathically asked.

He received nothing but silence in return.

As much of a miracle as it was that Cleo was able to elude such an enormous piece of flying timber with no harm coming to him, he now had an equally large object standing before him and his fallen mentor. Polyphemus was standing perfectly still, pointing his ears in each direction trying to catch the slightest sound from his newest adversaries.

"Did I crush your head like a melon, or are you trembling in fear in a corner?" Polyphemus taunted.

What am I going to do? Ramiel, now would be a really great time to wake up over there. – Cleo tried to will his friend awake.

Cleo's hiding spot would not last for long as the Cyclops slowly began to walk in his direction. He was swinging his arms out in a fanning motion hoping to make contact with Cleo's head. While the beast came closer and closer, Cleo came up with an idea.

Cleo closed his mouth, allowing just a slight crack between his lips.

Moment of truth. – He nervously thought.

"I'm over here you overgrown turnip!" he called out.

The giant stopped in his tracks, turned to his right and suddenly leapt headfirst towards the edge of the cliff. His body sailed through the air, before coming into contact with nothing but the solid earth resting three stories below.

"ARGH!?!" Polyphemus screamed out as his collision with the ground caused the mountain to once again tremor.

Cleo didn't waste any more time and sprinted over to Ramiel who was finally starting to come to.

"What's going on?" Ramiel asked groggily, as Cleo grabbed a hold of his arm.

"Come on, come on," Cleo said as he desperately tried to return them to reality. He thought of every detail of the bookstore as he could. His concentration broke with every snap of tree branch and choleric grunt from Polyphemus as he made his way back to them.

We will NOT die in here.

Cleo redoubled his focus. One by one, the details of the dusty old bookstore became clearer. He felt a tug at his body and opened his eyes. The last thing he saw was the hand of Polyphemus gripping the side of the cliff over which he had tumbled. Before the rest of the irate monster came into view, Cleo and Ramiel vanished from the story, and went crashing onto the floor of *Twice Told Tales*.

"Your exiting of stories really needs some work," Ramiel said, rubbing his sore back.

"Yeah sorry, I was too busy saving us from that one-eyed, tree throwing monster who was trying to eat us." Cleo said good-naturedly and breathing heavily from the exhausting ordeal.

"Thank you for that by the way. How exactly did you make him leap off the cliff?"

"You saw that? I was calling out to you and you didn't respond. I thought you were dead."

"It takes a lot more than that to get rid of me. Right as I opened my eyes, I saw him turn away from you and jump off the cliff. What did you do?" Ramiel asked, genuinely stumped.

"It's a trick I learned a long time ago. I threw my voice in the other direction. I made it sound like I was calling out from the other way. I intended to just get him to turn the other way, not hurl himself off the side," Cleo said rubbing the lump that had formed on the top of his skull.

"I must say, I'm impressed. At least you now know just how dangerous a power this can be. We were both nearly killed on that mountain," Ramiel said, immediately turning his praise into a teaching moment. "Who taught you how to do that little trick?"

"My mother did, sometime when I was younger. I don't remember when," Cleo said, struggling to recall the lost memory.

"She sounds like an amazing woman," Ramiel said.

"She was. She's sort of who told me to find you."

"Sort of told you?"

"She's the woman I met both in Oz and again in Verne's book."

"Really," Ramiel said with a mixture of concern and intrigue in his voice. "What's her name?"

"Her name...was...Calliope," Cleo answered after a moment's pause.

At the sound of her name, Ramiel's eyes widened.

"Calliope? Calliope Bailey is your mother?"

"Yes. You knew my mother? Does that mean that really was her inside of the books?"

"Yes, I know her. They would have been versions of her, obviously not the real thing." He picked up the copy of *The Odyssey* and opened it up to the chapter they had just exited. Throughout its pages, newly typed words had been magically embossed upon them, chronicling in perfect detail their excursion. "When we enter a story, we forever change it. We become a new character, permanently imprinted on the pages, as if the authors themselves wrote us, but that occurs only on the specific copy that we enter. Otherwise we'd have far greater problems to contend with."

"How exactly did you know my mother?"

"She was my...greatest student." Ramiel suddenly looked away from the book in his hands and into Cleo's eyes. "If she is your mother, why didn't she teach you how to handle this power?"

"Because she's dead. She died a little over four years ago." Cleo's chest ached as he spoke the words.

All of the color drained from Ramiel's face. The sudden paleness seemed to add at least a decade onto his already well-aged face.

"I am so sorry Cleo. How did it happen?" he asked.

"My grandma had passed away a few weeks before. She lived in Colorado so my mother had to fly to her home in order to retrieve some of her stuff. She was piloting herself in a little plane and it went down in the mountains. What is especially strange about the whole thing is that the authorities never found the body. When police searched the wreckage, they didn't find any trace of her at all. It was as if she vanished from the plane."

Ramiel pulled a nearby stool to him and sat down.

"You said she was bringing back your grandmother's belongings? Do you know what they were?"

"Yeah, just some of her clothes, jewelry, knick-knacks, also all of her books. My grandmother had a good-sized collection. Nothing to this scale, but it still had to be at least a hundred or so. Much of it was destroyed in the crash. I still have a few dozen books or so, a couple of the knick-knacks. Not much of a consolation prize for losing your mother though, is it?" Cleo tried to conceal his pain with an awkward laugh.

A twinkle came across Ramiel's eyes. He softly rubbed his beard, as he delved deeply into the recesses of his mind.

"You still have some of the books she was bringing back?"

"Yeah, but who cares. Out of everything I just told you that's what you're concerned about?"

"Cleo, I can say, with an almost absolute certainty, your mother did not die in that plane crash."

"What do you mean?"

"I mean, your mother may still be alive."

CHAPTER 5

Derrie's Caulfield

"Cleo, listen. It's not my intention to get your hopes up. But I think it's possible that your mother *is* alive."

Cleo's mind went blank at Ramiel's insinuation.

"What are you talking about?"

"There is a chance that your mother is not dead, but trapped in a story."

Cleo scrunched up his forehead, skeptical of the plausibility of this old man's idea.

"Let's look at the facts. Your mother possessed the same ability as we do. She was travelling with a box full of books. She was an experienced pilot, whom probably had known for at least a small amount of time that her plane was going down. I would be willing to bet that the reason why they never found a body was that there is no body to find. She jumped into one of those books just before the plane crashed."

"But..." Cleo tried to interject.

"Just wait, I'm not finished." Ramiel seemed to be saying his thoughts as they came to him, almost unsure of where the next one would lead. "It would have been an incredible risk. If the book she went into burned up, she likely would have died, but it would have been her only hope of surviving the crash."

"How do you, or she for that matter, know that it would work?" Cleo continued to try to suppress his growing hope over such a preposterous idea.

"I don't, and I doubt she would have either," Ramiel said coldly. "You have to realize Cleo, that all of this is purely speculation. Would she have really died if the book she retreated into were destroyed, or rather, would she be trapped in the book forever? Is the book she may have jumped into one of the ones that were indeed destroyed? Your guess is as good as mine, and likely hers as well. But in those moments, of her facing life and death, she would have had no other choice."

> *For me, for Linus, for dad…she would have taken any risk, no matter how dangerous. Do I dare let myself hope?*

Cleo had just recently accepted the fact that he would never see his mother again. Hope, it was both the thing he needed the most, but also what caused him the most pain.

"For argument's sake, let's assume your idea is true. Let's say that the book she went into is perfectly safe, sitting on one of my shelves at home. I should be able to simply find her name in one of them, go inside and bring her back home, right?" Cleo asked, beginning to give in to the idea.

"Well, it wouldn't be that simple Cleo. There are multiple problems with that scenario. First off, I imagine that there is no written trace of her existence in any of your books. She was my only pupil who ever mastered the ability of entering a story and erasing all evidence that she was there."

> *She always was an overachiever.* – Cleo thought about how his mom was the penultimate perfectionist.

"Why would she do that? And on a side note, if you can do it too, why have you left your name in nearly every book in this room?" Cleo asked, motioning to the collection around them.

"The first answer should be obvious to you, Cleo." Ramiel said, pausing to let Cleo try and work out the problem himself. When Cleo did not react, he continued. "How do you think your bedtime story readings would go if your mom's name kept coming up every time?"

"True, but at least I wouldn't have thought her name was so weird if I saw it in all of the other stories," Cleo rationalized.

"What's more is that even if she did not wish to erase herself from the book, it wouldn't matter in this case. Our presence in the books we travel into is not recorded until we leave. And your mother, still, would never have left."

Cleo took a moment to try to let everything sink in.

"Why didn't you erase your name then? Weren't you ever afraid of someone finding it odd for there to be a Ramiel character in all of these books?"

"I've always felt that it was more important to leave a record of my life than to worry about someone figuring out my secret from a handful of books in a room that is supposed to be off-limits," he raised his eyebrows at Cleo's rule breaking.

"What's the second reason you think this will be more difficult than I imagine?" Cleo said diverting the topic away from his transgressions.

"Given what you have told me, and imagining what I would do if I was in her position, I don't think she merely jumped into *one* of the books originally on the plane that day."

Ramiel's emphasis on the word one, made Cleo's stomach drop.

"She most likely would have grabbed a number of books and taken them with her when she disappeared from the plane."

Cleo was standing there with a dumbfounded look on his face. Ramiel noticed this and continued speaking.

"This way, in case she was for whatever reason unable to escape back to the real world, she could hop into the next book she had with her. Think of it as Russian Nesting Dolls. Inside of the first doll is one that is slightly smaller. Then when you open that one up, there is an even smaller one, and it continues until you get to the last one."

The analogy slightly illuminated a previously dim light bulb in Cleo's mind.

"So...you think she took a handful of books, and jumped into a story with them, and she kept jumping from one story to the next, creating a sort of literary soufflé?"

"That's precisely what I believe has happened."

"Why would she bother bringing more than one book in with her? That seems like an awful lot of unnecessary work just to save a few of her mom's books."

"It had nothing to do with saving the books Cleo. It would have been out of a necessity for survival. Assume she goes into the first novel. Then, sometime later, she gets into trouble. The problem is, she doesn't know if the copy back in the real world was destroyed, bound shut, etcetera. Either way she is unable to leave. Instead of being left to the mercy of whatever dangerous predicament she was in, she could jump into the next book at her disposal. Each additional book she brought with her could act as a failsafe until she was rescued."

The complexity of Ramiel's idea was absurd and the odds of it being true were astronomically low, but still, Cleo was hooked like a bigmouth fish. The idea that Calliope, his mother, had in essence been with him for the past five years, trapped inside of one, or many, of the stories currently sitting on his bookshelf hit Cleo harder than the dodge balls he failed to avoid in PE on a daily basis. Everyone had believed that she had died, himself included. The reality was, there was the most infinitesimal of chances that she was indeed alive, albeit in another plane of existence.

Ramiel leaned closer to Cleo and made sure Cleo heard every word.

"If I'm correct Cleo, and she still lives, then you can bring her home."

"I can bring her home?" He muttered to himself, the idea seeming crazy, irrational, and yet dangerously hopeful.

"Why wouldn't she have already left? What could have caused her to be trapped?"

"I'm sorry, but I don't have an answer to that. There are many reasons she has not been able to return."

Cleo had one final question. One that he was terrified of what the answer would be.

"What happens when she runs out of books?" Cleo asked.

"I think it's best if we don't think about what may happen when that time comes," he said gloomily.

Over the following days, Cleo had a very difficult time paying attention at school. His mind was constantly wandering to his ability, and Ramiel's revelation of his mother's potential whereabouts. On a daily basis, he was learning next to nothing. He was also managing to get in trouble in class quite a bit more frequently. Usually it was for blankly staring out the window instead of paying attention to the lecture or flipping through a book, hoping to find his mom's name miraculously inside.

Ramiel had given him multiple copies of *The Wonderful Wizard of Oz* to try to hone his skills. He told Cleo that, for now, he must always use a new copy when going inside. He refused to tell him why, just that he could never use the same copy twice. Cleo followed Ramiel's advice at first, going through the story from beginning to end. He made it a point to avoid the killer poppies, flying monkeys and evil witch. However, he quickly became restless at the same story over and over, and wanted to truly begin the search for hopefully finding his mother.

After merely a week from when he first met Ramiel, he decided it was time.

> *I need to start looking. I know enough about this power.* – He thought while packing his bag for school.

He decided to leave his borrowed copies of Oz at home and brought with him one of the books his mother had retrieved from his grandma's house.

Knowing what lay in his backpack, he had been extra anxious the entire day at school. It got to the point that ten minutes before the end of third period, Cleo began to pack up his things. As he was sticking his things into his bag, Bryce, who was sitting in the desk next to him, reached across and pulled something out of his backpack.

"Hey, give me that back!" Cleo stretched out and made an unsuccessful attempt at retrieving his stolen item.

"Peter Pan? I didn't know you were starting to borrow books from your little brother," Bryce said loud enough for the entire class to hear. He held it up for everyone to see it. Laughter disrupted the lecture and filled the room.

"I always thought you were into weird stuff, but boys in tights? That's odd even for you." Cleo whirled around and saw it came from Tristan, a lanky kid with spiky black hair and more piercings than fingers on his hand.

"Quiet down, quiet down. That's enough. We still have two minutes of class boys," their teacher said, trying to silence the laughter.

"Shut up Bryce," Cleo said, finally snatching the book back out of Bryce's hands.

Cleo could feel his face getting warm with anger and embarrassment.

> *Why the hell would you do that?* – He thought, glaring at Bryce. *You never used to be this way. When did you turn into such a jerk?*

Bryce used to stick up for Cleo, not try to ridicule him in front of his peers. The months following Calliope's disappearance, Cleo expectedly took it very hard. He often wore dark hoodies, secluded himself from the rest of his classmates and sometimes sobbed when he thought no one was around. One day in particular, Bryce came to Cleo's rescue when it was especially bad.

Cleo was looking through his locker for a textbook when a picture of his family lodged in the back fell to the floor. Cleo picked it up, and seeing how happy his family used to be, started crying. Later that day, an upper classman who had seen him began mocking Cleo in the cafeteria. Despite being considerably smaller than the young man, Bryce came to Cleo's defense and socked the bully in the jaw. Even the two-day suspension that Bryce received was not enough to stop him from telling Cleo he would, "Do it again, as many times as it took for people to leave him alone."

Now however, Bryce had more in common with the bully than his former self.

When the bell rang a few minutes later, Cleo did not waste any time sticking around class. He grabbed his bag and was the first student out of the door.

"Hey Cleo, class is this way. Where are you going?" Penny called out to Cleo as he started to walk in the opposite direction down the hall.

The two of them shared fourth period, Classical Literature. Even before Bryce's little outburst Cleo did not have any intention of going to class. He didn't want to merely *read* a book. He was on his way to become a part of one. Now that he was thoroughly embarrassed in front of so many other kids, there was no way he would stick around Bryce and the other mocking classmates.

"Um...I just left something in the library. I have to go pick it up real fast. I'll meet you there," Cleo said, only partially lying. In truth, he was going to the library. However, he also did not have any real intention of returning to class.

Penny shrugged her shoulders and continued toward her next class. In spite of it being located around the corner, Penny had never been late to a class in her life, and she was not going to jeopardize that streak by following him.

The library was located on the other side of campus. In fact, it was the most northern building on campus. Its location was one of the reasons why so few students bothered to go inside. The vast majority of the student body were too lazy to make the trek.

It's ridiculous that this is referred to as the Courtyard, considering it's the size of a four square court. – Cleo thought, walking across the concrete outside of the main building and over to the library. He did his best not to think about Bryce's teasing and only to think about his first non-Oz locale and the potential for finding his mother.

"Good morning," said the librarian, Ms. Steele, as Cleo entered the library. Ms. Steele was probably old enough to have witnessed the invention of books themselves. She spent the entire day sitting behind the front desk, rarely getting off her stool.

"Morning," Cleo responded courteously.

Over the previous week, the library had been Cleo's go-to spot for privacy. Lately, the interaction between Cleo and the librarian had become very cordial. The first few times he entered the library his presence was met with skepticism and cold stares. Very few students entered the library unless they were forced. When they did, Ms. Steele assumed that they were up to no good.

The combination of an ancient librarian with little to no mobility and no students, provided the perfect spot for Cleo to get his much-needed privacy. He was able to find secluded tables or booths with no trouble and disappear from the monotony of schoolwork into the unpredictability of literature.

Realizing that the library was empty, he quickly retreated to one of the corner booths and brought out a copy of the timeless tale, *Peter Pan and Wendy.*

> *It makes the most sense that she would be stuck in Neverland, the place where time stands still. Perhaps she hasn't realized just how long she has been gone.* – He hoped.

> *I wonder how many times after reading it to me at bedtime that she then traveled to Neverland herself.* – Cleo thought, studying the worn cover of the book that his mother had read to him all those nights while sitting beside his bed. He knew the story well enough that he could nearly recite the

entire thing from memory. Although his main reason was to search for his mom, Cleo could not help but get excited to see with his two eyes how amazing Neverland was. There were no less than twenty adaptations of the adventures of Peter Pan, Wendy and the Lost Boys in Neverland, but Cleo doubted that any of the interpretations could possibly have done the magical world the justice it deserved.

This particular copy had been in his family since his mother was a little girl. It was an exceptionally old copy and possessed a handmade dust jacket over its cover. Calliope constructed it herself, probably in an attempt to protect it from Cleo's constant chocolaty fingers. His hands, now clean, opened the book and he began reading.

Wendy, John and Michael stood on their tiptoes in the air to get their first sight of the magic island, and, strange to say, they all recognized it at once.

A moment later, the empty library was swapped with the clear-blue skies of Neverland. Around him were the siblings, Wendy, John and Michael Darling, as well as the famous Peter Pan himself. The three children were all still in their nightgowns and looked exhausted, clearly having had flown through the night.

> *Wait, something is wrong.* – He thought as the four children were quickly soaring out of sight. Wait, I'm not flying. I'M FALLING!

Cleo tried to propel himself forward, but nothing happened. He looked down and saw the ground becoming closer and closer with every second.

"AHHHH!!" he cried. His words becoming lost in the wind, never to reach anyone's ears.

Cleo fell into panic mode as he realized he was not wearing the magic pixie dust that the others were, enabling them to fly. He abandoned the spread-eagle form of a skydiver and plummeted in a head-over-heels tumble towards the earth. The sights constantly changing.

Sky. Ground. Sky. Ground.

Every time the ground momentarily came into view, it was closer than the last.

> *Alright Cleo. You need to focus. Try not to throw up and just focus on what is happening.* – He thought, struggling to keep his breakfast down.

He closed his eyes, desperately trying to draw his attention to something other than the pancake on the ground he would soon become. The sensation of tumbling around mildly diminished with his eyes closed.

> *Think of Neverland. Focus on standing on Neverland.*
> – He thought.

Unfortunately, his mind kept wandering on not the magical land of Peter Pan, but instead his family and friends. His dad, Linus, and Penny.

> *They won't ever know what happened to me. It'll be just like...*
> – With this last thought Cleo opened his eyes defiantly. *NO! I cannot let myself think that way!*

Cleo used every ounce of energy left to concentrate on the forests of Neverland. He couldn't afford to exhibit the same less than superior control of his fast forward technique Ramiel had attempted to show him in *The Odyssey.* Just before he was to impact the Earth, he dissolved out of the sky like sand in a southern wind.

Cleo went from falling to the Earth from above, to clamoring to its surface from below.

"AHGRGLL!!" Cleo tried to scream out but found his mouth full of water.

He had reformed in the middle of a freezing body of water. Frantically he swam his way to the surface, gasping for air as he finally broke through. Cleo wiped the water from his eyes and looked around, seeing that the body of water he found himself in was a lagoon. A lagoon that was already occupied.

"SQUAWK!!!" The famed Never Bird angrily called out as Cleo reached the surface. A rush of cool air blew across Cleo's face as he realized he knocked the bird from his nest, floating along the lagoon.

The Never Bird was similar to an oversized pelican. Up until the moment of Cleo's appearance in his lagoon, he led a peaceful and solitary existence.

"Sorry about that, I didn't see you there," he said to the bird, doubting it could even understand him.

The bird again squawked at him before flying back to protect her eggs, as they floated helplessly in the water. While the Never Bird flew off, Cleo felt something brush against his leg. Still shaking from both the shock of the water and his near-death experience, he hastily swam to the shore. Upon arriving safely on dry land, he looked into the water to see where the disturbance came from.

"So this must be Mermaid Lagoon," he said, noticing dozens of beautiful mermaids swimming and playing throughout the lagoon. Some splashed around with their tails shimmering in the pale moonlight. "And I'll bet that's Marooners' Rock."

Sitting on a giant rock in the middle of the lagoon were several mermaids combing their long, lovely, blonde hair. They made colorful bubbles and batted them back and forth to one another with their tails, a game, to keep the bubble from bursting.

> *They would dominate the synchronized swimming category at the Olympics. Perennial gold medal winners, guaranteed.* – He thought, watching them effortlessly move through the water. Despite his fear of water, their beauty and playfulness exuded an intoxicating aura that nearly caused Cleo to jump back into their cold waters.

"Excuse me," Cleo called out to one of the nearby mermaids, his voice cracking.

> *She looks a little like Penny.* – Cleo thought, feeling a little nervous as the mermaid swam up to him. *If you can look past the tail, she's positively stunning.*

"Yes?" she said, her voice soft and innocent.

"Have...have you...uh," Cleo stammered, unconsciously running his hand through his hair to straighten it. "Have you seen a woman, a human named Calliope?"

Her cuteness quickly disappeared as she scowled at Cleo and splashed him in the face, turning around and speeding off through the water.

"Yep, just like High School."

He decided to exchange the sudden cold environment for something hopefully a little warmer. After briefly consulting the storyline, he decided where he would go next.

The Fairy Forest in the west.

It lay just beyond multiple breath-taking waterfalls that rivaled even the most majestic on Earth. Cleo arrived in a small meadow in the forest. All around him, millions of tiny fireflies were zooming through the air, lighting up the night sky. Their miniscule size and lightning quick speed made it impossible for Cleo to get a good look at one up close. Their lights ranged from light pink and lime green to ruby red and sky blue, touching on everything in between.

Tinkerbell is able to talk, I wonder if these can also.

"If you can hear or understand me, have any of you seen a human named Calliope by chance?" Cleo asked the tiny fairies.

He waited for any sign that they had heard him, but was met with only the scurry of light zooming around the forest.

"Please, I just need a yes, or no answer. Have any of you seen or heard of a woman named Calliope that may or may not have come through here recently?" He pleaded with the fairies one more time.

This time he did receive a response. The response he got was surprising and not at all what he had hoped. Hundreds of the lights all gathered together and formed one giant, **NO,** right before his face, before scattering again in all different directions.

"So you do understand me. Do you know where I could look next?"

Again, the fireflies all gathered and formed a symbol. This time it was an arrow pointing off through the woods.

"What's out there?"

The miniature night-lights had already grown tired of Cleo's questions and ignored him, dancing about in the dark. Cleo became frustrated and plopped down on a nearby log.

He closed his eyes and, after a short struggle, brought the storyline up in his mind. It stretched out similar to a tape measure pulled to the end of its reel. He could see every chapter, every sentence, and every word.

> *Logically, there are really only two places they could be pointing. If she is here it will either be with Pan or Hook.* – He thought, analyzing his remaining options. *I will first go to Pan. With any luck, I'll never even have to meet the pirate tyrant.*

He withdrew his mind from the storyline and back to his body, resting on the log.

> *Besides, what's that saying. The enemy of my enemy is not my enemy, or something to that effect.* – He thought, before transporting himself further into the story.

Instead of arriving on the outskirts of the Lost Boys' camp and then carefully making his presence known, Cleo decided to have a little fun and pop up in the middle of everyone.

> *They're kids, how dangerous could they be?* – He rationalized.

"BOOO!" Cleo yelled out as he materialized in front of a dozen of the Lost Boys, including the famous Peter Pan himself.

Instead of being met with screams, or scared looks like Cleo thought would be the case, every "child" notched an arrow, drew back their slingshot, or hoisted a sword. Peter stepped forward and placed the tip of his rapier against Cleo's cheek.

"Umm...I was just kidding. Please don't kill me."

Wouldn't that be embarrassing? Killed by a bunch of kids. – He thought, nervously laughing off his predicament.

"What magic is this? Did Hook send you?" Peter spoke up, moving the blade down into Cleo's throat.

Cleo felt a small prick on his neck and a drop of blood slowly seeped from its source. He had to choose his words very carefully because he was one wrong sentence from being impaled by a pre-teen.

"No, I swear I don't work with Hook. My name is Cleo and I followed you when you took the Darlings here to Neverland."

"You're lying. You wouldn't have been able to fly with us. Nobody can go to Neverland unless I bring them," he said, taking one-step closer to Cleo.

"No, no, no, it's true. I have...other means of flying. That's how I was able to keep up with you."

Peter studied Cleo's face intently, searching for any evidence of him lying.

"If that is indeed true, then why did you come here? If you are not here on behalf of Hook, then why are you here?"

"I'm looking for someone very dear to me. My mother. Her name is Calliope."

"What makes you think she is here, in Neverland?" Peter asked in an accusatory tone.

"She told me a story long ago, about how she once travelled to Neverland."

"Impossible, no one knows of Neverland but those of us who live here."

Cleo glanced around at the trees surrounding him. The younglings around him looked closer to an army than a group of harmless kids. They all aimed a weapon at him, waiting for the word to let them fly at their target.

"I swear to you, it's true."

There is something different about this young man. He looks too desperate to be lying. – Cleo peered into the Peter's, the Lost Boys leader, mind. *He is also rather small and pathetic to be a pirate.*

"Please, I'm desperate. I don't know what else to do," Cleo said, playing off the boy's thoughts.

Peter withdrew the sword from Cleo's neck, deciding there was little harm in listening to him.

"Calliope, huh? That's a strange name."

"Yes, I know. Do you know if she is here?"

Why is it that everyone is always so caught up on her name? – He thought annoyed by Pan's comment.

"I've never heard that name before. But if she's here, she's likely with Hook by now."

Figures. Why couldn't she have been with the mermaids swimming around or building tree forts with the Lost Boys? – He selfishly thinking only of his own predicament.

A wave of fear and dread came over Cleo. If Calliope were with Hook then that meant he would have to confront the pirate to rescue her.

"Can you help me?" He solemnly asked Peter.

"You expect me to risk the lives of everyone here to save someone who may not even be held captive? Why should we trust you? For all we know you're planning to stab us in the back the first chance you get."

"I'm going to be honest with you. I couldn't care less about your quarrel with Hook. My only motivation is finding my mother. Not taking sides. Besides something tells me he's taken someone close to you as well."

He didn't need to read his mind this time. He knew that Peter's beloved Wendy was trapped on board Hook's ship at that very minute.

"Listen, I've never so much as been in a fist fight before, no less swung a sword. However, I will do everything I can to help you get her back. I swear to you. Wouldn't you like things to be over with him once and for all?"

Pan grinned at the thought of having everlasting peace in Neverland. He nodded at Cleo in agreement.

"You're right. It's time we end this." He turned to all of the Lost Boys in the camp. "Lost Boys, today we rid ourselves forever of Captain Hook!!" An eruption of cheers echoed throughout the trees. "Prepare yourselves! We leave in one hour!"

The throng of Lost Boys began going off in all directions to ready themselves for the impending battle. Cleo had no clue what he could or should do so instead he tried to keep his fearful mind on taking in his current surroundings rather than the potential outcomes of their looming fight. He walked around their camp, maneuvering between Lost Boys skittering about with their various weapons and survival gear.

> *I can't believe that children came up with all of this. It's like the world's largest playground, minus the parental supervision. Slides, rope swings, tunnels, they have it all. Linus would be in heaven here with all of these kids.* – He thought, squeezing into a hole carved into the trunk of a tree. The cleverly disguised entrance led straight into their living quarters.

All of the Lost Boys slept underground to provide further protection from sneak attacks by the pirates. They slept on small cots that hung from roots that travelled along the ceiling. Each boy did not have an overabundance of space, but as they spent most of their time outside it was not necessary.

Cleo continued to survey the underground parts of the encampment, slowly working his way back to the surface.

> *It's odd how all of this seems so...familiar* – He thought, finally arriving back to center of the camp.

"Cleo, are you ready to leave?" Peter startled him from his déjà vu". Here, take this. Just in case," he said, handing him a rapier similar in size to his own, but of clearly lesser quality. The blade was dull, and the hilt dented.

"Uh, yeah, I guess I'm ready." He hesitantly took the sword and its sheath and held it awkwardly in his hands. He sincerely hoped he would not have to use it. He had never used a sword before and was terrified of having to stab an actual human with it, fairy tale or not. Cleo began to walk towards, what he thought, was east, the direction of the sea.

"Where are you going?" asked Peter, sounding amused.

"Um...is this not the way to the ships?"

"Yes, but we're not going to walk. Do you know how long that would take? Tink, come sprinkle some dust on Cleo so he can fly with us." His little fairy friend flew over and dropped some of her famed dust on top of Cleo's head.

> *Well this certainly is a new sensation.* – He thought, suddenly feeling a little lighter on his feet.

"Now, just think happy thoughts and..." Peter effortlessly rose into the air. "You'll simply rise up into the air!"

The first thought that came to mind was the moment Ramiel said his mother could still be alive.

> *If this does not work, I don't know what will.*

"See, that wasn't so hard now was it Cleo?" Peter Pan's voice called from above. Cleo looked up and saw Peter smiling down at him.

"What are you smiling about?" Cleo asked.

"Look down."

Cleo looked at his feet only to find they were hovering at least four feet above the ground.

"Now, let us fly!" Peter Pan yelled as he and the Lost Boys ascended into the eastward sky. Cleo hadn't the faintest of clues as to what he was doing, but he aimed himself in the direction of his companions and leaned forward.

"Whoa!!" He cried out as he zoomed forward, causing a few of the Lost Boys to turn their heads and laugh at Cleo's lack of control.

Cleo felt exhilarated as the wind rushing over his face became nothing more than a refreshing breeze. He was weightless, soaring alongside the sun. The silence was absolute and total bliss (unless one of the boys talked into his ear, which happened on numerous occasions during their flight). At one point, a bird even decided to be his wingman, unaffected by the fact that he was sharing the skies with a wingless human.

> *Amazing, despite them having probably done this hundreds of times, every one of them looks like they are having as much fun as I am.* – Cleo thought, admiring the boys around him childishly giggling and doing loop-de-loops.

The beauty that encompassed him was extraordinary. Unspoiled lush green forests, water so transparent you could see to the very seafloor, and waterfalls that seemed to extend to the heavens. Everything was so perfect it made him feel as if he never wanted to leave. There was even a brief moment where the whole reason for him being inside Neverland was lost to him entirely.

It wasn't until Peter flew directly in front of him that his attention was snapped back to the task at hand.

"HEY! Stop lollygagging around. We're almost to Hook. You need to pay attention."

Sure enough, Hook's ship floated menacingly in the bay just in front of them. The ship hoisted tattered black sails, donning the customary skull and crossbones on its flag.

"Pan, what exactly is the plan? How are we going to do this?" One of the Lost Boys asked Peter.

"Hey, watch it new guy." One of the boys called out as Cleo's momentum sent him crashing into the young man.

"Sorry," he answered, blushing at his inability to control his new-found ability.

"They have no idea we are coming. We will take advantage of that with the element of surprise. We will all land on the ship's deck at the same time. Their shock will paralyze them and we will take the ship in no time. Cleo, you will watch from up here and keep an eye out for any trickery that Hook may try," said Peter laying out the battle plans. "Any questions?"

A dozen hands went into the air all at once.

"Alright, good," he said ignoring all of the outstretched arms. "We'll flank the ship on both sides. Wait until my signal and then we will storm the ship. Cleo, you stay here. Let's go!" Peter yelled.

Peter Pan and his boys flew off to their positions.

Cleo followed Pan's directions, but only for a moment.

> *I'm the biggest and oldest one here. There is no reason I can't get a little closer.* – He thought, getting antsy with his stationary position. *I'll hang out at the back of the ship. Nobody will even notice me.* ·

He slowly started to fly his way to the ships stern. As he got closer, he saw movement in one of the portholes.

> *It's more than likely just a coincidence. There is no way they saw me.*

He hovered high above the ship, watching for Peter's signal to begin the attack. The signal was simple. When Peter dive-bombed onto the ship, everyone but Cleo was to follow.

Cleo again noticed movement out of the corner of his eye, coming from his side of the ship.

> *I think I'll get a little higher...just in case.*

While Cleo gained altitude, Peter signaled their attack by rapidly plummeting down to the ship and blindsiding an unsuspecting patrol. Before the Lost Boys could follow suit however, pirates flooded to the deck from every door and every staircase. The advantage that Peter thought they would obtain with their sneak attack was gone.

Cleo took a deep gulp, feeling guilty for their failed opening attack.

I really hope that wasn't my fault.

The Lost Boys quickly rallied to their commander and joined the fray. Peter was fighting men twice his size on all sides. Cleo was amazed at the skill of the young man. He was faster and more graceful than anyone Cleo had ever seen. He slashed, parried incoming attacks and flipped around the horde of pirates with ease.

Although the buccaneers were ruthless and vastly superior in size and strength, the boys of Neverland had the gift of flight and had quick, agile frames. Any time one of them was thrown overboard, they escaped their fall into the frigid water below and flew right back into the fight. The pendulum began to swing in favor of the army of children. The pirates' numbers were starting to diminish due to their inability to remove the Lost Boys from the fight.

How odd, I don't see Hook anywhere.

Peter seemed to read Cleo's thoughts as he screamed for his archenemy.

"HOOOOK!! COME OUT AND FIGHT ME YOU COWARD!" He tried to draw the Captain from whatever hole he was hiding in. Still, there was neither sight nor sound of the most dreadful man in all of Neverland.

Cleo decided that he had stood by and watched the battle for as long as he could.

Besides, it is only a matter of time before the ship belongs to Peter and the rest of the Lost Boys. – Cleo cautiously glided around the ship searching for any sign of either the Darlings or his mother. Cleo knew there was no way he would find anything by just meandering about amongst the clouds. *I can't see anything from up here. If I'm going to have any chance of locating them I need to get in closer.*

He clumsily flew directly towards the ship. He traveled in a zig-zag-like pattern, still mostly unable to control himself.

"OOOOOF!" his full lungs expelled all of the air in them as he slammed into the side of the ship, nearly knocking himself out. Luckily, he remained floating in the air instead of the alternative...wet, numb and unconscious underneath the waves below. Cleo regained his composure and made his way through one of the ship's portholes, beginning his search through its supply area.

"God, this place smells horrible," he said, plugging his nose.

Crates nailed shut that, Cleo could only assume, were filled with whatever their most recent plunder consisted of. Barrels and barrels of gunpowder and rum scattered about. Hanging on hooks and rusted nails jutting out of wooden beams were swords and knives of various sizes. Two things that were noticeably missing however were the pirates and their captives. There was no sign of any enemies hiding beneath the deck, nor of Wendy or Calliope.

> She's not on deck and she's not down here. I bet they are in Hook's personal cabin.

Cleo was deathly afraid of having to engage in any real combat. Particularly if it was with their leader, Hook. He also knew he was his mother's only chance, and proceeded to the stairs that led to the ship's deck.

"WHOA!" Cleo hollered as the body of an unfortunate pirate suddenly tumbled head over heels down the stairs in front of him. Two Lost Boys peeked around the corner and smiled at Cleo as he stepped over the man's unconscious body.

When Cleo arrived back onto the deck, he noticed that the pirates had slightly evened the odds. They abandoned the notion they could toss their pint-sized adversaries overboard, and resorted to simply knocking them out instead.

Amidst the clashing of swords, Cleo saw a cabin at the far end of the ship. He took a deep breath in an attempt to calm his nerves, and took off in a sprint as fast as he could through the mayhem around him. His goal of staying out of harm's way had evaporated, he was now directly in the middle of the battle. The sound of metal crashing and howls of pain filled his ears. He dodged swords, pieces of wood shattering into splinters and bodies thrown in his way.

"OOMPF!!" He spurted as one of his allies was sent flying into him, causing them both to collapse to the ground. The boy resiliently got back onto his feet. He charged back into the fray without bothering to check to see if Cleo was all right.

Cleo rubbed the back of his head, feeling a bruise already forming, and crawled the short distance that remained to the cabin. He rose to his feet to see the battered exterior of what he hoped was Hook's residence. There were no windows for him to look through. The door was brittle and appeared as if he could break it with one swift kick.

> *I've always wanted to do this.* – He thought giddily, pulling off his best cop impersonation and thrusting his leg into the door.

The door didn't burst off its hinges like he'd hoped, rather his foot caused a small hole near its handle.

> *Wow, that was pathetic. I need to work out more.* – He shook his head and reached through the hole, opening the door from the inside.

The room was spacious but cluttered with an array of junk. There was a 19th century French bed made from natural walnut. The legs resembled Roman columns, but were chipped and badly scratched up. It was adorned with torn red ribbons and bronze floral ornaments that had long lost their shine.

In the middle of the room was an octagonal table made from redwood that housed an assortment of attachments for Hook's appendage-less wrist. There were attachments that could be used as eating utensils, hairbrushes, and even a flyswatter. There was also, of course, a large variety of his namesake, hooks. There were serrated ones, razor sharp ones, and ones as dull as a spoon. Filling out the rest of the room were parchments of paper, scrolls, maps, a wardrobe that would put Audrey Hepburn to shame, a cage with a parrot, Cleo couldn't tell whether it was dead or alive, and a box of books whose titles were obscured by a sheet draped over the top.

> *Books huh?* – He thought about making a beeline straight for the box, but before he could move, he noticed two women

gagged, sitting back to back and tied to one another in the far corner of the room. Wendy was a young girl, no older than Cleo was. She was wearing a once pearly white nightgown that had since been stained with the dirt and grime of the ship. She looked exhausted, her eyes struggling to stay open.

The other woman was the very one he had been looking for, and the very one he least expected to find.

"MOM!" he yelled at the sight of her.

She was much more calm and composed than Wendy, not exerting any energy against her bonds.

"Mom, Wendy, I'm here to help you," he said, jogging towards them.

"MMM!!! MMMMM!!!" his mom was trying to yell through her gag.

"Stay still. I'm not going to hurt you," he attempted to comfort them, removing the cloths that were tied around their mouths. He used his poor excuse for a sword to start sawing through the rope that tied them together.

"Behind you Cleo, look behind you," his mother coughed, her voice sounding far more tired than her body let on.

Cleo spun around, his sword raised.

"Well who do we 'ave 'ere? A new recruit to the Lost Boys?" said the infamous Captain Hook from behind Cleo. He was dressed in a pirate outfit that was closer to a Halloween costume than something you would imagine a Pirate Lord wearing.

"Nice feather," Cleo commented on the violet feather sticking from the top of his Monmouth cap.

"Why thank you. It's hard to find someone who appreciates good taste," Hook said, missing Cleo's sarcasm. "I must admit I rather hoped that Pan would be the one to try and free my guests,"

"Prisoners, not guests," Wendy blurted out defiantly.

"Semantics. Either way you are obviously helping Pan. Sadly for you, any friend of Pan is an enemy of mine. Now," Hook said, raising his sword in one hand and hook in the other. "You can get off my ship, NOW!" He lunged forward towards Cleo.

Cleo narrowly dodged his attack.

"AAHHH!" Both Wendy and Calliope screamed in unison.

Cleo backed away from Hook, comically holding his sword out in front of him and waving it back and forth.

"Hahaha, you might as well give that sword to one of the girls, boy. This is going to be fun," Hook said, sporting a sinister smile. He again lashed out at Cleo, this time with a fraction of the murderous intent that his first strike had. He was merely toying with the boy.

"Come on boy, you can do better than that."

This time Cleo tried to go on the offensive and waved his sword at Hook as if it were an oversized Japanese fan. Hook batted it away with minimal effort. Cleo was infuriated by Hook's nonchalance in what was, for him, a life or death fight. He channeled his anger into as powerful a swing as he could manage.

"AHH!!" he yelled, using all of his strength and swinging the blade like it were a baseball bat, aimed at Hook's head. Hook was able to get his rapier up in time, but the force knocked him into the box of books, sending them skittering across the floor. Despite Cleo being in very real danger, he could not help but snicker at Hook's balding head, now missing its characteristic hat. Then Hook regained his balance.

"So that's how it's going to be?" he said. The grin on his face replaced by a terrible look of malice. "Playtime is over."

Hook showed a surprising amount of speed given his age and repeatedly lashed out at Cleo. Cleo was able to deflect the first strike, but the second one knocked the sword out of his hand. Before it even hit the ground, a blinding flash of pain rang throughout Cleo's body.

"AGGHHH!!" He screamed as Hook slashed his face, leaving a gash streaking across his left cheek. He stumbled to his right, covering the cut on his face with his hands.

"Don't worry boy, it will only hurt for a moment for now you die," Hook said, rearing back his weapon for one final lunge.

Time seemed to slow down for Cleo until it nearly came to a complete halt. The sword rapidly closed the gap between its point and Cleo's heart and he was powerless to stop it. Just then, a figure leapt in front of him, absorbing the impact.

"Uahhh…" a slight gasp of air faintly escaped the lungs of Wendy, as she took the death strike intended for Cleo.

"NOO!!" Cleo yelled, grabbing hold of the body falling into his arms.

"I didn't mean to…she stepped right in front…" Hook stammered, briefly looking remorseful over what he had just done. "Foolish girl. She only delayed the inevitable." He hardened his expression. He raised his sword again for another strike.

"Ah, there you are Hook! You've been hiding from me." Peter Pan burst into the doorway, doing what Cleo could not, shattering the remaining pieces of the door. He confidently puffed his chest out in Hook's direction. His eyes moved towards the direction of Cleo and his fallen savior, Wendy.

"Wendy??? WENDY!!!" He screamed out, the boyish smile instantaneously replaced by a look of horror.

He flew across the room over to Wendy, lying lifeless in Cleo's arms.

"Wendy no, wake up. Please wake up, Wendy. Please," Peter pleaded, pulling her body close to his.

Peter looked up at Cleo who still had not moved a muscle or said a word. His eyes were full of a fury that Cleo had never seen in another human being. He softly laid Wendy's head back into Cleo's still outstretched arms.

"You've always tried to do whatever you could to get to me Hook," he calmly said, slowly rising to his feet.

Quicker than the blink of an eye Peter wheeled around and ran Hook through with his sword.

"You should have left us alone. You will not enjoy where you are headed Hook," Peter whispered into his ears before pushing his body off his now bloodstained sword. There was no one there to catch Hook's body. It collapsed in a heap to the cabin floor with a loud thud.

Peter somberly walked back towards Wendy.

"Wendy," Peter's voice cracked as he again pulled Wendy into his arms. The tears were streaming down his cheeks and could not mask the confusion in his eyes.

> *He doesn't understand what is happening. Death is a new concept to Peter. He has never had to deal with this before.* – Cleo thought, sympathizing with the everlasting boy who suddenly grew up before him.

"Cleo, is that really you?" Calliope's voice asked from behind him, all but ignoring what had just unfolded before her.

Cleo turned around, and without any maniacal pirates around, was finally able to get a good view of his mother. She was no longer the fearless teenager from Oz, or the young woman on the brink of 30 that he saw in Verne's world. She was the same caring, selfless mother that Cleo remembered on the last day he ever saw her alive.

"You're bleeding, let me help you." She used the scarf that draped around her neck and gently wiped the blood from his face. "I can't believe this. What are you doing here?"

He knew exactly why he was there, but he couldn't force out even a single word. All he could think about was the time lost and what he could never regain. It was a completely different set of emotions running through him than when he saw her in the center of the Earth. This time he knew for certain that she was no figment of his imagination.

"I'm here to take you home," he said, certain he had found her.

"Take me home? You can't take me home Cleo. I'm merely a recording of my previous trip into this story. I can't leave with you," she said. "Son, why do you need to take me home?"

Her response took the wind out of Cleo's proverbial sail.

So this isn't the correct version of her? She looks so similar though. How am I to figure out which one is the real one?

"It's nothing," he said not wanting to go through the same conversation of her disappearance with another version of her own self. He needed answers, but he did not know the questions to ask her. "Is there...did you bring anything with you when..." he stopped mid-sentence for without warning she began to disappear in front of his eyes. It wasn't gradual, moving from one body part to the next. It was happening all at once. Her whole body, eerily becoming ethereal on the derelict pirate ship.

"What's happening!?" Cleo asked worryingly.

"Cleo, my time in this story is coming to an end."

"I don't understand."

"When I originally came into this story I only stayed in for a finite amount of time. I eventually left. At the point of the story where I left, it must be the same point in which I always leave, regardless of what you may have or ever will change."

"Wait! I need an answer before you go. Did you bring any books in here with you!?" he asked, reaching for her now intangible hand.

"Goodbye son." It was barely a whisper as she vanished entirely.

Frustrated, Cleo picked up a nearby, darkened candlestick and threw against the wall. If Peter noticed the sudden evaporation of Cleo's mother, or his momentary tirade, he did not show it. He remained in silence, holding his loved one's limp body.

I can't stay here any longer. – The sight was heartbreaking and unsettling. The pain in his face from Hook's sword that had momentarily ebbed was flowing once again. He shut his eyes and began recalling the library from which he vanished, hours before.

"I'm sorry Peter. This is all my fault. I'm sorry," Cleo said to Peter right before he left Neverland.

He had a heavy heart as he finally returned to his own world where innocence and carefreeness were lost. Even though it was one character in one copy among millions, he still felt a profound responsibility for what happened on that ship. What was worse, it had all been for naught. He did not acquire any information as to where he could continue his search. To top it off, if it weren't for a fictional character, he would have far worse than a mere cut on his face to show for his failed efforts. He may have never returned at all.

He arrived back in the library, sitting in the same booth as before. He stared down at the book he just exited and watched as his name slowly scripted itself into the pages. As the final entry appeared, he closed the book. Dejected about his experience in Neverland, he got up to leave, but stopped midrise.

> *That's not good.* – He thought as he realized he was not alone. Standing directly in front of him, separated by only a few small strides was a very familiar young woman displaying a bewildered and dumbfounded look.

"What just happened to you?"

CHAPTER 7

Grimm's Wonka

Having fully materialized in the library, Cleo found himself face to face with Penny.

I eventually wanted to tell her my secret, but on my terms. Not like this. Maybe she didn't see anything. Maybe I can just play dumb. I'm usually great at that.

"Um, how...how's it going Penny?" he stammered.

He was trying very hard to avoid the typical signs of lying, but he wasn't getting off to a great start. He managed to stutter the first words he spoke and he could feel beads of sweat starting to form on his face.

At the very least, I need to maintain eye contact.

"What the heck happened to you?" she asked, pointing to his face.

Cleo reached up and winced at the smarting pain from touching the cut across it. His fingertips were painted red from his own blood.

I forgot about that. At least it wasn't sweat. – He thought, trying to see the bright side in the situation.

"Gosh Cleo, answer me. How did you get that huge gash on your head?" she said, going into her motherly mode again.

"Oh this, it must have happened when I hit my head on the bookcase over there," he lied, motioning to a random aisle.

"Why haven't you gone to the nurse's office? It's still bleeding," she questioned.

"I...I didn't even realize it was bleeding. I figured it was just a bump." Cleo couldn't think of anything else to say.

"What were you doing over here? When I first looked over, I swear there wasn't anyone or anything here except for your bag and that book. Then you just kind of appeared out of nowhere."

"Appeared out of nowhere? Are you sure you're not the one that bumped your head?" Cleo joked, trying to divert her suspicions. "I just came from around the corner is all. Nothing magical, I promise."

"I don't believe you, but I also don't know how else I could explain it." She studied Cleo as if they were in a poker tournament, trying to get any sort of read on him. "I don't know, maybe I was just seeing things. But...something wasn't quite right. I don't know, just forget about it." She grabbed a small tissue package out of her bag. "Here, put this on your face. Let's take you to the nurse. I'm not exactly a doctor, but that looks really bad. I wouldn't be surprised if you had a scar."

"Well then let's hope it's in the shape of something awesome like a lightning bolt and not just an off-colored line," Cleo said with a smirk.

Penny playfully shook her head and the two of them left the library.

"Why did you skip class to read Peter Pan of all things? Were you trying to find the resemblance between you and him?" Penny said sarcastically.

"I just needed a few minutes to myself. I guess I lost track of time."

Kind of ironic if you think about it. Losing track of time in a land where time doesn't matter. – The idea brought a smile to Cleo's face.

"Well lucky for you all we did was talk about Catcher in the Rye. And since you didn't read it, it's not like you would have added anything to the discussion," Penny teased.

"I'll have you know I read it a long time ago," Cleo said, hopping over a mud puddle.

"I kind of wish you were there though."

"Why's that?" Cleo asked.

"Because it would have been like having Holden Caulfield himself in the room," Penny said, laughing at her own comment.

"Wow, you're just hilarious today, aren't you?" Cleo said, throwing the sarcasm back at her.

They reached the office and Penny reached for the door before Cleo.

"Let's hurry up. By the time they finish cleaning you up lunch will be over," Penny pulled the office door open.

"Wait for me?" Cleo asked, walking down the hall and stopping at the slightly ajar door of the nurse's office.

"Of course," she said with a smile that took away the lingering pain that was still coursing through Cleo's face.

The weather was crummy again when they got out of school. Rain was coming down in buckets and at obtuse angles.

"You want a ride home?" Bryce asked Penny as they walked out of their last class. "You too Cleo," he added after the fact.

"No, I'm going to walk. I could use the fresh air," Cleo said, turning down Bryce's offer.

"It's pouring outside Cleo," Penny protested.

"Bah, this is barely a sprinkle," he said pretending not to notice the torrential downpour.

"Fine, then I'll join you," she said pulling out her umbrella.

Cleo wanted to have some time alone to think, but he welcomed her company.

"Whatever, it's your guys' loss. I'm out of here," Bryce said, looking slighted at Penny turning him down. He wasted no more time and left them.

"Well, you ready?" Penny asked with a smile, popping open her umbrella.

"When you were in the library today you missed Cassandra tumble into the trashcan in the Senior Hall. She had just finished yelling at someone, when her heel broke and she fell directly into it. The whole hall was in hysterics," Penny said trying to make small talk as they huddled together under her umbrella, walking down the wet sidewalk.

"Cassandra...She's the aggravating, pompous head cheerleader right?" Cleo wasn't a part of the "In-Crowd," so he only vaguely knew who she was talking about.

"Yeah, I felt bad afterwards for laughing at her. I couldn't imagine how embarrassing it must have been."

Cleo was being even quieter than normal. Usually he was a good conversationalist, but today he was too deep in thought.

> *Where should I look next? I could choose one of the more realistic tales, like Sherlock Holmes. What about another fantasy novel? There has to be some method to use rather than just randomly choosing a book on my shelf. This seems like such an impossible task. I don't even know what I'm supposed to look for.*

"Is everything alright?" Penny stirred him from his thoughts.

Cleo was tempted to tell her everything, every little secret he was hiding.

"Yeah, I'm fine. Things have just been...a little rough lately," he avoided eye contact with her. He stared at his feet and kept walking.

"You think about her a lot don't you?"

Penny had a unique talent for reading people. He stepped out from under the umbrella and stopped moving. He gazed off into the hills in the distance.

"Yeah, I do."

> Just not in the way that you think.

"Every day I do. Especially lately."

> About how she's alive. If she is alright. More importantly, about how I am going to save her. – He wanted to add.

"Everything's going to be alright Cleo. I know it will," she said, dropping the top of her umbrella to the ground, thus exposing herself to the cold rain. She reached out and grabbed Cleo's hand.

Cleo looked up into her eyes. They were sky blue, a stark contrast to the gloomy weather around them. Water was dripping from his unkempt hair down onto his face. Cleo wanted to keep it that way because he could feel himself on the brink of tears, and he had never let anyone see him cry.

"What if it isn't? What if I can't become the person I'm supposed to be? The person that I need to be. It's not just my life at stake."

"You don't need to put so much on your shoulders Cleo. I know you feel responsible for your brother, your dad, the whole world around you. But you're not alone."

> But I AM the one responsible. I am the ONLY one that can save my mom and reunite my family. It will be MY fault if she never comes back. I AM alone! – He wanted to shout at her.

But he wasn't ready to let her in. He wasn't ready to let anyone in.

"I guess you're right."

She raised her umbrella back up above both of their now sopping wet heads.

"What do you say we get out of this rain?" she said shivering. "Plus, now that bandage on your face is ruined. You'll need to replace it soon."

Cleo forced a cockeyed grin and nodded, before walking Penny the remainder of the way to her house.

Cleo was exhausted when he finally got home. The last week had been the longest of his life, literally. Twenty-four hour days were a thing of the past with the onset of his new ability. Time in the real world passed at a glacially slow pace when he traveled into a book. While Cleo's adventures would take him hours at a time, only minutes would go by back home.

He decided that he needed to take a catnap if he was to have any energy to continue his search. The nap only lasted a few hours, but that didn't stop the nightmare that deeply disturbed him.

He awoke, shaking and drenched in sweat. Even worse was, it was a nightmare that the moment he woke up, he had forgotten. Everything. He felt paranoid, looking in the shadows for beings that were not there.

> *How could something I don't even remember affect me so greatly?* – He thought, wiping his sodden face with his shirt.

He looked at the clock on his desk reading **8:14**.

> *Well, I'm certainly not going to be able to get back to sleep anytime soon. I might as well be productive.*

He got up and rifled through some of his grandmother's books on his shelf. He found one he liked, *Grimm's Fairy Tales,* and sat at his desk.

My mom's favorite movie as a kid was Cinderella. I could try the original story first.

He quickly found the tale towards the beginning of the book, found his entry point and began reading.

There she was obliged to do heavy work from morning to night, get up early in the morning, draw water, make the fires, cook, and wash.

"Miss Ella," he said in his most courteous manner. "By chance have you heard of a woman named Calliope?"

"Oh my, I didn't see you come in. Are you a friend of my stepmother?"

"Um...not exactly. It's complicated. So have you seen or heard of this woman before?" He tried to gloss over the fact that he did not belong in the young girl's house.

"Hmm, I might have, but I really don't have time to try and remember. I have a lot of work I need to get done," she said, dipping her mop in the nearby bucket. "If you would be willing to help though, it would give me more time to think about it."

Cleo hated to clean, but he needed information.

"Alright, hand me a broom," he said with a less than authentic smile.

Not long after Cleo began to sweep, he realized that Cinderella was not the sweet and selfless woman that everyone had believed.

"You missed a spot! If I get in trouble for your inability to clean up a small pile of dust, you will be sorry!"

She continuously berated his skills with the broom, dustpan and other cleanings tools.

After the grueling cleaning session, Ella finally consented to giving him all the information she had on Calliope.

"So, what do you know about her? Is she here somewhere?"

"I'm sorry. I have never heard that name before. But thanks for the help, and I wish you luck in finding her," her sweet tone returned now that her kitchen floor was spotless.

Cleo felt so used that he didn't say another word to her and vanished from the story.

"Let's hope this next one turns out a little better," he said flipping through the book until he found another story that he recognized, *Snow White and the Seven Dwarves.*

That choice didn't end up much better, for as soon as he tried to speak with Snow, he found himself being held down by a bunch of overprotective, bearded old men carrying pickaxes and shovels. Slightly more embarrassing was the fact that these bearded little men were not all that much smaller than Cleo was.

"Guys, I'm just looking for a young woman. I wanted to ask Snow if she had seen her or not," he said, struggling against the dwarves.

"We know you work for the queen. We will not let you harm Snow!" said the dwarf Grumpy, knocking Cleo on the top of the head with the side of his pickaxe.

"OUCH!" He said, struggling to wiggle his arms free of the little men.

> *Forget this, she's not in here. I don't have to take this from a bunch of old men barely larger than children.*

Cleo found it impossible to focus on his bedroom with the dwarves pulling and tugging on him. He suddenly had an idea.

"Fine! You are right. I do work for the queen. Release me and I will tell you everything about her plans."

The dwarves looked back and forth at one another before letting go of Cleo's extremities.

"Deal, but if you try anything we will be forced to harm you," threatened the one that Cleo assumed was Doc due to his wire-rimmed glasses.

The moment they let Cleo go, he retreated to the comforts of his house in the real world.

"Maybe I should just stop trying for the night. This clearly isn't getting me anywhere," he said aloud as he skimmed the remaining titles in the table of contents.

His stomach growled loudly as he came across *Hansel and Gretel.*

> *I doubt she's in Candy Land.*

He skipped the sugar-coma inducing story, hoping for one that may be a little more practical for his mother's whereabouts.

"Little Red Riding Hood, Rapunzel, The Frog Prince," he said trying to find the perfect one.

> *Wait, what if I bring him with me?* – He thought, looking back at the tale of Hansel and Gretel.

> *I could bring Linus. This would be perfect for him. What kid wouldn't like to go to a world of sweets? I'll tell him he's dreaming. We could go inside, eat some candy, and leave before anyone would know that we were gone.* – Cleo lit up at his plan of bringing Linus with him. I could finally share my ability with someone, and not have to worry about anything bad coming from it.

Cleo left his room, book in hand and crept into the living room. Lying in his customary sprawled out position and asleep on the couch was his father. Cleo could count on both hands the number of times his father had slept in his own bed since his mom disappeared. Cleo found it tragically heartbreaking.

Satisfied that there would not be any interruptions or untimely entrances by his father, Cleo proceeded to Linus's room. He approached the door and could make out a faint light flickering from underneath the door.

"Linus," he whispered, knocking on the door.

"I'm asleep, go away," his little brother responded.

Cleo opened the door and entered the room regardless of his brother's wishes.

"Can't sleep, huh?" he asked.

"Why knock if you're just going to walk in?" Linus said. "No, I can't sleep."

"You know, when I was about your age, and I couldn't sleep, mom would read me a bedtime story. She read me all kinds, from the classics like Peter Pan or the Velveteen Rabbit, to a special one that she wrote herself. I could do the same for you if you want."

"That's ok. I don't need a bedtime story."

"Come on, just give it a shot. Maybe listening to my voice will be so agonizing that it will put you to sleep."

When Cleo was younger, he had his mother around to make sure he had a childhood. Linus did not have that. Cleo felt responsible for making sure Linus had as normal a childhood as possible, given all the circumstances.

"Fine. How about mom's story?"

His mother's story was the one tale that Cleo was hesitant to tell. He alone had this special connection with his mother. He wasn't quite ready to share that link with anyone else.

"I don't remember too much of it. It's been a long time since I last heard it, and, I don't think I could recite how the story went." It was true that he didn't remember all of the story. Despite her reading it to him countless times, the story had become more and more a figment of his past.

"Bummer...well, whatever. Just read to me what you want." Linus finally gave in.

Cleo sat on the edge of Linus' bed and opened his copy of *Grimm's Fairy Tales.*

"You know this book has over 200 short stories in it and is almost 200 years old? A lot of them were even turned into Disney movies."

Cleo was far more interested in these tidbits of information than Linus.

"Alright then. Well, I'm going to read you Hansel and Gretel. How's that sound?"

"Hansel and Gretel?" Linus questioned in a whiney voice that reminded Cleo just how old his little brother was.

"Hey now, this is a good story. It can teach you many good lessons. I bet you have never read the original version. It's quite a bit different than the version that you kids read in kindergarten." Cleo said, trying to reassure Linus.

He cleared his throat loudly in an attempt to make his brother laugh. It didn't work.

Cleo began reading, "Near a great forest, there lived a poor woodcutter and his wife and his two children; the boy's name was Hansel and the girl's Gretel."

Cleo stopped reading to make sure to keep his hand on his brother's shoulder.

> *If this is going to work, I need for us both to go inside, not just me.*

"Why are you touching me? And why'd you stop reading?"

"Sorry, I was thinking about something. I want you to close your eyes before I continue. Alright?"

Linus looked at Cleo as if he was crazy.

"Just trust me, alright? It will make the story better. I promise."

Linus was skeptical, but he listened to his older brother. Once Cleo knew that Linus' eyes were tightly shut, he replaced his hand on his little brother's shoulder and continued reading.

Cleo continued, "The small little cottage was entirely edible. The walls were made of various kinds of breads. The roof was cakes of all shapes and sizes. The windows were a transparent sugar. The gutters were licorice, while the door knob was a massive gumdrop."

The feeling of being sucked into the magical world washed over Cleo. He could feel Linus squeeze his hand as they disappeared from Linus's bed and materialized in front of the gingerbread house he had been reading about just moments before.

"What happened? Where are we?" Linus asked, confused and startled by what just happened.

There they were, the two Bailey brothers standing side by side in the Grimm brothers' creation.

"Cleo, what's going on? How did we get here?" asked Linus again, this time his voice was quivering.

"Don't worry little brother. It should be obvious. You're just dreaming."

"Dreaming? I don't even remember falling asleep."

"What's the last thing you remember before you came here?"

Linus racked his six and a half year old mind.

"I remember you telling me to close my eyes."

"Well then, there's your answer. It's obvious. This is all your imagination. I don't even exist," Cleo said in an attempt to convince his brother.

"I guess you're right."

Cleo didn't know if Linus fully bought it or not, but figured it was good enough to keep going.

"Come on let's take a look around. We can see what this house tastes like. I'm starving."

The two of them walked over to the candy laden building and began gorging themselves. Linus, being considerably shorter, started with the maple bar windowsill and the chocolate and vanilla cake acting as the bottom of the outside wall panels. Cleo grabbed a hanging flowerpot constructed out of Rice Krispy Treats and filled with chocolaty dirt. He yanked it off its hook and began to devour it.

"Ohhh, this tastes amazing. It's so warm, like it just came out of the oven."

Cleo moved over to the corner of the building to take a sample of the licorice gutter. Just as Linus placed another piece of the sugar coated windowsill in his mouth, they heard a seemingly innocent old voice coming from inside.

"Nibble, nibble, like a mouse. Who is nibbling at my house?"

An old woman hobbled out of the house, leaning on a crutch. She was decrepit looking and the very definition of a wicked fairy tale witch. Her face was covered in warts, and her mouth was full of crooked, broken and horribly discolored teeth.

"Dear children, why don't you come inside and enjoy a nice meal," she said, beckoning them inside her home.

"Sorry, but we have to go. Linus, come here, we're leaving," Cleo made a move to grab Linus and take him out of the story. Before he was able to grab hold of his brother, the old woman pulled Linus into the house with reflexes so fast that Cleo questioned whether she really needed the cane by her side.

Cleo charged into the building after the two. She ushered Linus over to a table that had been laid out with a great meal of pancakes, waffles, fruit and milk.

"Sit, eat." She told the boys.

Cleo knew how this story played out.

> *I'm sure this food tastes amazing, but I'd prefer not to be cooked in her oven, or have to shove her in myself.*

"We are actually in a hurry. We really need to leave." He walked around the table in an attempt to reach Linus, but again she thwarted his advance, this time by stepping in front of him.

"Just have one meal and I promise I'll let you go after that, young man. What's the harm in that?"

"Besides being cooked alive?" Cleo muttered under his breath.

"What was that sonny?" The old woman glared at Cleo.

"Nothing."

> I need some sort of distraction to give me enough time to get us out of here. Unless I resort to shoving the old woman to the ground, I don't think she's going let me grab him.

"Fine, one bite. Then we're leaving," he conceded.

"Very well, now go ahead and sit down on the other side of the table there."

Cleo reluctantly sat down opposite Linus. He mouthed to him *'It'll be OK. I'll get us out of here'.* Linus was so bewitched by the food that he didn't even notice. The witch placed a plate of waffles topped with strawberry jam and bacon, scrambled eggs doused in melted cheese and crispy hash browns in front of Cleo.

"Alright, now eat up," she said, smiling devilishly.

> I can't believe this old hag thinks she can dupe me. This food is likely poisoned. If I eat it, we'll both be dead.

"How's your food taste Linus?" He asked, temporarily diverting the witch's attention to his little brother.

Cleo used the opportunity to dump the food off his fork and back onto the plate. When the old woman looked back, Cleo's empty fork rested in his mouth.

"Wow that is really something else."

"Yes, it is quite wonderful isn't it?" she said to him, her smile widening.

Cleo stood up from his chair.

"Alright, now that we ate it's time for us to leave." He walked around the old witch and grabbed a hold of Linus's hand. Linus looked at Cleo for some sort of guidance as to their next move.

"Just relax Linus, I'll take care of this."

He closed his eyes and began to picture his brother's bedroom. Before he could make out even a single detail however, he suddenly felt a horrendous pain on the left side of his head before he fell into complete blackness.

"A little bit of cayenne pepper, some paprika and maybe even some fresh basil will make you taste just perfect my dear." Cleo's ears heard the high-pitched, wicked voice of the witch before his eyes could register what was happening around him.

He opened one eye barely a crack in case the old woman was watching him. He felt the cold bare wood of the kitchen floor pressed against his cheek. He also felt an acorn sized bump near his temple.

> *This will go great with all of my other story-related injuries. When, or if, we ever get out of here* – He thought.

Cleo could just make out the feet of the old woman on the opposite side of the table. She was standing in front of her counter, rubbing spices on something, or someone. Cleo opened his other eye and carefully raised his head off the ground to try to get a better look at what had her attention.

> *Linus?* – He could barely make out his little brother, stretched out onto a four-foot long cookie sheet. The evil woman was sprinkling various seasonings all along this little boy.

"400 degrees for 90 minutes should do the trick," she said pulling open the door of her over-sized oven.

Cleo didn't take any time to formulate any sort of plan. Seeing his brother unconscious, or possibly worse, he jumped to his feet.

"WHAT DID YOU DO TO HIM?!?" He screamed out at the woman. The oven mitts in her hands went flying through the air.

"What? How are you awake? You ate my food, and do you know how hard I hit you with that frying pan? You should be out for at least another three hours," she said, anger filling her voice.

Cleo didn't bother wasting his breath with a response. He ignored the blinding pain in his head and jumped over the table.

She screamed out as Cleo grabbed her with a ferocity his body had never experienced before. Before his mind knew what his hands were doing, he shoved the woman into the oven.

"NOOOO!! YOU CAN'T!!" She screamed out in terror.

Cleo grabbed hold of the door and slammed it shut with all of his might before moving towards his motionless brother.

"Linus, wake up. Linus, are you alright?" He said, gently shaking his brother. The seconds ticked by without any sort of response from his little brother.

> Oh my God. I ignored Ramiel's warning and now look at what I've done. I've gotten my brother killed. What am I going to do?

A sickening pit formed in his stomach. His hands shook intensely with the fear and anger that was coursing through his veins "Linus..." Cleo said again, placing his hand on Linus's forehead.

"WHO DO YOU THINK YOU ARE?! USING MY OWN TRICKS AGAINST ME! I PROMISE YOU THAT WILL NEVER HAPPEN AGAIN!" The witch shrilled out as she struggled to pull herself out of the oven.

Boils and blisters already started to form all over her hands and forearms. Her face was a deep red from the combination of the intense heat of the oven and her volatile hatred of the two boys before her.

"Ugh...Cleo, what's happening?" Cleo spun around and saw his little brother slowly stirring awake.

"LINUS!" he yelled, reaching over and grabbing hold of his brother's hand.

He tried to block out the old woman's shrieks and curses. He envisioned the two of them back in his home. He could hear the clanking of pots and pans in the background.

"Cleo, that crazy lady is coming this way with another pan in her hand. DO SOMETHING!" Linus cried out, squeezing Cleo's hand.

Before he was blindsided by another frying pan, Cleo managed to remove them from the so-called *fairy tale*.

The devilish witch, the hellish kitchen and the nightmare were gone and replaced with the unused toys, children's books and a painters easel that made up the corners of Linus' bedroom.

"What just happened? How did you do that? Where did you take us?" Linus asked perplexed as to what he just experienced.

"What are you talking about? You've been asleep for a while. You must have been having a nightmare," Cleo said, panting as he tried to maintain the lie.

"You're telling me you seriously don't remember the candy house, or me lying on a countertop?"

"You were lying on a countertop? You really need some sleep. You're talking gibberish. Don't worry brother, you've been safe and sound in your bed the whole time."

Cleo turned his head towards the bedroom door as Linus' young eyes stared right through Cleo, not buying the lie one bit.

"I think it's time for bed. I'm about to pass out on my feet myself. Go to sleep, we can finish this story another night," Cleo walked out of his room.

Cleo groggily walked into the living room to lock up before heading to bed. When he got there, he tossed his book onto the floor. He was angry with himself for what transpired.

> *Ramiel warned me about bringing others with me. Just because it's a fairy tale, I have to stay on guard at all times.* – He thought, collapsing onto his bed. *I took on a 12-foot-tall, one-eyed, man-eating monster, yet a senior citizen armed with a spatula and a frying pan almost did me in.*

He massaged the bump that had formed on his temple.

> *What about what she said as we were leaving? That she'll never fall for that trick again? What does that mean for Hansel and Gretel? Did I just sign their death warrant?* – Cleo lay down on his bed, unable to look at the altered ending in the book. *Well,*

if something does happen, at least it is only one copy.

He finally forced his eyes shut, dreading what nightmares would come to him this time in the night.

CHAPTER 7

A Muse's Dream

"BEEEEEEEPPP!!!" The bell rang loud over the intercom, signaling the end of 5th period, and only one hour until they were free for the weekend.

Without letting their teacher even finish his sentence, the students all stood up to head to their last class.

"So Penny, you want to go up to Diamondback Ridge this weekend?" Bryce asked as they gathered their things.

"Yes! That sounds like it'd be great. Let me ask Cleo if he wants to come," Penny answered excitedly.

"Wait..." Bryce said, rolling his eyes.

She walked over to Cleo who was turning in an assignment at the front of the room.

"Hey, you want to come with Bryce and me up to Diamondback tomorrow? It's supposed to be gorgeous outside."

"Oh, nah. Thanks though. I think I'm just going to chill at home this weekend. Catch up on some of my reading," he responded giving her a half-hearted smile. "Plus, I really need to sleep. I was up all night writing."

"Writing? For the English assignment? It's not due for another couple of weeks," Penny pointed out, surprised that Cleo would even think of doing homework that far in advance.

"No, just something else I'm working on," Cleo said guardedly.

"Alright, then I'll keep you company," Penny said, not pressing him any further.

"What? Why? You're allowed to go without me you know?" Cleo said confused by her reaction.

"Because, something is going on with you," she said, lowering her voice so nobody else around them could hear. "I know you won't ask for it, but I'm going to help you figure it out."

Cleo opened his mouth to refuse her offer, but instead simply said, "Thanks."

"Cleo, can I have a word with you in private please?" Mr. Bergh, their history teacher asked while Cleo finished packing up his things.

"Sure. I'll catch up with you guys in a sec," he said to his friends. Penny nodded and walked out of the class. Cleo looked out the small window in the classroom door and saw Bryce shoot him a dirty look and shake his head.

I guess he doesn't agree with Penny's new weekend plans.

"Cleo, what's going on with you? You seem to be, be...disconnected from school lately," Mr. Bergh said after the door shut behind the last student exiting. Mr. Bergh was the only teacher that ever seemed to notice little nuances like this in his class. He could tell when someone was going through a rough patch, and never hesitated to offer guidance. "You no longer speak up, you show up late to class, and your mind seems like it is a thousand miles away. Talk to me," he said very earnestly.

"I'm just tired from fighting monsters, pirates and witches all the time now," Cleo said honestly.

"Well I'm not your father, but I think you need to spend less time on video games, and more time in books," Mr. Bergh said in a disappointed tone.

"You're right Mr. Bergh, I do need to spend more time in books," he said, suppressing a smile. "I'll try harder, I promise."

"You better. Now go have a good weekend," he said, ending his lecture.

"Thanks," Cleo said, hoisting his bag onto his shoulders and leaving the classroom.

"So you want a ride home after school today?" Bryce asked Penny as Cleo came into the hallway.

"No thanks, I'm going to walk with Cleo. We're going to grab a sandwich afterwards." There was only one place in town that sold sandwiches worth eating, *Which 'Wich You Goin' Wit'.* "I'll see you on Monday though."

"How much longer are we going to play this "pity Cleo" game? Because quite frankly, I have played more than enough of it over the last few years," Bryce snapped out suddenly, sneering at Cleo.

Cleo dropped his bag to the floor at his feet.

"If you have something to say Bryce then man up and say it. Otherwise why don't you just shut your mouth," Cleo's aggressive response took all three of them by surprise.

"What'd you say to me?" Bryce asked.

"You heard me. I'm so tired of your snide remarks about everything I do. Do everyone a favor and shut up for a change," his voice getting louder and angrier with every word.

"Guys, just cut it out. You're best friends, stop arguing." Penny, always the pacifist, tried to intervene as the two boys stood in the halls of the school. Their voices had reached the point where they could no longer be considered *inside voices*.

"Best friends? We're just acquaintances who happen to hang out with the same girl," Bryce responded, stepping closer to Cleo. "I couldn't be best friends with someone as sad as this."

"Funny, I've been thinking the same thing about you," Cleo said.

"You know I think I figured something out Cleo," Bryce continued. "Maybe your mom didn't die in that crash. I wouldn't be surprised if she left you and your whack job father," Bryce said with a sinister smirk on his face.

The words cut into Cleo like a dagger and struck the same chord in Cleo's psyche as that hag had done in *Hansel and Gretel.* Before Cleo could stop himself, he lashed out at Bryce, punching him in the face. His fist collided with the bridge of Bryce's nose. The sound of cartilage breaking deafened the noisy halls.

"AAAAAA!" Penny screamed as her friend fell back into the lockers, his face bloodied.

Typically, fights at school were met with "OOOHHH"s and "AHHH"s and the egging banter that High School teenagers toss around at one another. This time however, all that permeated the school halls was silence.

"Next time you say something about my mom, I promise you I won't stop."

Cleo looked around and saw all the open-mouthed faces staring at him. He could hear people whispering his name as if they were struggling to believe it was really him that just pulled off a Mike Tyson impersonation.

"Cleo...I..." Penny started to say something before Cleo pushed his way through the crowd and walked out of the building.

Bryce got to his feet to pursue Cleo. His eyes were watering and he was filled with rage as blood trickled down into his mouth.

"Just calm down Bryce. Leave him alone. Go get cleaned up," she said, stepping in front of Bryce's path. "I've got to check on him. I'm sorry," she apologized before leaving Bryce to tend to his injuries alone and sprinting off in the direction of Cleo.

Penny's loyalty to Cleo angered Bryce more than the punch itself. He was the one bleeding, yet Cleo was the one that Penny pursued. Bryce was tempted to chase Cleo down and beat him to a pulp. Instead, he opted for one of the lockers nearby to feel the brunt of his wrath. He turned and punched it as hard as he could, denting the pliable metal before storming off in the opposite direction of his friends.

Cleo was infuriated, a feeling he did not often feel. He didn't know how to deal with it. He had to get to a place where no one could follow him. He would only be able to find refuge in one of the many worlds at his disposal. For the first time he wanted to enter a book purely as a means of escape, not rescue. He needed an escape from his friends, his family, his responsibilities, his search, his life, everything.

He ran to the library in search of one of his usual booths, but paused when he reached the front door.

Damn, I forgot about SAT testing.

He looked around to gauge what other possibilities were available.

> *I guess there is always the photography room. Hardly anyone is ever actually in the classroom.* – The teacher, Ms. Green, frequently let her students leave early to "find inspiration around town to enhance their portfolios." In reality, most of the kids just left and went home. Ms. Green certainly knew about it, but she just seemed not to care.

He quickly came upon her classroom and found it characteristically empty. Based on the time, it may have been because Ms. Green was at lunch, but Cleo didn't particularly care. He reached for the handle, and, finding it unlocked, opened the door and entered the classroom. She had pictures that past students had taken plastered all over her class. There was a section for panoramic scenes, black/white ones of families and floral arrangements hanging from her ceiling, and abstract photos taken with a box camera taped to her walls. Cleo paid little attention to all of it, and walked straight to Ms. Green's desk and sat down. He opened up his bag to see what otherworldly options he had brought with him.

Glinda of Oz, book 14 in the series? I've had almost enough of Oz. It'll have to work for now. – He thought, opening up to a random passage.

They now climbed the bank and...

The door of the classroom swung open interrupting Cleo's sensation of being pulled into the book. He instantly slammed the book shut.

"What are you doing in here Cleo?" Penny said as she came inside. She walked to him and looked at the cover of the book in his hand.

"You are acting so odd. I don't understand, you break your friend's nose and run away to read the Wizard of Oz?" She asked, noticing the cover of the book he was holding.

"Um..." he was so surprised that she followed him, and relieved she didn't come in mere seconds later. "Technically, it's not the *Wizard of Oz*, that's the first book in the series. This is the last one. See, *Glinda of Oz*," he pointed to the title.

"Cleo, what's going on? Talk to me," she said concernedly, ignoring his smart-aleck behavior.

His heart pounded rapidly as he stared into her eyes. Maybe it was her mood or the dark ambiance of the room, but their color was slightly darker than normal, like smooth spherical sapphires.

I can't lie to her anymore. If I do, it could ruin our friendship. – He thought, weighing his options. I have to tell her the truth. It may lead to her recommending me to an insane asylum or never speaking to me again. It could also lead to... everything I want.

"You really want to know? Because once I tell you, there's no going back."

"No going back? You're making this sound like you're some sort of criminal on the run," she said, only half joking. "Yes, you can tell me anything."

"Alright, then follow me. We need to go back to my house. I can't tell you here."

Always wanting to follow the rules, she resisted, "We can't leave yet. We still have one class left."

"It's not like you've never skipped class before."

"I haven't," she said proudly.

"Come on, if you want to know, we need to leave now."

She was annoyed at his insistence to break the rules, but finding out why he was acting so distant and short-tempered was more important to her than perfect attendance.

"Fine, let's go. But I better not get in trouble for skipping school or Bryce's not going to be the only one with a messed up face."

Cleo doubted that Penny had ever hit a fly, but he also wasn't too keen on finding out the truth.

Ever since their stroll in the mini-monsoon a few weeks earlier, the two of them had walked home together every day. Their usual topics of conversation bounced from Cleo and his mother, to their plans for the future.

"I'm going to be a famous artist. What are you going to do Cleo?" She had once asked him.

"I'm going to travel," he said nondescriptly.

"Where to?"

"Everywhere," he answered cryptically.

However, on this walk from school, there was no small talk between them. There was no rain bouncing off the sidewalk, or water sloshing up from the tires of passing cars to drown out their silence. It was 1:00

pm on a Friday in a rural town. Barely a car could be seen on the road. Nevertheless, Penny kept looking back behind them, anticipating a school official to start chasing them down at any moment.

Cleo on the other hand was not worried about getting in trouble for truancy. His mind was on where he would take her and the impending repercussions of divulging his most precious secret.

> *I could use Glinda of Oz, or one of the other Oz books. I could take her into something from Verne. I think I'll stay away from Homer for the time being. I literally could take her into the creations of any author who has ever lived.* – He thought, trying to pick out their first destination. *Why am I even thinking about this? Of course, there is only really one choice. It has to be my own. Well not entirely my own. Mom deserves most of the credit. It is her story after all.*

Their walk to Cleo's house was brisk. Neither of them spoke, nor did they see anyone they knew. When they arrived at his home, the driveway was expectedly empty.

> *Good, that would have been unfortunate had he decided to stay home from work.*

They walked inside and Cleo locked the door behind him. He looked up at the clock made from a large slab of maple wood hanging on their living room wall.

1:25 pm. Linus doesn't get in until almost 4:00 pm. With Dad not getting back until at least 6:00, that's got to be like a week in story time. – He tried to calculate how much time they would have.

"Follow me," he said beckoning Penny towards his bedroom. He led her into his room and closed the door.

> *There's no point in me trying to simply tell her what I can do. She wouldn't believe me. I need to show her. I can explain everything once we are inside. Then she'll have no choice but to believe me.*

"This is not quite what I expected your room to look like," she said, looking around at the contents of his room.

"What are you talking about? You've been in here before." Cleo said, shuffling through various notebooks on his desk. "I've been in your room tons of times."

"You're right, you have seen my room lots of times, but I have never seen yours. We don't ever hang out in your house."

"Hmm, I guess you're right," Cleo was only partially paying attention until he finally found the notebook he wanted. "What do you mean it's not what you expected though?"

"I expected posters of women, music, sports. Dirty clothes strung everywhere. Maybe some empty pizza boxes and soda cans, but all this..." she said, pointing to the bookshelves filled to capacity with books, journals and spiral notebooks. There's a full-page booklist tacked to the wall above his desk. There were inspirational quotes from Ralph Waldo Emerson and Oscar Wilde written on a white paper nailed to his door. "I'm a little impressed."

"I guess I'll take that as a compliment. Anyway, go ahead and sit on the bed and I'll show you."

"You're going to show me what?" she said, skeptically raising her eyebrows at her teenage friend.

"Trust me. I promise you everything is going to be alright."

She reluctantly sat on the bed as he opened the journal a few pages in.

"Is that a journal? I didn't know you kept one. Is this what you wanted to show me? An excerpt from your journal or something?" Her tone was a soft mixture of sarcasm and genuine intrigue.

"Actually, yes...more or less. It's not exactly my journal though. It's a story my mother wrote."

He began to read the first sentence.

"*This magical world rivaled any other in the entire universe. It was as if the greatest qualities of every fantastical world that has ever been imagined, had been molded together to form the perfect world. It does not nearly do this paradise justice by merely describing its wonder. It truly is something that you should experience. And after just 1 visit, your life would be changed forever."*

Penny interrupted him as he started to read.

"Whoa, whoa, hold on a second. This has nothing to do with why you've been acting so weird lately, why you knocked Bryce to the ground, or why you decided to read a book afterwards. Really, this explains absolutely nothing."

"Please Penny, just listen. Trust me and I swear that you'll understand everything in a second."

He placed his hand on her knee and started to read again.

"When you finally make your first visit, start in the clouds. Because it is truly the closest to heaven you could ever be, without actually going."

As the last word rolled off Cleo's tongue, he saw out of the corner of his eye Penny jerk her leg away from Cleo's hand. It was already past the point that he could control his descent into the notebook and his bedroom dissolved around him.

Before Cleo could stop what was happening, he found his bed replaced by a white, puffy cloud resting in the sky. He also found that he was all alone.

"Crap," he said realizing that he left her behind.

> *That didn't go quite as planned. She is probably seriously freaking out right now.* – Cleo thought, closing his eyes and concentrating on his return home.

Images of his room and Penny sitting on his bed filled his mind. After a minute or two, he could see everything as clear as if he were looking at a photograph. Yet curiously, he stayed in exactly the same spot on the cloud. As the minutes passed one by one, he continued to try to leave his story. Yet he remained in the fantastical land of Terra Somniorum.

> *I don't get it. It feels like I'm running into a wall. I can't leave.* – He was confused, and began to worry. *Is it because I wrote this one? Does that change things? Am I stuck here forever?*

Cleo was so troubled by the situation that he was entirely unaware of his surroundings. He also had not realized he was pacing in circles on the cloud. That was, until his circle widened too far and he accidentally stepped right off the edge of the cotton swab platform.

I'm getting really fed up with free-falling at the mercy of gravity! – He flailed his arms as he again found himself dropping through the open air.

I could not have chosen a worse time to lose my ability to leave! How do I break through this wall? I need to think!

He squeezed his eyes shut tightly, ignoring the wind whipping at his tumbling body.

Should I try to skip ahead? I doubt I have the time to bring up the storyline. What I need is to stop falling. Where's a parachute when you need one?

He opened his eyes to try to get a look at how close he was to the ground. He expected to be falling head over heels, with views of the sky and water rotating every second. He found that he was not falling, but actually lying perfectly still, staring up into the sun. He sat up and noticed that the solid mass he was sitting upon was another cloud, softer than a goose-feather pillow but solid enough to jump on.

"It was clear skies. I'm sure of it," he said looking up at the cloud he had freshly fallen from, floating in the distance above him.

Was it because I wished to stop falling, or is it just part of the magic of my mother's story? I wonder... – Cleo smiled mischievously. He walked to the edge and hung one foot off the edge of the cloud. At least fifty feet below him he saw a cloud begin to form. *Now that is a neat trick. If leaving is not an option, I suppose I can have a little bit of fun.*

He backed up to the far side of the cloud. He crouched down in a sprinter's position and prepped himself to run.

Wait, the wall is gone. – He thought, standing back up. *That's odd. I'm not sure how I know, but I can feel that it's no longer blocking my escape. I can try this another time. I need to get Penny first.*

Putting his celestial game of long jump on hold, Cleo refocused on his bedroom and this time was able to return without any problems.

"AHHHHH!!!!" Cleo was met with a blood-curdling scream as he reformed back on his bed.

"Penny! Penny! Everything's alright. Please let me explain. You need to calm down."

Cleo may as well have been speaking Latin, as Penny did not hear a word he said. She jumped off his bed and had her back against his door.

"Penny, please. Calm down. Trust me, I know how this looks. Just relax and I'll tell you everything."

"What...what....what are you?"

> *Really? Not, what happened? Where did you go? How did you do that? You go with what are you? –* Cleo thought, mildly offended by her reaction.

"I'm not some sort of alien Penny," Cleo responded. "It's me. I'm no different than I was five minutes ago."

"Well, I don't know that. I just...I wasn't expecting that. What's going on here?" She asked, her shoulders releasing their tension and her wide-eyes shrinking to a normal size.

"I have a particular, ability, shall we say. I can travel out of this world and into any other world that I desire. I can...teleport myself into any story that sits in front of me. When I am reading books, instead of just imagining what is happening, or picturing the plots unfold, I can take myself into them and see them for real. I can experience them, become a part of them."

"You can enter into stories?" Despite having just watched him disappear as quickly as a lightning strike, she was not fully buying into his explanation.

Cleo sighed and realized that he was going to have to take this to the next level.

"I'm not lying. My mother also had the ability to do this. If you don't believe me, take my hand, and let me show you."

Penny was sure he was completely bonkers at this point. Despite her apprehension, he was her best friend and she trusted him with her life. Nervously, she grabbed his hand.

"This time, don't pull away or let go. Alright?"

She nodded her head. He grabbed the notebook again and started to read from the same passage.

"When you finally make your first visit, start in the clouds. Because it is truly the closest you can ever be to heaven, without actually going."

The moment the last word was spoken, the two of them were thrust down into the handwritten story, and the room around them disappeared. Although it only lasted the length of a few breaths, he was very aware of Penny's hand becoming tense and squeezing firmly until her nails dug into his skin. Her face reminded him of when they were at the amusement park the summer before and they went on the roller coaster together. She was holding her breath up until their car reached the top, before screaming at the top of her lungs as it turned into its speedy dive.

The two of them landed abruptly yet softly on the very same cloud that Cleo had recently fallen off.

"Welcome to paradise Penny."

Penny had yet to blink an eye. She wasn't sure if any of it was actually happening. She thought she must be dreaming or possibly going crazy. She even thought of the possibility that he slipped her something when she wasn't paying attention. What other explanation could there be?

"This is the world my mother created when I was a baby. It's called Terra Somniorum, The Land of Dreams. What do you think?"

Finally, she found her voice and spoke.

"You weren't lying. You really can...go into books. This is incredible. It's heaven. This can't possibly be real. This must be a dream. You put a psychedelic in my drink didn't you?" She said, uncaring even if his answer was yes.

"I didn't offer you a drink. No, I promise that you are not dreaming. Everything here is as real as either you or I. It is exactly how I described it with my pen and notebook. Whatever I am reading or imagining, I can take myself and whoever else I want, inside."

Now that Cleo wasn't worried about how to leave, he too was able to savor what he had created. There were sky-scraping, snow-capped mountains in one area. In another, there was a meadow covered with flowers of more colors than a crayon factory. Off in the distance was a purple and white castle, floating amongst the clouds. Directly below them was an ocean so crystal-clear that they could see down to its sandy floor.

Looking at the world his mother created brought Cleo back to all those nights she sat in her wicker rocking chair beside his red convertible-shaped bed. She would describe it in such detail that he always felt as if he were being transported into this world of bliss.

> Maybe she did take me here before. Maybe that's why I can remember how it looked so vividly. She could have done to me, what I did to Linus.

"How do we get down?" she asked.

"Take my hand."

She grabbed his hand and he led her to the edge of the cloud.

"Do you trust me?" Cleo asked Penny as she peered at what lay below them.

"Absolutely," she answered, her pulse going into hyper-drive.

Cleo bent his knees and leapt off the cloud, pulling Penny with him. Holding her hand, Cleo felt like their fall would last forever. He didn't think about the ground that could inevitably reach them. He felt as if they were encased in a bubble with the blue skies around them and a cool airstream controlling their descent.

Their exhilarating waltz with the winds ended as a new cloud formed instantly beneath them, providing a painless, cushioned landing.

"It's like a stairway to the stars," Cleo said, smiling at Penny, never releasing her hand.

"Unbelievable," Penny said, carefully leaning over the side of the cloud. Her face beamed as another pillow platform appeared beneath them. "Try and catch me," she said with a smile, releasing Cleo's hand and bravely jumping over the side.

Cleo ran to the edge to see Penny land beneath him. She looked up and waved, beckoning him to follow. That was all the encouragement he needed as he began chasing her through the sky. They hopped from cloud to cloud, each time their hearts stopping as they silently hoped another one would form. After at least a few thousand feet of descending, Penny finally came to a halt.

"Gotcha," Cleo said, finally reaching her.

"Cleo, look down there. What are those things?" she asked, pointing to an array of strange creatures flying around beneath them.

"Those are Griffins. They are half lion, half eagle. If I remember correctly, they are the king of all the creatures here."

"They're amazing. They look so...majestic."

Cleo walked over to her and took hold of her hand.

"Come with me."

I hope this works. It'll be very embarrassing otherwise.

Cleo put his fingers to his mouth and let out a whistle. One of the winged creatures flew up and landed right next to Penny. She gasped and jumped backwards, not anticipating its arrival.

"It's alright. He shouldn't hurt you. Do you want to try and go for a ride?"

"You've got to be kidding me. You want to ride that thing? What, like it's a horse?" Penny gave Cleo a highly skeptical look.

"No, of course not. That's a ridiculous comparison. Horses don't fly. I want to ride him like a Pegasus." Cleo said, sporting a charming smile.

The Griffin knelt before them. Cleo climbed aboard its back and held out his hand, beckoning Penny to accompany him. The great creature, possessing a 12-foot wingspan, appeared both regal and deadly. It could tear through anything in its path like paper, then curl up next to you and fall asleep like a newborn kitten. Penny finally worked up her courage, took Cleo's hand, and jumped onto to the animal's enormous back.

"Hold on tight." Cleo said as Penny wrapped her arms around his midsection. "Because I have no idea how to control these things."

"You what!?" She tried to say before the Griffin flew off into the sky.

Penny held on tightly to Griffin's back, gripping whatever feathers and fur she could find.

> *God I hope this thing knows how to pilot itself!* – Cleo thought while the Griffin dove, barrel rolling like a fighter jet towards the ocean.

With the skill and agility of a peregrine falcon, the Griffin pulled up at the last second, its claws grazing along the water. Cleo's mind could barely keep up with his body as they whisked across the horizon. Every so often, it wandered from their surrounding beauty to Penny's arms, clasped across his chest.

"I don't know if you can understand me or what, but take us around the island. We want to see the waterfalls, mountains, all of it," Cleo shouted into the feline/bird's ear.

It must have understood Cleo just fine, for it immediately banked a hard left towards dry land. It reached the shore and raced across the crab infested sandy beaches, further inland.

"Where's it taking us!?" Penny yelled to Cleo.

"You'll see!" He turned his head and yelled back.

The Griffin continued flying across the island. It glided over a hayfield, its wings flattening all of the four-foot high blades of grass that stood in its path.

"Look!" Penny shouted, pointing to a herd of unicorns racing in an opening in the field towards the incoming tree line.

The Griffin flapped its wings and raised high above the trees as they danced arm in arm to the music of the wind. Hidden within the forest was an alpine lake, upon which Sea Nymphs twirled about as if they were on an ice rink. Just beyond the lake was its main water source, a small river fed by a towering waterfall crashing down onto the rocks below with incredible force.

"AHHH!!!" Penny screamed as they became drenched from the mist of the waterfall, the Griffin angled through the spray of the falls. "You did that on purpose!"

Cleo shrugged his shoulders playfully as they finally came to a landing off the north bank of the river. Penny pushed Cleo off the bird's back, sending him tumbling into the mud.

"I guess I deserve that."

With the sound of the waterfall pounding the riverbed in the background, they sat along the bank to soak their feet in the cool, rushing river. The Griffin pranced off like a drunken deer towards a patch of flowers that resembled tulips.

"I guess he's a vegetarian," Cleo commented.

"How often do you visit this place?" Penny asked, taking off her shoes.

"Honestly, I've never been here before. The first time was when I disappeared in front of you. I wasn't even positive this would work," Cleo admitted.

"You know you should have warned me. You nearly gave me a heart attack. You were sucked into the notebook like it was a vacuum cleaner. I freaked out and threw your journal down. I ran around the house calling out your name. I seriously thought I was going crazy. When I couldn't find you anywhere I opened it back up, and POP, there you were sitting in front of me again."

Cleo laughed. "Do you really think you would have believed me? As it was, you didn't believe me until I brought you with me," he said dipping his feet into the near freezing water.

Penny turned and faced Cleo.

"So tell me everything. How long have you been able to do…this," motioning to everything around her. "How did you find out?"

"It was on my 16th birthday. Just before you and Bryce showed up, I was doing a book assignment on the *Wonderful Wizard of Oz.* I started reading it, and before I knew what was happening I was in Oz with Dorothy, Scarecrow, Tin Man, everyone," he recalled to her.

"So that's why you seemed a little distant that night. I just figured it was because of Bryce."

"Well, he certainly contributed," he said, frowning at the mention of Bryce's name.

"What happened between you two? You seem to hate each other."

"I really don't know. It probably started with something petty," he said, shrugging his shoulders.

"So what happened after Oz?" she said, changing the topic from Bryce.

"Anyways, a week or so after my birthday I started writing this story down. It's odd though. I can remember the way my mother described the look and feel of this world perfectly, but when it comes to the plot, the characters," he shook his head in frustration. "I can't remember anything. Like why is there an ancient tree standing alone at the top of a hill, or why is there a floating castle guarded by a Phoenix?"

"A Phoenix?" Penny asked.

"Yeah, a mythical bird of fire," Cleo answered nonchalantly. "She read it to me so many times. I just wish I could remember."

"This is really all that you have left of your mother, isn't it?"

Cleo just nodded his head. Penny reached over, gave him a hug and kissed him on the cheek.

"Are you blushing?" She asked, as his cheeks turned beet red after the friendly peck.

Cleo savored the moment of the two of them together. They sat and talked, and laughed about everything that had happened over the last few months. After over an hour, Cleo decided to reveal the last and most important detail of what he had learned.

"There's one other thing. My mother...she's not dead Penny," Cleo said, changing the mood of their conversation.

"Cleo, we already went through all of this," Penny tried to reason with him.

"I know, It's not like that. It's...different. You'll see what I mean. There is one more thing I have to show you," Cleo said, standing up from the riverbank.

Penny followed him back onto the Griffin, which was lying down after gorging on the nearby grass. Cleo whispered their final stop into the Griffin's ear. After stretching its powerful arms, it flapped its wings and flew off out of the forest.

Once it was clear of the forest, and back over the flowery meadow, the Griffin slowed its speed to a calm glide. The sun was beginning to set ahead of them when they came to a stop in the shadows of a single tree, standing by itself at the crest of the tallest hill.

The tree was unlike any other Cleo had ever seen. It was frosty blue, like an icicle inexplicably growing from the ground itself. Its roots extended deep into the Earth, holding the hill firmly in its grasp. It towered over them, its scatter-branched limbs spreading at least four stories off the ground. Despite not a single leaf hanging from any of its ghostly branches, it looked more alive than any of the Evergreens in Cleo's hometown. Sitting beside the tree was a woman, her back to the teens.

"Cleo, who is that?" Penny asked, dismounting the kingly bird.

"It's my mother," Cleo answered plainly, unmoving from his spot on the Griffin.

"What?" Penny said confused.

"I didn't tell you everything about my trip in to Oz. While I was inside, I ran into her. Well, a teenage version of her."

Penny clearly did not understand anything he was saying. Cleo narrated the whole story of finding his mother in Oz, then again in Jules Verne's, *Journey to the Center of the Earth.* He didn't stop until he rehashed his meeting with Ramiel and the old man's theory about his mother not perishing in the plane crash.

"So, that woman over there is really her?"

"Not exactly, she's another one of my creations. I wrote her in here, last night in fact." Cleo still had not moved any closer to the tree, or to the woman resting under it.

"I don't mean to sound harsh, but why would you do that?"

> *Because if I can't find her, maybe I can recreate her and bring her back.* – He thought, knowing he shouldn't say it out loud.

"Because if I don't find her, I don't think I can simply let her go again. It was too hard the first time. Plus, maybe I could even show Linus the woman his mother was."

"Are those the only reasons?" Penny asked.

"Of course," Cleo said, staring off at the secluded tree. He could feel Penny studying him for any insight into what he was thinking.

"You ready to go talk to her?" she finally asked.

"No, I don't need to. For now, it's enough just knowing it worked and that she is here." Cleo turned and started walking down the hill. Penny hesitated before following in tow.

"So after all of this, what do you think? Do you think I'm crazy or maybe a freak? If you never want to talk to me again, I would completely understand. I promise I won't hold it against you," Cleo said, offering Penny an escape from his weird life.

"A freak? How could you possibly think that? Crazy maybe, but that has nothing to do with your power," she said wryly smiling. She leaned in and stared directly into his eyes, forcing him to not look away. "Believe me when I say you are not a freak. In fact, it's the most incredible thing I have ever seen. The real question is, if you truly believe this Ramiel's theory, then when are we going to start looking for this trail of stories your mother is in?"

A great sense of relief came over Cleo as he smiled back at her.

"Soon. Very soon. What do you say we go home?" he suggested to her.

"I guess if we have to."

He again took her hand in his, this time feeling no fear in her grip, as they returned to the real world.

CHAPTER
8

Haggard's Treasure

"Cleo, did you look in this box of books?" Penny called out to Cleo from his bedroom.

Cleo came in from the kitchen, holding a plate with two grilled bacon and cheese sandwiches.

"You realize that reading one book doesn't constitute a *box of books*, right?" Cleo said, pointing out the singular book in her hands as well as the lack of boxes in the room.

"I'm talking about the one you came across in *Peter and Wendy*," she said showing Cleo the cover of the book she was holding. "I was looking through some of the books that you said you've already entered, and noticed a line mentioning there was a box of books covered by a sheet. Did you ever go back and check inside?"

Cleo racked his brain to try to remember the scene she was referencing.

"Uh...I really don't remember seeing a box of books anywhere in Neverland.

Here, I brought us lunch," he handed her a sandwich.

"Thanks," Penny took the sandwich before showing him the line from the book.

Filling out the rest of the room were parchments of paper, scrolls, maps, a wardrobe that would put Audrey Hepburn to shame, and cage with a parrot. Cleo couldn't tell whether it was dead or alive, and a box of books whose titles were obscured by a sheet draped over top.

"It was just before you fought Hook. That's the same day that I found you in the library with the huge gash across your face, isn't it?"

Cleo rubbed the scar on his cheek, which had become scarcely noticeable.

"Yeah, same day. Why exactly are you looking through those books?" he asked, taking a bite of his sandwich.

She handed over the copy of *Peter and Wendy* to Cleo.

"Because I was curious as to how the story changed when you went inside. Look inside, there is literally a dozen new pages magically added to the book, and your name is everywhere! It's really fascinating."

He flipped through the book, slightly thicker than it was a few short months ago.

> *It really is quite amazing. I never noticed it adds pages to the books.*

"I don't even remember seeing this box to be honest. I guess I was a little preoccupied with the two women tied up in the corner," motioning to the line describing the scene.

"Fair enough, but we need to check it out. It could be exactly what we're looking for."

"I agree. Just not today. I've spent more than enough time in Oz and Neverland. I want to do something new. I want to go somewhere I've never gone before," Cleo closed the book and replaced it on its proper shelf.

"Hmm..." she mumbled, running her fingers across the spines of his unexplored books. "We *do* have the whole afternoon to ourselves," Penny said to Cleo with a smile as they sat on Cleo's bed.

"Oh yeah, and what exactly did you have in mind?" Cleo asked, perking up a bit.

"Why don't we go into an adventure? Not one with dragons, or unicorns or wizards. Someplace real, where we could never go otherwise," she said giddily.

Cleo was a little disappointed as part of him was hoping that she was talking about something else.

"First off, we have yet to see a dragon. Frankly, I don't know if that's such a good idea Penny. Adventure is just another word for danger. Actively searching out a place where things go wrong would be very reckless of us. Above everything else I have to keep you safe," he said, finishing the last bite of his lunch.

"It wouldn't be reckless. You can zoom us out of there as soon as any trouble arises. Come on, it will be fun."

"It takes longer than a quick zoom to get us out. Are you sure that you're the same girl that would not even jaywalk a few weeks ago? Now you're all gung-ho on being a full-fledged action star."

"I don't know, I guess the idea of doing something that no one else will ever do, or has ever done, is somehow, exhilarating." Penny pulled a novel off a shelf. "How about *Dracula?*"

"That's a little bit of a morbid choice, don't you think? I really don't want one of us getting bit and coming back as a vampire," Cleo lightheartedly bared his teeth, before placing it back into its spot.

"Alright, let's see. How about this one?" She grabbed another one. Cleo noticed the title was *The Lost World*, by Arthur Conan Doyle, before she could reveal it.

"Don't you remember how Jurassic Park turned out? Are you sure you want to be chased by 40-foot-tall lizards this early in the day?" They both laughed at the prospect.

"Ahh, now here is one that could work great," Penny said, taking an older looking book down.

"King Solomon's Mines, written in 1885, by H. Rider Haggard. This could be interesting. I've never read it before though. I vaguely remember watching the movie at one point."

This one isn't one of my mother's books. It's impossible she'd be in here. – He looked at the joy in Penny's face. Searching for mom shouldn't be the only reason I use my power. I should be able to have a little fun occasionally.

"Me neither, but I think it's about some guys that travel through a jungle and found a bunch of gold. Doesn't sound too harmful, does it?"

Neither did a house of candy. I was able to get us out of that one unharmed. She is far more capable of protecting herself than Linus, and she will actually know what's going on. What am I supposed to do? Take her into Clifford or Dr. Seuss all the time to insure nothing ever happens?

As Cleo considered his options, Penny was skimming through the beginning of the book.

"Chapter Two, The Legend of Solomon's Mines," she began.

"Well, gentlemen, if you like I will tell you. I have never showed it to anybody yet except to a drunken old Portuguese trader who translated it for me, and had forgotten all about it by the next morning."

"It appears like one of the characters is showing two other guys a letter and a map of some sort that he received in reference to the mines." She again fell silent as she read to herself.

"With my own eyes, I have seen the countless diamonds stored in Solomon's treasure chamber behind the White Death."

"It talks a lot about countless diamonds in a treasure chamber," she said, conveniently leaving out the part about a *White Death*. "Doesn't that sound awesome?! Have you ever seen countless diamonds before?"

Cleo grabbed the book out of her hands and read the same passage to himself.

"Yeah, it sounds fantastic, right up until the part about the White Death."

"I'm sure it's just an exaggeration. This book is 200 years old. White Death is probably just a metaphor for something harmless," she said, trying to persuade him.

> *Fat chance. Still...I want this. I'm the one with the power and I'll be ready this time. I won't let some crazy old woman get the jump on me again.*

"Fine, we can go," Cleo agreed.

"Yay!" Penny cheered.

"But we need to be careful. You have to stay by my side at all times."

Cleo turned to the table of contents.

"I won't be able to get a look at the storyline until we are inside. To start lets meet up with Allan Quatermain and the others to tell them we will be coming with them."

"What does it matter? We're clearly not going to belong, regardless if we give them the heads up or not," she questioned.

"When I went inside of *Journey to the Center of the Earth*, I just popped in on them a couple of times. The first time nearly got me thrown into a mile-high pit, and the second time almost caused them to fall into a river of lava. All they had were some lanterns, backpacks and pick axes. The same thing happened in Peter Pan. I was this close to being a human pincushion for their arrows. This group looks like it's going to have guns. Trust me, it'll be prudent of us to make sure we don't get shot in the process."

"You're the expert," she said, sitting down on the bed next to Cleo.

He turned the pages until he came to a spot he liked.

"Chapter 3, Umbopa Enters our Service. Remember, hold on tight so I don't end up going in alone, ok?" Cleo joshed.

Her tiny hands squeezed his with all their might. Her fingers interlinked with his own, caused Cleo to ignore his intuition, warning him that what he was about to do was a horrible idea.

"Mr. Quatermain," said Sir Henry presently, "Have you been thinking about my proposals?"

Within seconds, Penny and Cleo found themselves rid of the surroundings of Cleo's bookshelf, desk, bed and pet hedgehog. They were standing on Captain Good's ship, as it lay docked at the shores of Durban Point, in South Africa. A sweet yet spicy smell came from the land and filled their noses, while the drunken, off-key music coming from the sailors raising the ship's anchors filled their ears. Standing near the wheel of the ship was Mr. Allan Quatermain, Sir Henry Curtis and the Captain of the ship, Captain Good.

Cleo pulled Penny close to him and they crouched beneath one of the windows to the cabin. Cleo put his finger to his lips, indicating to Penny to stay silent.

"Ay, what do you think then, Mr. Quatermain?" said the Captain, echoing Sir Henry.

"Yes gentlemen," Quatermain said, sitting down again, "I will go, and by your leave I will tell you why, and on what conditions. First for the terms which I ask:"

Cleo peeked into the window to get a look at his soon-to-be fellow adventurers.

Quatermain was a man of small stature in his mid-50s. He had a deeply grayed beard and short hair sticking straight up. He wore a beige fedora, presumably made from one of the many big-game animals he had hunted over his lifetime. Sir Henry Curtis came from the other end of the physical spectrum. His physique was closer to that of a professional surfer, towering over Quatermain with long blond locks reaching down to his shoulders. Captain John Good was a commander in the Royal

Navy, but obscured by the other two men so Cleo could not get a good look at his appearance.

"You are to pay all expenses, and any valuables we may get is to be divided between Captain Good and myself," Quatermain began to relay his service requirements. He also asked that in the event of his death, his son would be compensated handsomely. "You may perhaps wonder why I would undertake such a journey. First I am a fatalist, and believe that if I am to go to Solomon's Mountains to be killed, I shall go there and be killed."

> *Why would he go if he thought he would be killed?*
> – Cleo thought.

"The average life of an elephant hunter is between four and five years. So you see, I have lived through about seven generations of my class, and I should think that my time cannot be far off, anyway," he continued his reasoning for accompanying them on their dangerous trip.

Cleo lowered his head back down beneath the window, completely out of sight.

"I can strangely relate to him, you know," he whispered to Penny. "When I die, I hope it happens in a story."

"Cleo don't talk like that. Everything is going to be just fine," Penny whispered, upset with his grim prophecy.

"I know that. I'm just saying that if one day something happens to me, I hope it happens in some wonderful world. As much as I am trying desperately to hold onto the fact that I am normal, I can't ignore the fact that I am different. If my destiny is special, why can't my fate be as well? I don't want to die in a blaringly loud ambulance speeding through the city to some gloomy and depressing hospital."

Penny gave him a sympathetic look, but didn't say anything in return.

The Captain spoke louder and took Cleo away from his morbid thoughts. "Now I vote we go down to the saloon and take a few swigs, just for luck, you know." The three gentlemen stepped out of the ship's cabin together, about to make their way to get their fill of spirits.

Cleo held up his hand at Penny, signaling for her to stay put. She nodded in agreement and Cleo stepped out from around the corner, causing the three treasure seekers to all jump like scared children.

"You're not a part of my crew. What's your business here and how did you get on my ship?" Captain Good immediately spoke up, placing his hand on the hilt of the sword sheathed at his side.

"My name is Cleo, and this here is Penny," Cleo beckoned to Penny to stand up. She obeyed but looked quite flustered.

"We just came here to tell you that we will be accompanying you on your journey. Due to prior engagements, we will not join you until much later. However, when the time is right, we will present ourselves again. We require no payment, except for the opportunity to see the mines of King Solomon with our own two eyes."

The three men stood speechless with various expressions of shock on their faces. None of them could explain how or why these two young people, dressed in strange clothing, just appeared on their ship and somehow knew of their impending journey.

"Who are you again? How do you know of our plans? Are you a spy?" Mr. Quatermain finally spoke up. His tone was not threatening but it was clear that he was serious and would not hesitate to do what was necessary to preserve the group's secrets and protect everyone onboard the ship.

"Let's just say we are from far away, in a land you've never been to, nor heard of. We have been keeping an eye on you for some time. I swear to you, we do not mean you, your crew, or your treasure any harm. We must leave now, but you will see us soon."

Cleo held onto Penny's hand and began to visualize his home.

"You look like children. How did you manage to get aboard this ship with nobody seeing?"

Cleo ignored their questioning and continued to pull up the details of his room in his mind. Just as he felt like he had enough to return them home, he pulled Penny around the corner, out of the three men's sight, and disappeared from the ship.

The Captain, Mr. Quatermain and Sir Henry soon realized that they needed a few stiff drinks, for when they rounded the corner to pursue Cleo and Penny they found themselves standing alone on the deck, no teenagers in sight.

As soon as Cleo and Penny reformed back on his bed, Cleo walked straight to his desk.

"Shoot, I forgot to take a look at the storyline. I don't want to chance anything, so let's read a summary of the book before we go back inside," Cleo said, turning on his laptop.

"Why? Is that really necessary?" Penny asked. The process of teleporting to and from books was still quite jolting to her. She took deep breaths to relieve the nausea and repeatedly checked over her body for any missing or wrongfully placed pieces.

"Because, I know in the movie there are some pretty gruesome scenes. There was one where somebody is killed by an elephant. Then there is a big war towards the end. If I'm remembering right, I want to make sure we go in after that happens, not accidentally during."

Penny sighed, becoming a little impatient with Cleo's caution.

Cleo scanned the internet until he found a satisfactory book summary.

"Here's a good one, let's see which chapter will be the safest to return at."

The two of them read through the synopsis of each chapter.

"See, I was right. One of the men hired to accompany them is stomped to death by an elephant. Another one freezes to death in a cave. A cave which apparently was already inhabited by the rotting corpse of a hundred year old dead explorer," Cleo pointed out on the screen.

"A wild elephant! That would be so much more exciting than one in a zoo. We could watch it from a distance you know. The person that froze probably wasn't wearing enough clothes. We could put on a few extra layers and be perfectly comfortable in that cave. Oh, and for the record, if it's really been that long it would really just be a skeleton at that point, not a rotting corpse," Penny said, reciting some of her minimal Anthropological knowledge.

"Ok then, Tarzan, how about this next one? They then come upon a tribe, where it just so happens that the slave they brought along with them is actually the long lost King who was driven out into the desert. A furious battle subsequently occurs, including the Tyrant King, Twala, being beheaded."

"Well, I'd actually be Jane. You'd be Tarzan," she said, playfully batting her eyes at Cleo. "Listen, I know you're trying to protect me, but I'll be fine. I promise. We can go in after the battle. At that point, they are on their last leg and heading towards the mine. We'll be out of danger, and still get a nice little adventure."

Penny reached over and closed the laptop shut before Cleo could delve any further into the story. She then reopened the book up and flipped to the latter half.

"We can go back inside right here." She noticed the chapter name was "The Place of Death" and sneakily covered the title with her hand.

"First sign of danger and we leave. Non-negotiable," Cleo said firmly.

"Deal," she agreed, handing the book over to him.

He nodded his head in agreement, took her hand and began to read.

"We camped in some huts at the foot of the Three Witches, as the triangle of mountains were called to which Solomon's great road ran."

Immediately they whizzed into the story, arriving at the foot of the mountains in the exotic African Jungle.

Allan Quatermain walked out of his hut and stared up at the extraordinary mountain that stood before him.

"Please do not be alarmed sir. We mean you no harm.", Cleo said immediately.

The expert explorer was startled by Cleo's sudden arrival at their camp. Quatermain had obviously just woken up, for he was barely dressed and did not have a weapon on his person. He spun around and reached to his belt for protection that was not there.

"CAPTAIN GOOD! SIR HENRY! COME TO ME QUICKLY!" Quatermain shouted to the huts behind him.

Within moments, the two men came out followed by a small handful of guards.

"It's you two again. I remember you from the ship, just before you disappeared like specters. Explain yourselves. Now," Captain Good ordered, holding a long rifle in his hands. While Good possessed the only firearm, the armed guards were still sufficiently armed with throwing spears.

"We're just two fellow explorers looking for an adventure. Like I explained to you on the ship, we've been keeping an eye on you from afar."

"You're lying. There is no way you have stayed out of our sight this entire time. What are your names? How did you really get here without us knowing?" Captain Good was all business as he walked straight up to Cleo, unafraid of the teenagers before him.

"We have been..." Cleo started to continue with his same story that he and Penny were both just exceptionally sneaky. Frankly, he was also tired of lying to every character he came into contact. "We aren't from this world. We travelled here from a different Earth so we could go on an adventure with all of you. You're quite famous where we come from."

Penny looked at Cleo in horror at what came out of his mouth.

"Great, these ones are even crazier than Gagool over there," said Captain Good to his men and motioning to a haggardly looking woman huddled by one of the tents. Gagool was the oldest creature Cleo or anyone for that matter had ever seen. She looked to be as old as the very mountain they were standing on. She was a devious woman who on multiple occasions tried to kill Quatermain and his party. The only reason she was still alive, was that she knew the exact location of King Solomon's treasure, and without her there was no hope they would ever find it.

"Whether you believe us or not doesn't really matter. All that matters is you trust us enough to let us tag along. We're not going to take all of your treasure, or somehow stop you from reaching it. As you can see we are completely unarmed, and about half your size. If at any point you decide you can trust us no longer, we'll leave. Sound good?" Cleo put on the most trustworthy smile he could muster up.

"Why should we bother letting you come? What could you possibly add to our company that we do not already possess? You are, after all, children."

Penny sensed that Cleo was not going to succeed in persuading the skeptical adventurers so she stepped in.

"Clearly we have something to offer as we've managed to follow you up until now without any of you suspecting a thing."

Captain Good wasn't bothering to consult Quatermain, Sir Henry or any of his soldiers. He sized up the two teenagers.

> *They aren't telling us everything, but they are just kids. I doubt they pose any threat to us. Especially the boy.* – Captain Good thought.

Having heard the Captain's thoughts, Cleo was about to respond to defend his masculinity and so-called lack of being a threat, but realized nobody else had heard a thing.

I'll show you no threat. – Cleo vented to himself, knowing full well he was both incapable and unwilling to do anything to the Captain.

"Very well, you may accompany us. However, we will not be responsible for you. You are not welcome to our rations nor will we go out of our way to protect you. We have enough to worry about."

Cleo noticed out of the corner of his eye Mr. Quatermain and Sir Henry exchanging looks of concern at their Captain's decision, but kept their opinions to themselves.

"Awesome, let's head out then," Cleo suggested before they could change Good's mind.

While the men did not look overly thrilled about their new companions, the native girl that they had picked up at a nearby village named Foulata, whom had become quite attached to Captain Good, seemed quite excited to have another female to walk with.

CRACK!

The sound of a branch breaking stopped Cleo and caused him to whirl around in its direction.

"Did you hear that?" he said, slowly walking towards the jungle.

"It was probably nothing Cleo. We just got here. You don't need to start worrying about every little sound. Ok?" Penny said, softly grabbing his arm to stop his advance.

He wanted to investigate the origin of the sound, but the thick vines and razor sharp branches dashed any hope of seeing anything.

"Fine, but if a tiger jumps out of the jungle at us, it's not my fault," he said, not spotting any danger.

They set off in the direction of the three towering mountains that lay before them. The man made path that led to the base of the mountain was about five miles long and surrounded by magnificent beauty. It was a white ribbon of clay, hidden and barely discernible from the majestic and boundless jungle around them. The vines intertwined across their path as freely as they did across the jungle floor. Rainbow lizards skittered along the ground, while chimpanzees cackled to one another in the trees.

"I can't believe places like this exist," Penny said to Cleo as the three of them, Foulata included, took up the rear of their mini-caravan. Quatermain, Good and Sir Henry took up the lead, followed by a handful of guards keeping watch over Gagool.

"These are the Three Witches. Three mountain peaks that all come from the same base," Foulata explained to Penny and Cleo as they took in the incredible sights around them.

Their trek lasted about two hours until they reached the bottom of the furthest peak. At its base, the road split into two paths, each circumventing an enormous hole in the ground.

"Can you guess what this is?" Quatermain asked the group as they looked down into the pit.

"It looks like a huge crater to me," Cleo answered.

"This isn't a crater. It's what our entire trip has been for. This, my friends, is the diamond mine of King Solomon," Quatermain said excitedly.

Everyone held their breath as they looked into the crater. Gleaming white diamonds shined like stars in a night sky.

"I always hoped it was real, but I don't think I ever truly believed it until now," Captain Good spoke.

Cleo leaned over to get a closer look. His stomach rose to his throat as he thought about all of his recent misfortunes with falling.

I'm quickly starting to hate heights.

"You have a hard enough time with ladders, maybe you should stand back a bit," Penny said, thinking the same thing as Cleo and tugging on the back of his shirt.

"I think you're right. I'd like to keep my feet on the ground for a while," he said, stepping back. "How are you going to get those out? There aren't any paths to follow into the mine," Cleo said, turning his attention to Good and Quatermain.

"We aren't. This mine has been thoroughly excavated. There isn't nearly as many jewels down there as it appears. Let us continue. If the tales are true, then this is only a small taste of Solomon's treasures," Mr. Quatermain called out from ahead of everyone.

Quatermain took point and urged them forward in the direction of three towering objects standing tall on the opposite side of the chasm. As they grew closer, they could see that the objects were indeed three substantial statues sitting on the road twenty feet apart from one another.

"If I'm not mistaken, and I highly doubt I am, those are the Silent ones. They are believed to be the deities that Solomon and his people worshipped, serving as the protectors of his treasure," Sir Henry educated everyone as they carefully walked around the gap.

The road widened where the statues stood. In the middle was a woman, entirely nude with a crescent moon arcing up from either side of her head. Flanking her were two men, appearing as her yin and yang guardians. One had a malicious and devilish face, while the other's was angelic and serene.

"What's the matter?" Penny asked Cleo, catching his eyes darting from the statue of the woman back to Penny.

"Oh, it's nothing," he said, his face suddenly beginning to feel hot.

"Can we move on? I don't like these statues," Foulata said, looking away from them.

"I agree, there is something about them that is troubling," Good said, echoing Foulata's trepidation.

Cleo sensed that the unnerving statues were staring at him, trying to give him a dire warning as he proceeded into the giant temple that lay before them. The temple, whose name, according to Gagool, was "The Place of Death".

"You go ahead of me. I'll stay back with Foulata. She looks terrified," Penny insisted to Cleo as everyone continued on, two abreast into a pitch-black chamber.

Moments after they all entered, the two girls screamed and Good shouted, "What's that? Somebody hit me in the face!"

"Don't worry, it's only bats. On you go!" Quatermain assured them.

The darkness did not persist for long as they quickly came upon an illuminated cavernous cathedral so large that anything in Rome would pale in comparison. All throughout the jungle basilica were pillars, appearing to be columns of solid ice.

"These are stalactites, not ice," said Sir Henry. "But how can light make its way in?"

"A small amount of sunlight is let in through the ceiling, then bounces off and magnifies off the pillars," Gagool answered, creeping her way around.

In the middle of the cavern, Penny was conversing with Foulata.

"You are so lucky to live here Foulata," Penny said.

"I guess I've never thought about it. It's all I've ever known. What's your home like?" asked the native girl.

"I also live near mountains, but it's nothing like here. We don't have the exotic animals like you do. Our trees are a lot different too. They're taller, but yours are so much prettier, and I've never seen anything close to this. This is incredible," she said, running her hands across the shimmering pillars.

"Cleo, look at these!" Penny excitedly pointed at the carvings and sculptured figures in some of the pillars. Some were in the shape of the beasts of the jungle, elephants, leopards and gorillas. Others were of likeness to the Egyptian Gods, Horus and Anubis.

Cleo continued gaping at the appearance of the stalactites around him.

> I'm glad I listened to her. Of all the places I have travelled to, this is certainly near the top.

Cleo suddenly felt two hands shoving him from his back. He went sprawling face first into the ground, just as a four-ton piece of stone crashed to the ground behind him. The impact caused the whole room to shutter and the rock shattered into pieces, showering him with shards of stone.

"Aghh," he said, wiping the fragments from the top of his head. He looked around to see who pushed him and saw only Gagool standing over him. She looked just as mystified at he was.

"CLEO! Oh my God, are you alright?" Penny screamed running to him.

"Yeah, I'm fine," he said, turning his attention to his scraped up elbow.

"Careful boy, you wouldn't want something to happen when we're so close to the end," Gagool said, offering a hand to help Cleo to his feet.

Cleo looked at the hands of the old woman. Her fingers didn't seem human. They were unnaturally long and bent in directions that should not have been possible. He shunted her aid, and pushed himself up from the ground.

> That was too close. If that would have hit me, not only would I have been killed, but Penny would have been trapped in here forever. – He thought, looking at Penny standing over him concerned. We're too close to the treasure. We'll stay in a little longer. Maybe I'll even find a little something to take back home for her.

"Very well. Are you prepared to enter the Place of Death?" Gagool asked loudly to the group, sadistically smiling.

"Can we skip that part and go straight to the treasure?" Cleo joked, trying to ease the tension and erase the narrow escape from his mind. Gagool looked at him and broadened her smile.

"Lead on, but I am keeping my eye very closely on you," Good said, following behind her.

One-by-one everyone followed the witch's directions through a dark passageway at the far side of the cathedral. As Cleo stepped over the threshold, he entered into a room much smaller and far dimmer than the previous one. He struggled to see into the darkness and only noticed, what appeared to be a large dining table made of stone.

"What is this place?"

He slowly moved his hands along the wall and took small, precise steps as to not trip. After carefully moving halfway around the table, his eyes adjusted to the blackness and he could see who was dining at the oversized dinner table. At the far end was a fifteen-foot tall statue of Death. A cloak draped over his head, and in his long, jagged fingers was a scythe twice the size of any human in the room. Sitting around in the chairs at the table was a giant, spear-wielding, skeleton that was grinning as if he were gleefully about to strike down anyone who came before him.

That is super creepy, but the detail is quite remarkable.

"Umm...is it just me, or is that one not made of stone?" Cleo said, pointing towards the center of the table. Sprawled out along the table, with his head resting on his knees and not attached to his shoulders like it should have been, was a very lifelike man.

"Isn't that Twala, the last king of the Kukuanas that you beheaded in the battle, Sir Henry?" Captain Good asked.

"Yes it is. How did he get here?" Henry turned to Gagool.

She didn't answer but smiled deviously.

A shrill scream rang throughout the room as Penny and Foulata both entered the room. The sight before him had Cleo so entranced that he hardly turned his head towards the girlish screams. He could see the slow dripping of water, falling slowly onto the corpse. All around the table were giant pieces of stalactites, shaped as if they were sitting around readying themselves for supper.

"Is he being turned into a stalactite?" Cleo asked Gagool who began to pray to the statue of Death.

"He he he he," she cackled. "Very perceptive aren't we young man?"

There has to be thousands of years of kings, all of whom have been mummified in this manner.

Cleo backed away from the table, tripping over a frozen king in the process.

"Come now boy, into the treasure room." Gagool beckoned him over to the far end of the room where the wall had somehow been magically raised into the ceiling, revealing a tunnel to a secret room.

Cleo hesitated, looking back to Penny who was deep in conversation with Foulata.

"Come see what they found. I think they may have found enough to share with even you," she said, urging him through to another shroud of darkness and towards a loud commotion coming from inside.

"Wait, I need to grab Penny and Foulata," he said, trying to push himself back into Death's dining room.

"She is fine young man. Let her look around. Go bathe in Solomon's riches," she said, this time forcing him through the doorway with a strength that Cleo was not expecting.

The entryway, as it turned out, was much longer than your typical doorway. Instead of a few inches thick, it was a thirty-foot long tunnel. Deciding it would probably be worse to resist her, he followed Captain Good, Sir Henry and Mr. Quatermain through the newly revealed doorway to see what all of the fuss was about.

"Wow..." was all Cleo could muster when he walked into the room.

The chamber was filled with more treasure than Cleo knew existed in the world. Piles of gold were strewn about the room like leaves in a front yard after a long autumn day. Gem encrusted crowns and tiaras hung from the walls. Golden weapons that looked more beautiful than deadly, stuck out from the ground.

"Take a look over in those chests there. You don't want to forget anything," urged Gagool.

Cleo opened the first chest he came across and revealed it packed full with countless diamonds, rubies, and flawless pieces of ivory tusk.

"PENNY, Come quick!! We found it! You'll never believe it, but we found it all." Cleo's shout echoed off the walls. Although he promised Captain Good he didn't want any of their treasure, he couldn't help his imagination begin to wander.

> I take even a few of these back and it will change my family's lives forever. What if, aside from finding mom, this is the reason I was given this power?

As Cleo mentally spent jewel after jewel, he heard a shrill scream followed by a bone-crushing crunch come from behind him. He spun around, terrified by what he might see. The light in the room dimmed and he sprinted in its direction.

"PENNY!!!" he yelled, praying to God with every step that his worst fear hadn't come true.

Lying on the ground was Penny, clutching her chest with blood-soaked hands. Her eyes were unfocused, pained and fearful.

"Penny, stay with me. I can...I can fix this. You're going to be alright," Cleo tried desperately to instill a false sense of hope into his dear friend as he carefully took her head in his hands.

"Cle...Cleo...I..." It was a struggle for her to choke out even the smallest of words.

"Just don't speak, just lie there alright?" Cleo was panicking. He looked around, searching for anything resembling an answer.

A stone wall blocked where the tunnel used to be.

"What happened?" Cleo yelled to Foulata.

"It was Gagool, she tried to close the door and flee. Penny saw and grabbed ahold of her to stop her. We tried pulling her through the tunnel to you. Then she stabbed her. Gagool ran off back out of the tunnel, but I don't think she made it," Foulata was sobbing into Captain Good's chest.

Cleo's cheeks became pint-sized waterfalls as tears streamed down them uncontrollably. His normally reserved emotions flooded out without regard for the grief-stricken treasure hunters that had run to his side.

"Penny, I'm so sorry. I shouldn't have left your side. This is my fault. I'm... I..." he stopped, knowing nothing he could say would bring any comfort to either of them.

Penny didn't respond as she struggled to keep her eyes open and lungs full of air.

"What can I do?" Cleo said as his tears fell from his eyes onto Penny's forehead. "I can't lose you Penny." He began to pray silently to a deity that he wasn't even sure he believed in, begging for her to be spared.

Penny looked into Cleo's eyes, and put the rest of her strength into one last beautiful smile.

"Goodbye Cleo," Penny's words were barely a whisper as her enchanting eyes closed forever.

CHAPTER 9

Well's Butterfly Effect

I have to talk to Ramiel. He'll know if this is even possible and he can help me if it is. Either way I need as much time as I can get before anyone becomes suspicious of her being gone. First thing I need to do is call her parents.

Cleo took one last look at the altered pages in the book. He dared not reread the scene that had just unfolded. Instead, he focused on his own final spoken lines.

"I'll come back to you Penny. One way or another, I will bring you back. I promise." Cleo gently placed his best friend's motionless body onto the cold, stone floor and vanished from the mountain temple.

He shut the book and tamed his emotions as much as was humanly possible. He grabbed his house phone and dialed in Penny's number.

Ring...

What am I going to say?

Ring…

Will they be able to see right through my lie?

Ring…

   Maybe they won't answer. Then I could just leave a message.

Ring…

   But then what am I going to say to a machine?

"Hello?" A female's voice came on the line. It was Penny's mother, Barbara. Cleo had always gotten along very well with both of Penny's parents. They frequently said he had an open door to come to them with anything, anytime. Cleo's only hope was to take advantage of their trust until he could somehow make things right.

"Hi Mrs. Jackson, it's Cleo."

"Oh hello Cleo, how are you? How's Penelope doing?" Her mother was the only person who ever referred to her by her full name, Penelope. From the day she was born everyone else, including her father, called her Penny.

"Penny's doing great. Myself…not so much."

"Oh I'm sorry to hear that. Is there something I can help you with? Do you need to talk about it?" Mrs. Jackson said, genuinely concerned.

"Well that's kind of why I called actually. I know this may sound like an odd request. I don't want you or Mr. Jackson to take this the wrong way. But I was wondering if Penny could stay the night tonight."

"Stay the night?"

Cleo could picture her mother raising her bushy eyebrows in skepticism.

"Um…yeah, I really need someone to talk to. It's about my mom…and my dad. I've just been having a really hard time lately and I would really like it if I had someone to talk to. Don't worry there won't be any funny business if that's what you're worried about."

"Ha-ha, don't worry Cleo, that's not what we're worried about." The way she said this made Cleo wonder what Mrs. Jackson really thought about him.

"My dad will be here later tonight. I'll make sure she's home in the morning." Cleo paused, as both of them remain silent. "I'm sorry to even ask you, but I really need this."

I'm a terrible person for lying to her and abusing her trust. What other choice do I have? Tell her that her daughter was stabbed to death and that I left her body in the African Jungle?

"You're really a great young man Cleo. You know that right?"

You won't be thinking that soon.

"If you need her that much...then yes she can stay with you."

"Thank you so much Mrs. Jackson. We'll stop by in a little while to pick up some things."

"Alright sounds good. Tell her I love her. I'll see you two in a bit."

"Will do, goodbye," he said before hanging up the phone.

Cleo was thankful to end their conversation before it was prolonged by small talk.

Now, time to go see Ramiel. He'll know something.

Still relegated to only having a bike for transportation, he looked all around his room for his helmet. It wasn't on his floor, in his closet or under his bed. He looked in the living room and garage to no avail.

Fine, I don't need a helmet. It's not that long of a bike ride. – He decided, putting on a jacket and running out of the house. His bike was chained to the front deck.

It has to be possible that this can work. Why shouldn't it? – Cleo thought as he struggled to remember the combination on his bike lock. *If I can bring a normal person with me into a story, it seems logical that I could go back in and bring them out. That means I can go in before she was killed and bring her out of the book, alive and unharmed.*

Finally, after multiple tries he was able to unlock his bike from the deck.

"Where is she?"

Cleo jumped and spun around at a voice coming from the bottom of the steps.

Cleo had been so deep in thought he didn't notice the black BMW pull into his driveway.

"Bryce? What are you doing here?" he said, shocked by Bryce's arrival.

"Where's Penny at?" he said in an accusatory tone. He still had two black eyes and a bandage covering the bridge of his nose where Cleo had punched him.

"Why should I know? She's probably at home," Cleo lied without hesitancy.

"Because you two are never out of each other's sight anymore," Bryce said jealously. "And she told me that she would be with you today."

Cleo tensed up at Bryce's interrogation.

"Well something else must have come up, because she's not here. I don't know where she is," Cleo continued his ruse of ignorance.

Bryce looked over Cleo's shoulder towards the windows of his home, trying to get a glance at what may or may not be inside.

"I guess I'll just have to head over to her house and ask her mom if she knows then," Bryce said, attempting to intimidate Cleo into revealing whatever information he may have known.

"Go for it," Cleo responded, pretending not to care.

Bryce didn't move from the bottom step of the deck. He shot daggers at Cleo while squeezing the rail.

"You have anything else to say? If not, I have things to do, so you can leave," Cleo stood his ground, returning Bryce's stare.

Bryce briefly moved onto the second step before whipping around and returning to his car. Without bothering to check his surroundings, he peeled out of Cleo's driveway.

Why did he have to come here? On today of all days. This is bad. When he tells her mom that she's not here then both of them will know I'm lying. I only have a few minutes before he gets to her house. Nowhere near enough time to go to talk to Ramiel. – He thought, throwing his bike to the ground in frustration. *I have no choice. I have to take the chance and go inside now.*

He left his bike on the deck and rushed back into the house, locking the front door behind him. He ran back to his bedroom, grabbing the copy of *King Solomon's Mines*.

This is her blood. – He paused, noticing the edges of the pages were stained red. He immediately bottled up the swirling emotions that had been about to surface and opened the book, ignoring the discolored paper.

Normally, Cleo strived to be a meticulous planner. He looked at all the angles before making any decision. As a result, his mistakes only resulted in broken glass, porcelain, or on rarer occasions, bone. However, if his assessment of the impact of Bryce's visit to Penny's mother were correct, then he would not have the luxury of time to formulate any sort of plan.

Look what happened the last time I acted on impulse. I got her killed. This has to go perfect. It could be my only chance to save her. – He thought, looking for the point where he and Penny entered into the story for the second time, at the base of the mountain. *This will work. It has to.*

After finding their point of entry, he concentrated on the gritty, wrinkled pages of the book, and began to read.

While the men did not look overly thrilled about their new companions, the native girl that they had picked up at a nearby village named Foulata, whom had become quite attached to Captain Good, seemed quite excited to have another female to walk with.

As he felt himself detach from the real world, Cleo imagined being crouched off the path and within the jungle, hopefully out of sight and sound of everyone.

The moment Cleo materialized a loud **CRACK** rang out.

A branch had snapped underneath Cleo's foot as he arrived much closer to the trail than he intended.

"Did you hear that?"

Cleo froze as the questioning voice was unmistakable. It was his own.

"It was probably nothing Cleo. We just got here. You don't need to start worrying about every little sound. Ok?" This time the voice made Cleo's heart skip a beat.

"Penny," he whispered, struggling to restrain from jumping out and running to her.

> *No, I can't lose my head. I don't know what could happen if the other version of myself sees me. For all I know I could cause some sort of butterfly effect and really screw things up.*

"Fine, but if a tiger jumps out of the jungle at us it's not my fault," the storybook Cleo said, stepping back to the group.

> *Interesting, I remember saying that. Am I the reason I said that? Or is it just a coincidence? –* Cleo thought, trying to listen in as they started up the trail.

Once he could no longer hear the clay path crunching beneath their feet, Cleo crept out from behind the bushes and proceeded to follow them, making sure to keep a considerable distance between them.

The five-mile trek from their camp to the mountain was mentally and physically exhausting for Cleo. He not only had to keep up the swift pace of the group, but also could not make a sound in the process.

It would be so much easier to just teleport to the diamond mine, but I can't take another chance of them hearing me pop in. I already almost screwed up once. I shouldn't test my luck. – He thought, wiping the sweat that was streaming into his eyes. *Too much more of this and they'll be able to smell me coming. I reek.*

They finally stopped when they reached the diamond pit. Cleo could see Quatermain addressing everyone, but was too far away to hear what he said.

I'll have to wait until they go inside. Everyone is too bunched up here. – He stopped, making sure to keep a safe distance.

After another brief stop for their history lesson on the three guardian statues, they continued into the mountain.

If there is going to be an opening, it'll be in here.

His first trip into the cathedral he couldn't have been more awestruck. This time, not even its grandeur could divert his mind from why he was there. He scuttled about in the shadows, looking for any moment where she was alone and he could save her from her ill-gotten fate. Everywhere she went however, Foulata or the other Cleo was close behind.

"Look at these!" Penny said, pointing to the same carvings in the pillars.

This is where I was almost crushed. That rock is going to fall from above soon. Which means Gagool must be nearby. Although, that's strange, I don't see her anywhere. – Cleo thought, inching closer and closer to his other self to get a better look. He squinted through the darkness and finally saw Gagool hovering about on the opposite side of the room. *She's not moving towards me. If she doesn't leave soon, there's no way she'll make up that distance in time.*

Cleo looked up at the top of the pillar while his other self, analyzed the base. A crack formed and quickly spread like a spider-web ten feet from its tip. He again looked towards Gagool who hadn't moved from her position.

> *She's not the one that pushed me out of the way. If she isn't, then who does?*

The crack finally expanded all the way through and the large stone toppled from its peak. Without thinking, Cleo took off in a full sprint towards his literary twin. Just before the falling rock reached them, Cleo shoved his other self from behind.

"UGH!" cried the storybook Cleo as he was sent crashing to the ground.

The real Cleo immediately rolled behind the nearest pillar.

> *It was me all along! Gagool never pushed me. I pushed me!*

"CLEO! Oh my God, are you alright?" He heard Penny scream, running towards them.

"Yeah, I'm fine," said the other Cleo in pain.

"Careful boy, you wouldn't want something to happen when we're so close to the end," Gagool said.

This time as she spoke, Cleo could hear the evil in the woman's voice with every word.

> *I should have seen it all coming. It's obvious she was scheming something devious the whole time.*

Cleo could hear everyone begin to make their way to the dark passageway and carefully moved from his hiding spot.

"I know you're there stranger." The voice made Cleo's heart and movement stop. A lump in his throat prevented him from responding. Gagool was standing where the light of the cavern only illuminated half of her face. "It was you that saved that young man. I don't know why you wish to stay hidden. Nor do I care. Stay out of my way and I won't alert the others." With half of her face concealed in the darkness, Cleo couldn't get a full look at the expression on her face.

Why would she say that? What reason could she possibly have for not blowing my cover?

Despite the woman's promised secrecy, it still took every ounce of Cleo's strength not to lash out at the old witch. The woman responsible for Penny's death was standing mere feet from him, vulnerable and exposed. His blood boiled and in the blackness, his face turned bright red. He wanted so badly to reach out and strangle her with his bare hands.

How dare she just stand there! Smiling as if nothing has happened. Pretending she doesn't know that she will soon kill. It won't happen this time. If it comes down to it, I'll kill her myself. I swear to God I will.

As his mind focused on his intense hatred of Gagool, he realized that he missed a perfect opportunity to potentially reach Penny. The other Cleo had gone into the next room leaving Penny with only Gagool and Foulata nearby. Unfortunately, she did not linger any longer and they quickly proceeded into the mountain's dining room.

"Damn, I need to pay attention," he scolded himself in a whisper.

His time, or more appropriately Penny's time, slowly ticked away second by second. He moved with a greater sense of urgency, not bothering to tiptoe to the next room, almost daring someone in the next room to hear him. He waited by the door and ever so slightly stuck his head into the room.

"Is he being turned into a stalactite?" he overheard book-Cleo ask Gagool.

The second I go into that room, I need to act. It's my last chance at saving her.

"He he he he," she cackled. "Very perceptive aren't we young man?"

Cleo watched himself trip over one of the frozen bodies.

Idiot... – He thought, criticizing himself.

"Come now boy, into the treasure room," Gagool said to the other Cleo.

He could see himself pause briefly at the doorway before Gagool assuring him that his friend was perfectly safe where she was.

I was blinded by the promise of riches. I can't believe I left her alone.

Storybook Cleo moved into the next room while Gagool slithered towards Foulata and Penny, standing in somewhat of a stupor, staring at the permanent guests sitting around the dinner table.

"Come, come, do not waste any more time in this room," she sounded very irritated by their lethargic pace to the treasure room. Gagool turned in Cleo's direction, placing her hand on the small of Penny's back in an effort to usher the straggling girls to the door.

They reached the threshold of the tunnel and Gagool slowed down. While the girls continued on, she slowly backed up until she was at the entrance.

"Hey, what are you doing?!" said Foulata, noticing she was no longer right behind them.

Gagool reached up and pushed in on a stone jutting out from the wall, causing the entire tunnel to begin closing.

Penny ran back and grabbed the crazed woman's robe, exposing a small glinting piece of metal within, and pulling her back into the doorway.

"The dagger," Cleo said aloud, no longer bothering to quiet his voice.

Seeing the blade that was about to end Penny's life sent Cleo into a fury. He abandoned all reason and logic and sprinted across the dining room. Penny and Gagool tugged and struggled against each other as the tunnel slowly descended. Gagool managed to get one of her hands free and reached into her robe for the hidden dagger.

"NOOOOOOO!!" Cleo yelled, it echoing through the cavern as he charged forward.

"What? But you're in there..." Gagool began, noticing Cleo just before he slammed her. The force sent the old hag crashing to the hard, unforgiving cavern floor, unconscious.

"AHH!" A scream squeaked out of Penny as her would-be assailant fell at her feet.

Gagool's dagger dislodged from her grip and slid across the ground, its jagged steel and ivory handle coming to a stop underneath Cleo's foot.

"Cleo?! Why would you...How did you get there?" Penny asked, perplexed and pointing back and forth, to where Cleo came from to where the other Cleo had just gone.

The stone ceiling was only a few feet above them.

"PENNY! What's happening?" shouted storybook Cleo from the treasure room. The kicking around of rocks could be heard as he ran back towards the commotion.

Cleo grabbed Penny by the arm.

"What are you doing?" she said, trying to pull her arm away.

"Move!" he jerked her over Gagool's body and into the adjacent room.

"Ouch! Cleo!" she shouted.

"Penny!?" the other Cleo yelled, entering the far end of the tunnel.

"Get away from the door! Quick!" Cleo said, stepping in front of Penny and obscuring her view of the nearly sealed tunnel.

Cleo looked back, hoping his literary twin had turned back. He saw not himself, but something far more terrifying. It was the horrific sight of Gagool regaining consciousness, just as the tunnel's ceiling finished its descent, crushing her underneath. The voices hollering from the treasure room silenced and were replaced by those of bone crushing under the weight of the rock.

> *Oh God, I'm going to throw up* – He thought, turning his head away from the grisly image.

"What was that?" Penny asked in horror.

"She had a knife, she was reaching for it. I don't think she made it out,"

Cleo said.

"Is she dead?" she asked, already knowing the answer.

"It was an accident," he assured her.

Was it really? I was ready to stab her myself a minute ago.

Penny's hands were trembling.

"Let's go home," he said, trying to calm Penny's nerves by holding onto her shaking body.

What if she's now just another character in a book? What if when I open my eyes I'm alone on my bed? I won't be able to live with myself. – He started to picture his room, hoping to bring both of them back home. *Please God, I don't ask for much. Only that you let her come with me.*

He barely noticed the sensation of leaving Haggard's creation. He didn't feel the stone floor become replaced by a shaggy carpet. He only felt the touch of warm skin on his fingers.

"I can't believe we killed her," Penny's voice came from beside him.

He opened his eyes and could not have been happier by the sight before him.

"Penny," he said, unable to hold back an ear-to-ear smile for seeing his friend, sitting next to him, alive.

I can't believe it. It worked. I saved her. She's alive. I brought her back from the dead.

"How can you be smiling after what just happened?" she asked, oblivious to what Cleo had just accomplished.

"I'm just happy you're ok. She was going to stab you. It's sad what happened to her, but it was either her or you." He was trying very hard not to become overly emotional in front of her.

"Oh, well thanks for that," she said, not having any idea as to her previous fate. "How did you get behind us? I saw you walk into the other room, and on top of that, I swear I heard your voice coming from the other room *after* you tackled her."

> *How much of the truth should I tell her? She deserves to know what happened, maybe just not now.* – He thought.

"I circled back around when you guys entered the tunnel. You must have been talking to Foulata and didn't notice," he said, deciding to keep everything to himself. "And my voice must have echoed off the wall, that's why you thought I was in the other room."

"Foulata...I hope she made it out of that tunnel."

She reached for the book resting on the bed next to Cleo.

"I want to read what happened. See what happened after we left."

Before her hands were able to reach the book, Cleo yanked it off his bed.

"No, we can look later." Cleo stood up, holding onto the book tightly.

"Why are you acting so strange?" she asked.

> *There has to be something different. There are always repercussions for changing the future. At least as far as Science Fiction has always gone.* – He thought, studying every inch of her face. *She looks the same. She sounds the same. She's alive. That's all that matters. For now...*

"Hey! What's going on with you?" she said snapping her fingers in Cleo's face.

"Sorry, it's nothing, just thinking is all."

"Uh..." Penny started to say when the phone rang.

"One sec," Cleo cut her off and answered it.

"Hello?"

"Oh hello Mrs. Jackson," he responded cheerfully. "Hmm, that's odd. I don't know what he's talking about...She's right here if you want to talk to her...Alright here you go."

"Yeah actually, that'd be great."

Cleo held the phone out to Penny.

"It's your mom. She wants to talk to you."

Penny grabbed the phone from Cleo.

"Hi Mom...Yeah I've been here the whole time....He did? I didn't even see him come over," she answered her mom's questioning. "No everything is going great...When am I coming to get what?...Oh yeah, uh, we'll be over soon...Um, ok...Yeah I will...I know...See you soon," she finished before hanging up the phone.

She looked at Cleo for some sort of explanation as she was baffled by the conversation with her mother.

"Can you explain to me what that was all about?" she asked, frowning.

"Explain what?" Cleo played dumb.

"She said Bryce came over looking for me? She also asked when I was coming to get my stuff for the night. What's going on Cleo?" Her questioning came across more as an interrogation.

"Yeah Bryce came over when I was making sandwiches. Sorry, I totally forgot to mention it. I didn't feel like talking to him so I said you weren't here."

She looked a little upset by the lie.

"Alright, then why does she think I'm spending the night tonight?"

Cleo was not particularly adept at thinking up lies on his feet, but he found himself having to do it quite frequently as of late.

"You already know the answer to that," he said, placing the blame back on her.

"What are you talking about?"

"Don't you remember you were going to stay the night tonight? You asked your mom a few days ago. That way we would have more time to go into books. We were going to spend all night looking for my mom."

"That never happened," she said defiantly.

"Penny, yes it did. I was the one that asked her. I told her I needed someone to talk to and your mom was just fine with it," he said, holding fast to his fabrication. "Call her back and ask her, if you don't believe me."

She looked at her feet, trying to recall even a trace of a memory of the incident.

"If you don't want to stay anymore, that's fine. Just stay until dinner and then head home afterwards."

Cleo felt terrible about pulling the wool over her eyes, but he didn't think he had a choice.

> *It's for her own good. I can't tell her the truth. Not yet.*

"Um…alright, we can do that," she finally agreed, unconvinced that she must have forgotten something.

"Great. Why don't we take a break for a little? Let's go grab a pizza or something for dinner," he said, gesturing to the door.

"Ok," she said, still puzzled at what just happened. She got up and walked to his door.

Cleo dropped the book on the floor by his feet.

> *I need to get rid of this. I can't let her read what really happened.*

She grabbed the knob and then suddenly stopped.

"Are you sure there is nothing that you need to tell me?" She asked, wondering if he was hinting that he actually *was* needing her help.

"No, everything is perfect," he said, kicking the book underneath his bed and following her out of the room.

CHAPTER 10

The Boy Captain

It was Sunday night and Linus and their father were both home, which made Cleo reluctant to go into any stories. However, his potential ignorance that Penny pointed out before their debacle in *King Solomon's Mines* bothered him greatly.

> *Not only did I push off my search, but I also potentially overlooked the very thing I was looking for. I cannot make those same mistakes again. I have to pay more attention to every detail. Until I find something of importance, I will only go into books that she could be in. No exceptions!*

He held *Peter and Wendy* and analyzed the scene that Penny had shown him.

> *Even though Linus and dad are home, I wouldn't be gone for long. I could go in the same moment I left before. Hook would be gone, so it would be harmless for me to go inside and look through the box.*

He looked over the last line before he previously exited from the story.

"I'm sorry Peter. This is all my fault. And I'm sorry." Peter's only response was persisted silence as Cleo eventually was able to leave Neverland.

> *I shouldn't have said that. It wasn't my fault. Peter will understand.* – Cleo thought, hoping he was right.

He closed his door and sat back down on his bed.

> *I'll make this quick and easy. I'll go in, look through the books, and leave. Nice and simple.*

He reread the same line and traveled back into Neverland.

Cleo arrived in the ship's cabin at the precise moment he departed a few months earlier. Everything was exactly as he remembered it. Peter was still sitting on the floor, with his dearest Wendy lying dead in his arms, and his arch nemesis Hook, lying lifeless at his feet. While for Cleo it felt like a lifetime ago, it was but one continuous event with no pause or break for Peter.

"You're right Cleo. This is your fault. You should have listened to me. None of this would have happened if you would have stayed out of it," said Peter, not batting an eye at Cleo's departure nor his instantaneous return. His head still hadn't risen from looking down at Wendy.

"I'm sorry about what happened, Peter. I was wrong, it's not my fault. It's not yours either," Cleo said looking around the room for any sign of the book his mother may have entered. "If there is anyone to blame, it is Hook. He has already paid for his mistakes."

"Hook...hahaha," Peter's laugh was as maniacal as Hook himself. He looked up from his Darling at Cleo. Cleo could see that the young boy had changed. An intense hatred of the world around him was forming inside of him. "I guess I'll never have to worry about him again, will I Cleo?"

> *This isn't going to be as safe as I thought it would be. This is about to get ugly, fast. I need to find that box.*

Cleo quickly tried to scan the room. His eyes darting back to Peter, afraid of what he might do. If Peter made any movement, Cleo needed to make sure he could counter without hesitation.

"I'm telling you Peter, I did everything I could to stop it from happening. I'm not a fighter though. There was only so much I could do against a Pirate Lord."

Peter gently placed Wendy onto the floor of the cabin, sending chills up Cleo.

It is like Penny and I all over again.

"I know what you're going through. Exactly what you're going through actually," he said, trying to defuse the situation. "Peter, think about what you're doing. Hook's blood is already on your hands. You don't want another body on your conscience. Wendy doesn't want that."

"Wendy doesn't want anything anymore. She's dead!" Peter suddenly lunged at Cleo with his sword.

Cleo just barely managed to dive out of the way. He got to his feet and scrambled backwards. They were now in opposite positions, Cleo kneeling beside the two bodies with Peter facing him.

"Peter stop!" Cleo pleaded with the crazed fairy boy.

"You can't dodge me forever, boy," Peter said again swinging his sword in Cleo's direction. Peter was normally a master swordsman but his blind rage caused him to flail his sword aimlessly, with little accuracy.

"Boy? I'm older than you are." Cleo said, narrowly blocking another strike with a nearby bronze candlestick from Hook's desk. Cleo kept moving around the room, tripping over Hook's belongings in an attempt to put any sort of distance between him and Pan.

"I should have killed you when you showed up at our camp. Then Wendy would still be alive."

"You're not making any sense! Just stop and think for two seconds!" He said, rolling over Hook's bed as Peter slashed the drapes hanging down.

He grabbed an attachment for Hook's missing hand off the nightstand next to the bed.

With the bed separating the two boys, Cleo stole another glance around the room.

> *I see it! The box!* –The box he needed, spilled all over the floor right behind where he had entered back into the story. *Of course it would have been right there. Now how can I get back over there without Peter killing me?*

Peter hovered off the ground so his head was almost touching the ceiling.

"You think a bed will save you?" He floated through the torn drapes and over the mattress.

"You're really starting to piss me off, you green tight wearing ballerina. Why don't you just BACK...The HELL...OFF!" Cleo took the small weapon he had picked up and hurled it over the bed towards Peter's face. Peter was caught off-guard and didn't move. Unfortunately, Cleo's aim was horrible and it crashed harmlessly against the wall beside Pan.

> *Damn, I really should have thought that through.* – Cleo thought, as he stood in front of Peter defenseless.

"Did you just call me a ballerina?" Peter said smiling at Cleo, realizing he was now helpless. Peter nonchalantly floated closer and closer to him.

Cleo's composure started to evaporate. He looked around the room for some sort of escape when he noticed the wall behind Peter. Even Peter's shadow was slowly changing. It no longer had the childish, carefreeness for which it was famous. The shadow was larger, rougher and more sinister.

"You're not Peter anymore. You've turned into the pirate lord himself." Cleo said. He realized he had managed to circle the entire room, for out of the corner of his eye Hook's body lay next to him. Cleo got an idea and reached down, grabbing the Captain's feathered hat off the ground. "Why don't you see if it fits?"

Cleo threw the hat in the air towards Peter's head. Instead of simply ducking, Peter reached up and snatched it out of the air. His reaction was exactly what Cleo was hoping it would be. His advance ceased as he examined the headpiece.

"This man plagued me for longer than I can remember. Odd how... comfortable this hat feels."

Cleo used the momentary distraction to sprint across the room, slide underneath Peter hovering in the air, and roll towards the pile of books. He desperately crawled the remaining feet and grabbed a hold of the small box.

> *Great, most of it is all over the floor.* – He panicked, sifting through the books scattered about in front of him.

Without looking back, he could feel Peter turning his attention back upon him.

"Screw it, I'll take all of them and figure it out later," Cleo said aloud, pulling in as many of the books from the floor as he could with one arm while holding onto the box with the other.

He turned his head to see how much time he had before Pan was upon him. Expecting to see the boy about to strike, he was shocked when Pan had not advanced another foot. Rather, Peter was no longer floating in the air, but standing upright over Hook's body.

> *He's no longer a Lost Boy. He can't fly anymore.*

Peter wore Hook's hat at a crooked angle, and laughed out triumphantly.

> *All he's missing is the eye patch.* – Cleo thought as he turned his mind to his own room in order to escape Neverland.

A box in one arm and a pile of books cradled in the other, Cleo abandoned the pirate ship and its new captain.

> *Is that what I would have become if Penny wasn't saved? Would I have turned into a monster?* – He wondered dumping the contents of the box along with all that were in his arms out along his bed.

This better be worth it. – He thought, spreading the books out.

Most of the books seemed to belong to his mom. Although there were a few titles that Cleo dearly hoped were a part of Hook's personal collection, and not his mother's.

*Mom, if you're inside **Blackbeard's Guide to Being a Pirate**, or **Arrrrrren't You Glad You're a Pirate,** then I might just be forced to leave you inside.*

Overall, there were no more than twenty books staring him back in the face.

> *Even if half of these are hers, that would mean a lot are missing. How many did she say she was bringing back from Grandma? Fifty? Sixty? I wish I could remember. Does that mean the rest were destroyed, or did she really take that many with her into the next book? If she did, who knows if I'll ever find her.* – He thought, picking up book after book and flipping through them. *No, I can't worry about that. I only need to find the first book she went in. I'll worry about the rest later. Suddenly Cleo's door flung open.*

"Hey bro," said Linus as he walked into his room unannounced. "What's with all the books?"

"LINUS! You can't just walk into my room whenever you want!" Cleo yelled.

"Why not? You do it to me," he sniped back. "Why are you looking through all these books?"

"Not that it's any of your business, but I bought the box from a yard sale," he effortlessly fibbed to his little brother.

"As long as none of them are Hansel and Gretel," Linus said, shooting a look at the Grimm fairy tales on his brother's shelf.

"I still can't believe you had a nightmare about that story."

Ever since Linus was almost baked into a human casserole, Cleo had managed to convince him that it was just a bad dream.

Linus mumbled something incoherent under his breath and walked to the box, picking books up with no regard for Cleo's privacy.

"How about you ask before you just grab my stuff?" Cleo said, now thoroughly annoyed and second-guessing his decision to save his little brother.

"Nah, that's ok," Linus responded, continuing to rifle through Cleo's newfound texts.

> *Gah! It's pointless to get into an argument with a six-year-old. It's not as if he can find anything out by looking through these anyways.*

Cleo decided to ignore his annoying little brother and kept on searching the pages of the books himself. He had no idea what he was looking for, or even what he hoped to find. Nothing stood out from one book to the next. *Brave New World, Dr. Jekyll and Mr. Hyde, The Aenead, Hamlet, Cat in the Hat.*

> *God help me if she is in that one. Venturing into Dr. Seuss's mind is an experience I don't want to have.* – Cleo shuddered at the thought. He didn't see her name in any of the stories, not that he expected to. *I doubt she would purposefully go to fight Greeks, play with a mischievous cat, or test whether or not she had some sadistic alter ego. That likely means she was rushed, and chose at random.*

"Oops, a page fell out of this one," Linus said, holding up *Alice's Adventures in Wonderland.*

Cleo was so frustrated that he had no idea where his next move should be, that he didn't pay any attention to Linus.

"Cleo, uh...this piece of paper has your name on it," Linus said, picking the piece of paper off the ground.

That grabbed his attention. He took the page from Linus's hand. It was not in fact a page of the book. It was a handwritten note, inscribed in black ink upon an old piece of parchment.

Dearest Cleo,

If you are reading this then what I feared has indeed come to pass. Not only have you now discovered what you are capable of, it means that I was not there to help you. I cannot express to you how sorry I am for everything that has happened. I do not know just how much time has passed since I was forced to disappear into Neverland. I must hurry in writing this down for I do not have much time left before he comes back. Soon I will be heading into Alice in Wonderland, but I do not know where I am to go after that. The only advice I can give you is to never give up, for I know I certainly won't. I love you more than words can describe son. I hope to see you soon my sweet, sweet boy.

Love, Mom

P.S. I understand if you probably cannot tell your father and brother about any of this yet. It will be difficult for them to know the truth. Take care of your brother. Make sure he knows how much his mother loves him.

Cleo had to read it a second time just to make sure of what it said.

"Ramiel was right. She's alive," Cleo said without regard of Linus standing in the room.

"Who's Ramiel?" Linus asked, standing on his tiptoes to try to look over Cleo's shoulders at the letter.

"It's...a friend. I've been looking for this letter for a long time Linus. I can't believe you found it," Cleo lifted his little brother off the floor in a bear hug.

"Let...go...of...me," he squirmed out of Cleo's hold. "You're weird. I'm going to my room."

Linus straightened his disheveled shirt and left Cleo alone.

Cleo picked up *Alice's Adventures in Wonderland* where Linus left it.

> *She could be in there, waiting for me right now. I could go in and bring her back. Bring my family back together. Everything I have wanted could be right here in my hands.*

He read the moment Alice went down the rabbit-hole herself.

The rabbit-hole went straight on like a tunnel for some way, and then dipped suddenly down, so suddenly that Alice had not a moment to think about stopping herself before she found herself falling down a very deep well.

> *What if it's that easy? What if those words are all that stand between being reunited with my mom?*

He shook his head and quickly shut the book.

> *No, I said I would learn from my mistakes. It's not going to be that easy. I don't even know if she is in there. It could take me days, even weeks inside of Wonderland to find her. Linus and dad are sitting in the other room. I can't go while they are around. One of them will walk in for sure while I'm gone. — He stuck the book inside of his backpack, right next to The Iliad and zipped it shut, as if to seal away any temptation it may cause. I can be patient. I'll tell Penny tomorrow what I found. I'll see what she has to say first. Then go from there.*

He ran his fingers over his mother's handwritten words before placing the letter in his desk, right on top of the single page from Terra Somniorum.

Penny had barely stepped foot on the school's campus when Cleo ran up to her.

"We need to talk. Now," he said grabbing her by the sleeve of her jacket. He pulled her away from the crowds of teenagers until they were mostly by themselves.

"You're acting like a crazy person. What's so important?" She asked, straightening the sleeve that Cleo tugged out of place.

"You were right. It was in Peter Pan all along," he said excitedly.

"What was?"

"The first book my mom went into. She's alive Penny. This proves it," he said louder than he intended. "I finally found where she went. It's all because of you. Without you, I don't know if I ever would have found it."

Penny blushed at Cleo attributing all the credit to her.

"I didn't do anything. I just happened to read a random sentence. So where did she go?" she said, diverting the conversation back onto Cleo.

"Alice's Adventures in Wonderland," he said, pulling the book out of his bag and showing it to her.

"You haven't gone inside yet to look for her?"

"No, not yet. Linus and my dad were both home last night. Plus, I didn't want to make any brash decisions," he replaced the book back into his backpack.

"When are we going to look then?" she said, not hesitating to offer help.

"*I* was going to go inside after school today. But alone, not with you," the moment he said it, he could see his words hurt her feelings. "At least, not at first. Penny, I don't know what to expect inside. She could be sitting there waiting for me, she could be in trouble, I just don't know. I need to find out what we're getting ourselves into before you come with me."

The morning bell rang loudly, drowning out Penny's response.

"Let's talk about this later," he said as students began to walk around them.

"Ok." Penny was clearly disappointed in Cleo's decision, but left it at that, as the privacy they needed to continue the conversation was gone.

"Thank you Penny," he said backing away from her. She smiled and walked off towards her first class at the far end of the campus.

He backed up a few more paces, keeping his eyes on her as she walked away from him.

"Why don't you watch where you're going?" a boy said as Cleo walked into him with his backpack.

Cleo turned to apologize when he saw that he had bumped into Bryce.

How long have you been here? – Cleo thought as Bryce glared at him. *Did you overhear anything?*

"Aren't you going to say sorry?" Bryce asked him.

"That would imply I actually was," Cleo said.

"You think you're so tough after that sucker punch don't you?" Bryce said, taking a step towards Cleo.

"What, are you here to get revenge? You gonna hit me?" Cleo said, almost daring him to take a swing.

Bryce laughed in Cleo's face.

"No, all that would get me is a suspension," he said, noticing a few students had begun to congregate around them. He leaned in close so only Cleo would hear. "But don't worry, we're not through yet."

Bryce patted Cleo on the head condescendingly and walked away, leaving the small gathering crowd who were anticipating an altercation disappointed.

Cleo struggled mightily the entire school day. He was only a physical presence during his classes and certainly not a mental one. He was perpetually daydreaming about his mother having tea with the Mad Hatter, or playing in a very odd game of croquet with the Queen of Hearts, just waiting for him to bring her out.

When the bell finally rang to send everyone to their sixth and final period of the day, Cleo had had enough. He left the classroom first and waited outside its doors for Penny, perpetually one of the last students to leave.

"Penny," he said with a "come here" motion of his finger when she walked out.

"Yeah?" she asked, readjusting the shoulder straps on her bag.

"I know I said I would wait until I got home today, but I just can't wait any longer. I need to take a peek, just a quick one. I'm going to the library to go inside," he said in a hushed tone.

"Cleo, we still have one class left. I want to go with you. Just wait until after school," she urged.

"Like I said before, I want to make sure it's safe before you come with me. I don't want another...anything to happen. Alright?"

She clearly did not approve of his decision, but she knew he wasn't going to listen to her.

"Be careful."

He appreciated her concern and walked out of the hallway to the school's quad. When he reached the door, he saw an unwelcomed body standing by it.

"Skipping class huh? I didn't think you had it in you," Bryce said as Cleo approached him.

"You just won't go away today, will you? For the record I'm not skipping. I have something to take care of. Now get out of my way," Cleo said abrasively, not in the mood to deal with Bryce.

"Of course, I wouldn't want to keep you from your books now, would I?" Bryce said, stepping aside.

Bryce's comment unsettled Cleo, but he stopped wasting his time and continued on his way to the library.

Once inside, he noticed it was customarily empty.

"What are you doing in here? Aren't you supposed to be in class?" Mrs. Steele asked.

"It was too loud in there, so I got permission to do my work in here," he lied.

Cleo had been such a frequent visitor of the library that Mrs. Steele didn't question the falsehood.

There wasn't another student in the entire library, so he was able to get the booth that was furthest from the door, and its librarian.

I'm only going in for a minute anyway. I'll check one scene, ask a few questions and then leave.

He pulled the hard copy of *Alice's Adventures in Wonderland* out of his bag and opened it up to a random page. He took one look around to make sure nobody was around and began reading.

"Hector, now you'll learn, once and for all, in combat man-to-man, what kind of champions range the Argive ranks, even besides Achilles, that lionhearted man who mauls battalions wholesale."

Cleo was so preoccupied with the prospect of finally locating his mother's book trail that he wasn't paying any attention to the actual words he was reading. By the time he realized what he was about to get himself into, it was too late. It was not the nonsensical world of Alice and the White Rabbit, but the bloody battlefield in front of the impenetrable city walls of the great ancient city, Troy, to where he was headed.

This isn't Wonderland...

Completely surrounding him were the battling armies of the Trojans and the Macedonians.

Hector? Achilles? Why did I end up in the Trojan War? – He tried to remember which book he grabbed out of his bag in the library. *I'm positive I didn't grab The Iliad. I can figure it out later. I need to get OUT of here!*

Before he could exit the most famous battle ever waged, he felt a blinding pain in the back of his head. He fell, face first to the ground, unable to brace for the impact.

So this is what it feels like to die? – Was the last thing that ran through his mind before he was once again consumed by total blackness.

CHAPTER
11

Homer's Deception

A blistering heat burned Cleo's body. The horrific sound of metal grinding and men screaming in pain filled his ears. The darkness subsided and was replaced by a searing bright light. He tried to raise his arm to shield his eyes but found it heavily weighed down. Unable to see, he tried to sit up, but found that whatever was on his arm was also draped across his whole midsection. Cleo wasn't the strongest of kids and struggled mightily to push the mass that was slowly crushing his chest. He put all of his strength into one mighty heave and forced the weight from his body.

He used his free hand to veil the sun from his eyes. He looked over and saw that the object that lay on top of him was actually the armored body of a grown man.

> *Where the hell am I?* – He thought with his sight and ability to move no longer constricted. *Oh God. This isn't even close to Wonderland. Why did I end up here?*

He was in the middle of a vast, endless desert and all around him was the grisly carnage of a battlefield. There were bodies, bloodied, hewn and scattered about. Two armies of an incalculable size were standing around, no longer fighting. The cries of pain and sounds of clashing metal had stopped. It had become eerily silent.

> *Why is everyone standing around?* – He thought confused. He was standing in an almost entirely empty circle while the soldiers looked on.

"Were you sent from the Gods?" A man who was standing to his left spoke up. He was one of two men, aside from Cleo, that all of the soldiers had their attention on.

Despite his armor looking largely the same as many of the soldiers surrounding him, Cleo could tell he was kingly. He commanded respect without uttering a word. He held a gold sword with a purple hilt at his side. On Cleo's right stood a man of the opposing army. This man was of colossal size. He wore no armor over his clothes, save for a golden girdle around his waist. His shield looked to be made of bronze and cow hide. It was bigger than the entirety of Cleo. His spear dwarfed all of those around him.

> *Is this a duel? On second thought it doesn't matter. I need to leave now!* – He thought, focusing his mind on the library and his little booth, which proved to be nearly impossible under the given circumstances. To his horror, nothing happened. The same mysterious wall he felt the day he showed Penny his power, blocked him.

> *Why is this happening? Why did I end up in The Iliad, and why can't I leave? The book was sitting open on the desk. Did Mrs. Steele come over and close it thinking I had accidentally left my things behind? There was nobody else in the library. Was there?*

He didn't have any time to brood over the answers for the smaller of the two men stepped forward, his sword raised.

"You are clearly not a soldier. What kind of garb is that, that you wear? Are you a messenger of the gods?" he asked again.

Cleo was petrified as he was surrounded by a throng of armed men, all who could kill him in the blink of an eye. He knew that he had to escape immediately before he was cut in two by one of the armed warriors. Even the sorriest of excuses for a soldier could crush Cleo like a piece of Styrofoam. Forget a hundred thousand strong.

> *Well if I can't leave, then I at least need to move to a safer point in the story. I'll pull up the storyline and speed out of here.*

Cleo tried to close his eyes and move through the book. He failed straightaway however, as his concentration was broken by Hector calling out to him again.

"I am Hector, Prince of Troy. Speak now or I will strike you down!" He extended his sword out in front of him to emphasize the sincerity of his promise.

> *Cleo's mind was racing.*

> *I can't focus with all of these swords and spears aimed at my face. If I can't focus, that means I can't escape. If I am stuck, then I need to say something fast. Otherwise, I'm dead.*

Cleo mustered up the courage to hurl out a warning.

"You dare threaten a God!" he yelled at the top of his lungs. His voice cracked and the warning was nothing more than a squeak.

This time the gargantuan man to his right spoke up.

"I am Ajax, the mightiest warrior save for Achilles in all of Greece. What God may you be?" Ajax could have been mistaken for one of Polyphemus's cousins he was so massive. Still, even with his unnatural size, Ajax seemed hesitant to the young man.

> *I can crush his head with one hand, but in case he is a God, I shall be careful not to anger him. —Cleo read Ajax's thoughts.*

> *That is my only chance. I have to make them believe that I truly am a God. They must fear me. —Cleo decided.*

"Soldiers of Troy and Achaea!" Cleo yelled as his voice cracked. "I am Cleo, God of Stories!"

"God of Stories?" Ajax addressed him. "There is no Cleo, God of Stories. You are a trickster. You must be a servant of Hermes, or maybe Hermes himself."

"A servant? Of that cowardly thief nonetheless? I should destroy you now for mentioning us in the same sentence. I am far more powerful than Hermes. Don't believe me?" He said somehow forcing his feet to take a single step closer to the barbaric man. "I will prove it to you. Continue with your little war. When I feel I have seen enough of your fighting I will show you the power of Cleo." Cleo was desperately trying to pull off his best "God-like" imitation. His ability to keep the cracking in his voice in check literally meant life or death.

Some of the soldiers looked legitimately frightened of Cleo. Unfortunately, Ajax was not one of those soldiers.

"You lie. You are no God. You look like nothing but a scared child to me. I will not let you get the chance to cause any of your mischief. I will kill you with my own hands first," he called out to Cleo. Any concern with Cleo being an actual God had all but disappeared.

> There is no rationalizing with or tricking Ajax. He knows only bloodlust. My only hope is to talk with Hector. Buy myself as much time as possible until a miracle can possibly come. What do I really expect to happen though? – Cleo thought, trying to keep his cool and formulate a plan.

"If you doubt my Godliness then I will prove it to you. I challenge Hector to a duel," Cleo said turning to the Trojan Prince.

"What!? You challenge him over me?" Ajax was furious at the disrespect. He became enraged, swinging the colossal sword in his hands high above his head.

"He is the Trojans' greatest warrior. If I defeat him, then nothing will prevent you from sacking the city," Cleo said, trying to convince Ajax that his plan would actually benefit the Greeks.

Ajax was a proud man. He would never admit to being a lesser fighter to anyone aside from Achilles. He also happened to be one of the more brilliant generals in either army, and the new strategy that Cleo presented him sounded appealing and foolproof.

"Very well, have your duel. But if somehow you are victorious, you will have to get past me next." Ajax was seething as he stepped out of the open circle and joined in with the on looking soldiers.

"I accept your challenge." Hector was not as arrogant as his counterpart was, and would not underestimate any opponent, even a scrawny 16-year old boy. He raised his shield and tapped it with his sword. "Give the boy a shield and spear. He will die an honorable death."

A random soldier in the ranks behind Hector ran up to Cleo and handed him a long wooden spear and bronze shield.

> *I can barely hold one of these by itself. It'll be impossible for me to hold them both at the same time.* – Cleo thought as his arms and shoulders ached at the weight of his newly acquired gear. He decided to drop the spear on the ground and hold the shield only. *It won't do me any good to go on the offensive. I'll block his attacks and try to reason with him.*

"Let us begin." As soon as the words came out of Hector's mouth he lashed out at Cleo, slamming his sword into Cleo's shield. The force of the blow sent Cleo flying through the air and onto the desert floor. It only took one attack and Cleo was already lying flat on his back, his shield detached from his grip and lying several feet out of his reach. Cleo wiped the dust from his eyes and his heart rose to his throat as his harbinger of death approached to finish the job.

> *If I somehow survive this, the first thing I'm going to do is learn how to fight.*

Cleo sat up to see Hector, the glorious Trojan War hero slowly walking to finish off his victim.

"Hector! Before you kill me, first listen for a moment. I can win you this war. It is true I am no War God. My powers are not in fighting, but in prophecy. I know what becomes of you and your people," Cleo held out his hands and pleaded with the Prince.

Hector stopped, his spear pushing against Cleo's throat.

"What do you know?" Hector spoke up.

"I know you lose this war. Achilles himself strikes you down. He falls into a murderous rage after you kill his nephew, Patroclus, and becomes unstoppable. He desecrates your body, maiming it and dragging it back to the Greek army on the beaches."

Cleo still couldn't bring the book's storyline up in his mind, but he knew exactly what Hector's fate was.

"Even if I died, the whole Achaean army could not breach our walls. Achilles is but one man. Even he could not breach this city," Hector said, gazing at Cleo through the eye slits in his helmet.

"You are right, he cannot. However, the Greeks trick your father and his advisors. Odysseus, the King of Ithaca, creates a wooden horse as large as a ship, and disguises it as a gift from the gods. Once brought into the city their army will pour out of it in the night. They will burn your city, kill your people and win this war."

"And you know this? Why should I believe you? If you are truly the God of Stories, this could be just another one of your stories." Hector was wary to believe in the prophecy of a teenager. He was also one of the greatest military tacticians ever to grace a battlefield, and he would take any advantage he could get.

"This is no tale. I promise you. I swear on Zeus himself, that if you do not listen to me, you and your entire city will come to ruin," Cleo issued the grave warning.

> *What if the boy is not lying? He could have just ruined the war for us! With the knowledge of foresight, Hector will be unbeatable. Well if he will not strike him down, then I shall do it myself!* – Ajax's thoughts popped into Cleo's head unexpectedly. He dove to his right just as the mighty warrior *lashed out at him.*

"AGHH!!" Cleo screamed as an excruciating pain came over him.

Miraculously, though Ajax's spear was no less than eight feet long, only the last inch was able to graze across Cleo's left shoulder blade. That inch was still more than enough as it cut through his shirt and into his flesh.

"See, you are no God," Ajax pointed at the red stain on Cleo's back.

Hector walked over to Cleo and touched his wound, sending a painful shock through his spine. Hector looked intently at the blood on his fingers.

"You do not bleed the golden ichor of the Gods. You are nothing more than a Speaker of Lies. I cannot help you," Hector said, sheathing his sword and backing away from Cleo.

"You will not turn the tide of this war with your falsehoods and deceit. Now Cleo, *God of Stories*, you will die like a powerless mortal," Ajax said with a baleful smile coming across his face.

The sand was rough and gritty under his fingers as Cleo crawled backwards away from Ajax.

"HAH! Now the God runs away like a coward!" Ajax mocked.

Cleo felt his hand come across metal, the shield that Hector had knocked out of his hands.

> *Maybe I can tire him out by blocking everything.*

He stood up, held onto the shield, this time with both hands, and braced for an impact. Cleo weighed a little over a hundred pounds sopping wet, and was nothing but a ragdoll to Ajax. He slammed the side of his spear into Cleo's shield, knocking him back to the ground.

"Is that all you got?" Cleo panted, picking the battered shield up again.

His upright stance lasted for only another second as he was tossed through the air yet again by a violent swing into his shield.

"HAHAHA... pathetic! You call yourself a God?" Ajax said, this time kicking the detached shield back towards Cleo.

Cleo was rapidly running out of energy. He barely had the strength to lift it up in front of him.

> *I cannot die in here. They have to have a body to bury* – He thought of his father and brother.

Ajax thrust the spear forward so powerfully that it pierced through the shield. The point came within a fraction of an inch of entering Cleo's skull. Cleo did not have time to reflect on his close call , as Ajax yanked back on his spear, pulling the shield and Cleo with him.

"Stop...please..." Cleo begged, face first in the sand.

Ajax kicked the destroyed shield off his spear, smiling triumphantly. Cleo was exhausted. His vision doubled, he was bruised and scraped everywhere. He knew he didn't have the capability to dodge another strike. He used the last of his strength to sit up on his knees and wait for his Grim Reaper. Cleo took what he assumed would be his last breath and closed his eyes. He did not want to see the final stroke of the spear.

> *How strange, I always thought if I was dying I'd spend my final moments thinking about my family. Yet here in the end, all I can think about is you Penny. I can't believe Bryce was right. I do love you, and you're never going to know it.*

He kept his eyes shut tightly. He wanted the last picture in his mind to be that of the girl who would never know his true feelings, not of the barbarian that was ending his life.

"How dare you come onto my battlefield and pretend to be a God. I am the greatest warrior these fields have ever seen. And now you will see why," Ajax continued to taunt Cleo. "Say hello to the Gods for me."

Cleo barely heard the jeering voice of the man four times his size. He continued to shut his eyes. He didn't need to open them to know exactly what was coming. It was a long piece of hardened steel, coming with enough force to cut through wood, metal, and most importantly, bone.

> *Goodbye Penny.*

Just when Cleo expected his head to be separated from his shoulders, he felt a familiar, fragmenting sensation, followed by a small tug. He reopened his eyes to see the bloodthirsty expression on Ajax's face exchanged with a look of bewilderment as he vanished.

Since the day of his 16th birthday, Cleo had entered and exited books more times than he could remember. Yet he was never more surprised than the moment when those blood-soaked battlefields of Troy were inexplicably replaced with a rusted bridge, spanning across a raging river, and Penny sitting beside him.

"Oh my god! Cleo, you're covered in blood!" Penny grabbed hold of him and helped him to his feet. "We need to get you to a hospital. Just hold on. Don't give up on me."

He could hear the squealing of tires peeling off the bridge. He appreciated her dramatic response, but the reality was the only blood that belonged to him was from the cut on his back, and that had already begun to clot.

"I'm ok Penny, none of this is mine," he said pointing to the front of his shirt. He grabbed a hold of her hand. "Can you tell me what the hell happened? Why are we on a bridge? How long was I inside?"

She calmed down slightly as Cleo held onto her hand.

"We're on the bridge at the edge of town. It was Bryce. He is responsible for all of this."

"Where is he now?"

"He drove across the bridge and up Old Mountain Highway. Are you sure you don't need a hospital?" she said, looking at the cuts and tears throughout Cleo's shirt.

"I promise, I'm fine. If he's heading up Old Mountain Highway, then I know exactly where he's going. Whose car is that?" he asked looking at a station wagon parked on the bridge.

"Oh that," Penny blushed. "It's a long story."

"Can we use it to follow him? You can tell me what happened on the way," he said, pulling himself to his feet.

"You want to follow him? Why?" she asked.

"Because, I have to know why. Can you drive?"

Penny was visibly worried about Cleo's condition and the idea of pursuing Bryce.

"Yes," she said softly.

Cleo got into the passenger side, moving Penny's backpack aside. Once she got in, they drove off down the same dirt road that Bryce had.

"Just follow this road until I tell you to stop. It should only take a few minutes," Cleo instructed.

"Ok. I have a jacket in my bag. Can you put it on? All that blood is making me queasy," Penny said rubbing her stomach.

"So tell me everything that happened," he said putting on the windbreaker that she had stuffed into her backpack.

"It started when you left to go to the library. I saw Bryce go after you, and something seemed off. He looked...well like he was about to start trouble, so I followed the two of you. I went in the library just a few seconds after you and Bryce did. Right away, I knew something was wrong. Bryce was running from the back, where you said you like to go when you need privacy, and he had a book in his hands. He didn't even notice me say his name when he ran past me," she recounted as she cautiously drove them through the twists and turns of the winding mountain road.

"It was the book I went into," Cleo said.

"Yes. I realized that when I saw your booth, empty except for your bag sitting on the one of the chairs. I ran after him, which, by the way, I'll probably get in trouble for by Mrs. Steele when we get back to school. He then hopped in his car and drove off."

"Did you steal this car to follow him?" Cleo interrupted.

"No, I borrowed it," she defended. "I saw Matthew Giacomi walking through the Quad and asked to use his."

"Matthew Giacomi? That the kid that's asked you to every dance since 8th grade?"

"Not every dance, just most of them, but yeah, same kid. Anyways, he agreed rather quickly and I kept following Bryce."

"Wait a second," Cleo said, trying to get a clear picture. "You're telling me you sped off through the city, in someone else's car, trying to catch up with Bryce?"

"Yes, and I was terrified. Cars were honking at me, giving me the finger. It was horrible," she said, flustered.

"I must say I'm impressed. So what happened next?"

"I finally found his car parked on the bridge. Thank God there is only one road in and out of the town, out that way. I may have never found him otherwise. Anyway, he was standing outside of the car next to the railing of the bridge. He had the book with him. It was bungeed shut with a small piece of rope."

"He bungeed the book closed? That explains why I couldn't leave. How'd you get the book from him?"

"He was about to throw it over the edge into the river. I jumped out of the car and surprised him. He had no idea I was following him. I didn't have any idea what I should say, so I asked how he knew about you. He said the day you hit him he followed us to your house. Apparently you should start closing your blinds."

> *I hope that nobody else has seen me through those blinds.*
> – He thought.

"He then called you some pretty foul and hurtful names. He said he was doing the world a favor and reared his arm back to throw the book over the edge. A logging truck crossing the bridge was none too pleased with our parking jobs and honked his horn. It startled Bryce long enough for me to run up and tackle him."

"You tackled Bryce?" Cleo asked disbelievingly.

"Why do you sound so surprised? I can be feisty when I want to be."

Even under the circumstances, the visual caused Cleo to chuckle.

"I didn't have a clue as to what I was doing. The book flew out of his hands. I grabbed it and started to undo the knot that he tied. That's when he grabbed a hold of my feet and called me a very inappropriate name. I don't know what came over me. Maybe it was him calling me that...that name. Maybe it was you being stuck in the book. Whatever it was, it caused me to kick him as hard as I could right in the face, right in the same spot where you punched him. He let go pretty fast after that."

Cleo's jaw was almost even with his chest. He was beyond shocked that Penny the pacifist, could be pushed to violence.

"It only took me a few more seconds to pull the rope off. I opened the book, and then out of nowhere you popped out!"

Cleo's chest ached worse than it did during his fight with Ajax.

"I can't believe he'd try something like this. We have obviously had our problems for a long time now, but nothing to the extent that should have warranted this. I mean, it would have been murder." Although they were certainly no longer friends, and really hadn't been for quite some time, the idea that his best friend for so many years had just tried to kill him cut him far deeper than any ancient Greek sword ever could.

"What do you think we should do? Should we call the police?" Penny's intentions were good, but she could be very naïve at times.

"Telling the police won't solve anything. You think they would believe that he trapped me in a book and tried to throw me into the river? There's a better chance we'd be tossed in the loony bin and he'd get away scot free," Cleo shot down the idea.

"Where is this place you think he'll be at?" Penny asked, continuing to drive with little direction.

"It's a place in the woods that we found a couple of years ago. We were riding our bikes up here and just happened to come across it. We spent quite a few weekends up here, back when we were kids and still friends," Cleo said somberly.

As Penny was focusing on the dirt road ahead of her, Cleo snuck a book out of her backpack and shoved it into the jacket Penny let him wear.

I'll make him understand if I have to.

They drove further and further into the mountains. The area became more and more remote. There were no buildings, cars or any signs of human life.

"Stop there," he said pointing to a trail, hardly visible and questionably wide enough for a single car to fit down.

"Are you sure this is the right place Cleo? There's nothing out here," she said, pointing out the lack of cars at the path's entrance.

"It's the only place I can think of that he'd be. Go ahead and park," he instructed her.

Penny turned the car off and reached for her seatbelt.

"No, I need you to wait here," Cleo said, putting his hand on her belt buckle. "Just stay in the car, alright? I need to talk to him alone."

"What? No, you can't go back there by yourself. He just tried to kill you Cleo. I'm not leaving you alone with that psycho," she fervently resisted his request.

"I promise I'll be careful. This is between him and me. I can't have you come along. If I need you, I'll yell out, alright? But I need to talk with him, alone."

"But..." Penny started to resist again, but Cleo interrupted her.

"Listen, I owe you my life Penny. You saved me. I'll never be able to thank you enough for what you've done, but this isn't a request. I'm sorry. I need to do this part alone."

He leaned over and gave her a hug, then kissed her on the cheek.

"I'll be back before you know it, I promise." He didn't give her any more time to protest for he got out of the car and walked down the dirt path.

O'Dell's Solitary Confinement

The dirt path extended deep into the woods until there was neither sight nor sound of the road behind. Cleo walked around a soft bend where it culminated in a small cul-de-sac.

> *The train. We never did figure out how this got here.* – Cleo thought as he came across the early 20th century train car that sat in the middle of the cul-de-sac.

The passenger car extended almost 30 feet from end to end. It was constructed of mainly steel and was heavily rusted inside and out. It looked like it had lain at the bottom of the ocean floor for the last century. Inside were rows of vinyl seats, some missing, almost all ripped or torn. Above the seats were small compartments for luggage, most of which were missing their doors. Littered around the car were aluminum cans, gallon milk jugs and soda pop bottles, all of them containing multiple punctures.

> *How long has it been since I was last here? A year? Maybe more?* – He stopped at the dead end's edge. Seems like

forever. *I feel like I was just a kid back then, playing stupid make believe games.*

Built amongst some large branches that overhung the train was a tree house. It was a simple one room, shoddily constructed square fort. It took an entire summer of the boys sneaking supplies from their fathers' garage up into the woods. Dragging 2x4's, hammers, nails and saws up into the mountains on their bicycles proved to be the easy part of their task. After multiple smashed fingers, a nail through the foot and nearly cutting off Cleo's hand, the finished tree house proved to be one of the greatest accomplishments of their young lives.

Parked alongside the hundred-year-old train was the two-year-old BMW that belonged to Bryce.

"Bryce!" Cleo called out.

Suddenly two small patches of dirt shot up at Cleo's feet. He looked into the fort and noticed the barrel of a BB gun pointing out of the window of the tree house.

"You've been practicing. You used to be a terrible shot. You couldn't hit the side of the train from 20 yards before," Cleo said, unafraid of the air-powered rifle still aiming at him above the train car.

"I still am one. I was aiming at you," Bryce answered.

Cleo snickered nervously, unsure if Bryce was being sincere or not.

"Why don't you drop the BB gun and come down here? I just want to talk," Cleo said, bravely taking a few steps closer.

Bryce peered through the sights at the top of the air rifle. His pointer finger softly bounced on and off its trigger. Even with the open window frame to help steady his aim, the barrel of the gun waved back and forth in Bryce's unstable hands.

"Come on man. We can't do this if you're trying to shoot me."

Cleo held his ground but was fearful their reunion in the secluded impasse was about to become a confrontation.

"Fine," Bryce said in a muffled tone. He placed the air rifle down beside the window and slid down a rope that hung from the bottom of the tree house. He came to a stop on the roof of the passenger car, and stared down at Cleo. There were holes in the knees of his jeans and his windbreaker had a tear across the left sleeve.

"So talk," he said from his perch.

"I want to know why. Why would you do it?" Cleo asked bluntly.

Bryce began to pace back and forth along the roof.

"You remember when we used to come here?" Bryce asked, avoiding the question.

Cleo did not particularly want to reminisce about their past, but did not know how else to get Bryce to talk to him. He decided to humor him.

"I do. We had a lot of fun up here."

"Yeah we did. Every week this train was something different. One week we would be on a government train gone missing. The next it was an old bank train carrying millions of dollars that was once stolen by a band of vicious thugs. Do you remember that time we pretended it was a giant mechanical robot? Hah!" he laughed loudly. "That was a fun day."

"It was. So what happened?"

Bryce turned away from Cleo and looked off into the woods.

"Enough stalling Bryce, how did you know what I can do?" Cleo demanded.

Bryce stopped pacing and turned to Cleo.

"That day you sucker punched me in front of everyone. The day you made me the laughing stock of the school. I saw you and Penny walk off campus. I didn't understand why you would just run home together after what happened, so I followed you. I couldn't believe how dumb the two of you were. You were so worried that someone would see you ditch school, yet you left almost every blind in the house open." He was jumping from thought to thought with no clear direction. "I watched you a couple more times, when you weren't looking. I eventually figured out that if the book was closed, you couldn't get out. So I waited, just buying time."

"Waiting for what?" Cleo asked.

Bryce looked away from Cleo, ignoring the question.

"Why did it have to be you?" he spoke through gritted teeth.

"Why did it have to be me, what?"

Bryce hopped off the train and onto the ground, landing just in front of Cleo.

"Why are you the one that gets to be different? Why are you the one that gets to stand out and be...whatever it is you are? You've never been anything but ordinary. Boring, a ghost, invisible, unimportant," he said resentfully.

"Why do you care what I am, or what I can do?"

"Because nobody has ever wanted to be *you*. I'm the one that everybody wishes they could be. I am the one that everyone wants to be with!"

Cleo was shocked at where this was all coming from. "What are you talking about? Nobody wants to be me."

"Now it's like I don't even exist," Bryce continued, ignoring Cleo.

"Don't exist? Nobody, except for you and Penny even know that I'm different. In whose eyes exactly do you not exist?"

Bryce remained silent. He stood, staring at Cleo with a cold malice in his eyes. Bryce's silence spoke volumes to Cleo. He suddenly realized precisely to whom Bryce was referring.

"Penny? That's why you did all of this, isn't it? You tried to kill me because you like her? You committed attempted murder over a petty school-boy crush?"

"I like her?" Bryce looked at Cleo as if what Cleo said was the dumbest remark he had ever heard. The hatred on his face had morphed into a mild amusement at the comment. "I like chocolate. I like my car and my clothes. Like doesn't even begin to describe it. I shouldn't have to compete against someone like you for her. Yet, I have always had to. It doesn't make any sense."

"Always had to compete for Penny? How long have you felt like this Bryce?"

Bryce shook his head as if he couldn't believe Cleo didn't already know.

"As if you don't remember. It was when I bought us those tickets to her favorite musical, but she refused to go because of you. "

Cleo couldn't believe what he was hearing. All of this pent up anger and hostility all over Penny.

"When was this?"

"There's a shocker," Bryce said sarcastically. "When it doesn't revolve around you, you don't have any clue."

Cleo made sure to keep an eye on Bryce's hands. The look in his eyes suggested he was likely to try to strangle Cleo at any moment.

"Last year. The anniversary of your poor little mom." Bryce put his hands up, pretending to ward off Cleo and keep him at bay. "Oh that's right, touchy subject. Wouldn't want you to snap again," he said mockingly.

Cleo felt like lashing out at Bryce, but knew it wouldn't solve anything.

"What exactly did you hope to accomplish by killing me?" Cleo asked.

"I didn't know if it would necessarily kill you or not. I just figured you'd at least be out of the picture," he answered nonchalantly.

"So then what was your plan? After I was gone you thought she'd come running into your arms?"

"More or less. If she hadn't followed me out to that bridge, then you would have disappeared forever. She would have thought you died in one of your stupid books and I would have been there to comfort her."

They stood face to face, neither giving up any ground to the other. Despite Bryce's size advantage, he no longer seemed intimidating to Cleo.

"It doesn't make any sense Bryce. Why does my power make you hate me so much?"

"It's unnatural. You're a freak Cleo, a stain upon a world of normality. You are a danger to society."

"You're right, I'm not normal, but being different doesn't make me a freak. It doesn't make me dangerous. Let me show you Bryce. You'll see that what I can do is amazing." He reached back and pulled the *Island of the Blue Dolphins* out of his pocket.

Bryce looked down at the book in Cleo's hands. He backed away, suddenly terrified at the very sight of it.

"Cleo, put that away, now."

"What are you so scared of?" Cleo took a step forward.

"I'm not scared of you if that's what you think," Bryce said unconvincingly.

"Then come with me," Cleo implored.

Cleo opened the book immediately to the precise page he wanted. It was easy to find, for it was the final page in the book. It provided Cleo the gate to the perfect destination for Bryce and himself. He raised it up in front of Bryce's face.

"Cleo, I'm warning you." Bryce continued to back up until his head pressed up against the side of the train. He had nowhere to go.

Cleo approached Bryce carefully for he looked like a feral cat in fight-or-flight mode. He moved until he was within an arm's reach of Bryce.

"Trust me Bryce. This will be beyond your wildest imagination. You'll see."

Cleo lifted the book up, holding it in front of him. Bryce reached out and shoved the book away from his body.

"Get away from me Cleo!"

Cleo looked down at the book and started to read silently.

For a long time I stood and looked back at the Island of the Blue Dolphins. The last thing I saw of it was the high headland.

The moment he felt himself begin to change, he reached out and grabbed hold of Bryce. The shift happened so quickly that Bryce had no time to get away and was sucked into the book alongside Cleo.

> *We need to be on the island itself, not the ship.* – Cleo concentrated in order to ensure they would not be setting sail into the open seas with the island's last inhabitants.

Faster than the flap of a hummingbird, they were transported to the cliffs overlooking the recently abandoned island beach. The two of them towered above Desert Fan Palm Trees clustered together just inland from the sandy shores. Western Gulls soared through the skies while Brandt's Cormorants dove into the waters to retrieve their next meal. Prowling through the scrubland that peppered the coast were Island Foxes, gray, red and miniature sized compared to their mainland counterparts.

"Where have you taken me?" he finally spoke up. His voice contained an emotion he had not heard before in his friend, terror.

"Isn't it amazing? I brought you to the *Island of the Blue Dolphins.* Funny enough this actually happens to be a real island. It's the San Nicolas Island off the coast of California. Can't you see Bryce? What I can do, it's a gift. It's not a curse." Cleo tried to reason with him. "We can go and do almost anything we want. Just imagine all the places we could go, imaginary or real."

Even from their height above the ocean, Cleo could see dolphins just off the coast leaping in and out of the water, at times soaring parallel to the horizon.

> *If Bryce has any appreciation for what is around us, and what is possible, then he has to understand that my power should be seen as a blessing, not something worthy of casting me out as a pariah.*

However, a sense of understanding was not one of the feelings conveyed by Bryce's face. He reached into the pocket of his windbreaker and pulled out another firearm. This time it was a small handgun.

"Uhh...Bryce, that's just another BB gun right?" Cleo asked anxiously.

Bryce turned the gun over in his hand.

"No, this one is perfectly real. Cleo, I swear I will use it if you do not get me out of here."

"Where did you get a gun Bryce?" Cleo asked, backing away from his armed and unstable friend.

"It's my dad's. I took it from his safe yesterday. I thought you did something to Penny. I saw her go inside your house. Then you lied about her being there. You were acting funny. I was positive that you did something to her. I was going to make you tell me the truth. I was going to make things right."

"Make things right?! What, by shooting me? That was going to make everything ok?"

"I didn't know for sure if I would shoot you or not. I wanted you to confess to whatever it was that you did, but if it came to it, then yes, I suppose I would use it." Despite holding the handgun, Bryce sounded as fearful as Cleo was looking down the barrel of the gun.

"Bryce, it doesn't need to go down like this. I understand you are scared. I was terrified when I first found out about what I could do. I still am," he said, trying to relate to Bryce. "Listen, I'm not naïve. I know we can never go back to the way we were, but we can at least try to put all of this behind us. We can try to start over."

"No, we can't." Bryce said coldly. He held the gun with both hands and aimed it at Cleo's heart. His finger rested on the trigger, on the cusp of sending a bullet hurling through Cleo's chest.

"If you shoot me, you'll be stuck here forever. You know that, right? I'm the only way you'll ever be able to leave." Cleo threw out in desperation.

Bryce moved his trigger finger back onto the gun's grip.

"What are you talking about?"

"What did you really think would happen? You would shoot me and then magically go back home? You need me to get you out of here. Unless I take you out, you're stuck. You can never leave."

Bryce took aim again at Cleo, this time at his knee.

"Get me out of here right now. I don't have to aim to kill. Remember that."

Despite Bryce's horrible accuracy, Cleo knew even he could hit his target at five feet. It would only be so long until his threat became a reality. He had to keep Bryce talking and not thinking about using the weapon in his hand.

"How do you expect this to play out Bryce? What happens when we get back home?"

"We'll go our separate ways. For good," Bryce said flatly.

> We'll both just forget you tried to kill me and then pulled a gun on me? Somehow I doubt that.

"Why don't you leave the gun here then? If you plan on holding up your end of the deal then you won't need it," Cleo offered.

"Not going to happen. Remember, it's my dad's. I have to bring it back. Now do we have a deal?" Bryce said, extending his hand out.

Cleo looked at Bryce's tainted peace offering, knowing his excuse was likely complete hogwash.

> I'd be a fool to blindly trust him. There is one way to know for sure. – He decided to look into Bryce's thoughts.

Ever since his trip into the *Odyssey* with Ramiel, Cleo knew he could read the minds of those he brought with him. He would never cross the line with Penny. He trusted and respected her far too much to commit such a breach of privacy. With Bryce, such boundaries no longer existed.

What an idiot. The second we get out of this story, I'm going to shoot him. I'll leave his body in that train. I doubt anyone will ever find him. He thinks he is special. Let's see just how special he is. He won't even see it coming. The only loose end I'll have to tie up is Penny. I'm going to have to. – Bryce thought.

Cleo couldn't listen anymore. He closed the link into Bryce's mind. His heart broke over Bryce's intentions. He had tried so desperately to save some trace of the relationship between Bryce and himself. He tried to welcome him into his world and mend their broken fences. He was willing to overlook the betrayal of trying to trap him on an ancient battlefield and share his ability with him. It had become obvious that things were beyond repair and had reached a lethal level. This realization hurt Cleo more than the bullet in the chamber of Bryce's pistol ever could.

"Cleo," Bryce's voice contained a hint of concern. "Are you going to shake my hand or what?"

Cleo forced a smile, reached out and shook Bryce's hand.

"Fine, we have a deal. This is how it is going to work. I am going to place my hand on your arm. You'll feel a slight tug, and before you know it, we'll be back home. Once we are back, you are to leave us all alone, forever. Understand?"

Cleo's voice was on the brink of cracking. Bryce didn't notice and nodded, still holding onto the pistol.

"Yes, now do it."

Cleo slowly stepped closer to Bryce and placed his hand on his shoulder. He blinked his eyes and a single tear rolled down his cheek.

"You know what makes this book about deserted islands so different from many of the other classics? The ending. Unlike *Robinson Crusoe, Swiss Family Robinson, Treasure Island,* and so many others nobody ever returns to this island. Everyone leaves, and it is left entirely uninhabited."

"Why are you telling me this? Why do you think I would care? What are you doing?" Bryce said, sensing something was very wrong.

Cleo opened his eyes and looked at the boy that at one point in his life was as close to him as his own brother. A boy that welcomed him into a new city with open arms. A boy that stood up for him when no one else would come to his aid. A boy that committed the ultimate betrayal.

"Nothing...I'm not going to do anything to you." He closed his eyes and began to focus on the wooded cul-de-sac. Just as his body started to lose its anchor on Scott O'Dell's creation, he released his grip from Bryce's shoulder.

I'm sorry my friend. I never wanted it to come to this. This is your fault. You left me with no other choice. – Cleo projected the thought into Bryce's mind.

Cleo's transition back to Earth came to a momentary standstill. He opened his eyes at the last possible moment to get one last look of his former friend. The scene was a look of bewilderment and horror on Bryce's face as he realized the impending outcome and his complete inability to change it.

Although the scene came and went in an instant, the image was forever burnt into Cleo's memory. He arrived back in the real world, his conscience heavier than ever.

"WHYYYY!?!?!" Cleo screamed out, kicking the train repeatedly. "Why did you have to force me to do that Bryce? Why!?"

This is the second time in as many days, that I've left a friend behind.

His head hung low and he walked dejectedly back to the car.

I can't tell Penny the truth. She would never forgive me for leaving him to such a horrible fate. I'd probably be arrested. Maybe I should be. – He thought as their borrowed car came into view. *I didn't have a choice. He left me with no other choice.*

He repeated the sentiment again and again to himself until he got back into the car.

"What's wrong? Was he there?" Penny asked.

Cleo looked at the clock on the car's radio.

It's only been ten minutes.

"Cleo," she asked, leaving the car in park.

"No he wasn't. I thought for sure he would be, but there was nobody there," he said, avoiding any eye contact with her. "I don't know where else to look for him. Honestly, I doubt he ever comes back after what happened."

"You're sure there was no sign of him? You took kind of a long time." Penny seemed a little skeptical about Cleo's story.

"I'm sure. I looked around everywhere. It looked like no one had been there in a long time. Can we just go home? I don't want to be out here anymore."

Whether or not she fully believed Cleo, she could see how emotionally and physically exhausted he was.

One day I'll come back for you Bryce. I promise. – He assured himself as they drove off back down the Old Mountain Highway.

CHAPTER 13

Shakespeare's Happy Ever After

It had been exactly one month since Bryce's banishment and Cleo had yet to follow his mother's trail into *Alice's Adventures in Wonderland*. His confrontation and subsequent abandonment of his ex-best friend had a traumatic effect on him. He needed to talk with someone about it, but was afraid to tell anyone.

> *I obviously can't tell dad any of this. I still can't tell Penny. She'd never talk to me again. She might even call the police on me. It's not as if she wouldn't have good reason to. What would the charges be? Kidnapping? Maybe they'd create a new law just for an albatross like me.*

It was the first Saturday after the school year ended. He should have been like all of his peers, thrilled to start his summer and one year closer to graduation. Instead, he was spending his first day of summer mulling over his actions.

> *If there is one person I can tell, it's Ramiel. He can help me. He'll understand. He's got to.*

It was warm and muggy outside when he biked across his small town and entered Ramiel's secluded bookstore. Like his previous visit, the shop was void of any customers, but strangely enough, it was also missing its owner. Nowhere in sight was Ramiel tending the aisles of his shop.

"Ramiel?" he called out as he walked by the front counter. There was no sign or trace of the old man anywhere. Cleo briefly looked around, but knew that there was little point in searching for him. Aside from himself, there was not another person that the phrase "he could be anywhere" more appropriately fit. There were dozens of books lying around the store that were open and he could have been in any one of them. He walked behind the front counter and noticed an antique hope chest resting on the floor. Piled on top of it were various vintage books and manuscripts. Attached to its face was a handwritten NOT FOR SALE, DO NOT TOUCH sign.

> *Hmm, what could he be keeping in here?* – He wondered, moving the pile to the ground.

He flipped up the latch and opened the lid. A loud creak squealed from its ancient hinges, further highlighting the augmented age of the box. Inside was a considerable amount of extremely old looking texts. They ranged from leather bound books to manuscripts written on brittle parchment and fragile papyrus.

"These look hundreds of years old." He picked up each of the historical pieces with extreme caution.

He had heard of many of the titles, but read none of them. Dante's *Divine Comedy*, Dumas' *Three Musketeers* and *Count of Monte Cristo*, *Don Quixote* by Cervantes. There were centuries upon centuries of literary masterpieces in the chest. There was one title in particular that especially drew his interest.

"The First Folio, by William Shakespeare."

He turned the cover, which was in surprisingly great condition for its age (or any age for that matter). The first page's title was *The Tempest*.

> *I think this one has something to do with a crazy magician stranded on an island with his daughter.*

He had never bothered reading it before, and didn't feel the need to do so at that moment either. He continued flipping through the book. He quickly realized that it was not just the single Shakespearean play, but it appeared to contain his whole life's work.

> *Comedy of Errors, A Midsummer Night's Dream, Much Ado about Nothing. Are they all here? I'm not exactly a Shakespeare connoisseur, but this is quite a find.*

He skimmed the pages of the ageless tales until he came to the one Shakespeare story that he had actually read before, *Romeo and Juliet*. Coincidentally it was the subject for his English final the previous week. It was a story that he enjoyed far more than he would ever admit to anyone.

"What's the point of signs, if no one follows their directions?" Ramiel's deep voice startled Cleo to the point that he dropped the book into the chest quite ungracefully. "No please, there's no need to follow the rules strictly on my account. Please, feel free to look in whatever drawer, cabinet, or chest you feel the need to."

Shamed and embarrassed at being caught snooping around again in Ramiel's personal things, Cleo's face became flushed.

"Hi Ramiel. Um...I'm really sorry I looked inside," he quickly apologized.

Ramiel walked over to the chest and carefully picked up the fallen book. Cleo's heart was racing at both his recent discovery, as well as, the old man standing silently analyzing what was clearly a prized possession.

"It's probably my own fault. Having a sign like that on the outside of the box is just begging someone to look and see what is inside. Well, it doesn't appear that any harm has come upon the book." Ramiel said, replacing the book into the chest far more delicately than Cleo had just done.

"How old are these books?" Cleo asked, referring to the chest.

"Many of them are hundreds of years old. *The First Folio* here is over 500 years old."

"How in the world did you come across it? In this condition no less," he said, shocked at how something could look so immaculate after that many years.

Ramiel stroked his beard as he studied the chest's contents.

"There's something I think you should know Cleo," Ramiel began. He walked over and locked the front door of the shop before continuing. "I possess this book, because I was there when it was written."

"But you just said it was written 500 years ago."

"I was born sometime in the 5th or 6th centuries Cleo. I don't remember the precise year. My memory isn't quite what it used to be. Fifteen-hundred years or so will do that to a person."

"I'm quite impressed that you're able to talk, walk and you know, breathe after so many years," Cleo said with a laugh, assuming the old man was attempting to make a joke.

"Long, long ago I died inside one of my stories. Someone...very close to me went back inside the pages, before my death, and saved me before it could happen again," he continued, ignoring Cleo's attempt at being witty. "Her intention was to give us a few more years together. She unintentionally gave me the curse of immortality."

The smile faded from Cleo's face.

"Wait, you're not joking are you?"

"I don't joke. Not about this." His expression was hard and unwavering.

"So you can't die? Ever?"

"I can be killed. At least, I think I can, but, I cannot age. Nor can I ever get sick. I am immortal."

"You're immortal? Why do you see it as a curse? You get to live forever."

Ramiel looked offended at Cleo's comment.

"Live for as long as I have and then see if you think that. I have been forced to watch my family, my friends, everyone, die with no hope of joining them. I have lived through wars, famines, even the very plague itself. I have seen more death and tragedy than anyone has in all of human history. Trust me when I say that immortality is nothing but a curse."

Ramiel's admonition made Cleo sick to his stomach. It wasn't because he felt sorry for Ramiel. It was because of what he did for Penny.

Have I doomed her to the same fate? Is she going to live forever? Do you have to have our ability to be able to become immortal? She would be trapped, forever, in the body of a 16 year-old girl. What have I done?

"You are troubled by something. Is it what I said?" Ramiel said, correctly sensing a bit of an internal conflict in Cleo.

"So you mean to tell me that you were around when Shakespeare wrote his plays?" Cleo changed the subject back to the books, hoping to take his mind off the potential eternal mistake he made on behalf of Penny.

Ramiel let out a jovial laugh.

"I may as well be Shakespeare himself."

"How so?"

Ramiel reached back into his hope chest and pulled *The First Folio* out.

"You know the ending of *Romeo and Juliet,* right?"

Cleo received a B+ on his final, but he still knew the story well enough.

"Of course. Their families hated each other. They made an elaborate plan to run away together. Then the plan goes south. Romeo ends up killing himself with poison while Juliet dies by stabbing herself."

Ramiel turned to the tragedy in his book.

"So you've only read the remake."

"That's not the remake. Everyone knows that story. It's what happens."

"That's my version of *Romeo and Juliet.* The William Shakespeare originally wrote the two of them running away together and eloping. They lived together in the country. Romeo became a successful carpenter, while Juliet was a homemaker and gave birth to three wonderful children."

"Let me get this straight," Cleo held his hand up to stop Ramiel. He had to take a moment to absorb everything. "You're telling me, that you changed Romeo and Juliet, so long ago, that the story that the entire world knows today, is a farce? That it's your version of Shakespeare's work?"

"Yes." There was a small amount of pride in the tone of Ramiel's voice.

"How did you even get a hold of one of the original copies?"

"Believe it or not, I knew Shakespeare."

"WHAT!? You knew Shakespeare? *The* William Shakespeare?" The statement flabbergasted Cleo. "How many of his stories did you change?"

"Let's just say that he didn't write nearly as many tragedies as everyone thinks. He was much more of an optimist than people today believe. He always thought of himself as a hopeless romantic. I always thought he was somewhat of a sap honestly."

"Why did you do it?"

"Well, I didn't mean for it to happen like it did. I never dreamed his work would become the greatest works of literature the world has ever seen. I did it, because I felt that people would benefit from tragedies more than they would fairy tales. You cannot expect everything to work out in life. If you only read happy endings, then that's all you will ever expect in your own. It is not fair to give someone unrealistic hopes and expectations. I thought that if I gave them a sad story, then everyone could appreciate their lives that much more. That they would realize their life isn't as bad as it could be."

> *I never pictured him as the cynical type. I guess that is what living for fifteen-hundred years will do to you.* – Cleo looked at his elderly mentor with pity.

"What about all of the other books in the chest? Did you change the original copies of all those as well?"

"Some. None of them to the extent as Shakespeare's works, however. I think that is enough about me. Let us talk about you. Have you made any progress on finding your mother?" Ramiel said, shutting the lid to the chest.

"Yeah I did. I found…" he hesitated to tell Ramiel the truth.

"What'd you find?" he pushed.

"Well, my friend Penny helped me find what book she went into when the plane went down."

Cleo looked down at his feet. He did not want to see the disappointed look on the old man's face.

"You shared your ability with someone? That takes a lot of trust."

Cleo was surprised. He expected Ramiel to scold him for his lack of secrecy about their ability.

"You're not mad?"

"Of course not. You think I haven't told people over the last ten or so centuries?"

I guess I never saw you as a rule-breaker.

"Just be careful with her. It can be very dangerous bringing a normal person into a story."

It is a little late for that advice. – Cleo thought, feeling guilty about what he had done. He tried not to reveal any sort of emotion in his face.

"I'm curious, what story did you take her into?" Ramiel sounded genuinely interested and not prying.

"It was a story my mom wrote. She called it *Terra Somniorum*."

"*Terra Somniorum*? In Latin that would be The Land of Dreams, if I am not mistaken. I'll have to read it."

Cleo looked towards the empty store pensively at the mention of his mother's story.

"Unfortunately, that won't be possible. She only ever wrote one copy, just for the two of us. I only have one page of it left. The rest of it is gone."

"Gone? Gone where?"

"I don't know. Probably with her. She usually took it with her on long trips," Cleo said, shrugging his shoulders at its disappearance.

"Interesting..." Ramiel said, going back to massaging his beard.

"What's that?" Cleo asked.

"It's nothing. What book did you say she went into?" Ramiel said, sidestepping Cleo's inquiry.

"I didn't." Cleo was a little annoyed with Ramiel's unwillingness to divulge whatever he was thinking. "She started in Neverland and then jumped into Wonderland."

"Oh, Lewis Carroll. That is one of my least favorite minds to trek into."

"Thanks, that's really reassuring," Cleo said sarcastically. "Speaking of which, I should really go start searching for her again. Thanks for the chat."

"You're welcome. Come back when you find something else." Cleo made his way towards the shop's exit. "Cleo, are you sure you don't have anything else that you want to talk about? For instance, what your original reason for coming here in the first place?" Ramiel questioned.

> *What, you mean like the fact I may have doomed the girl I love to an immortal life? What about the fact that I trapped my childhood best friend all by himself on a deserted island? No, it won't do me any good to tell him. I'll make everything right after I find mom. No one will ever have to know anything.* — Cleo thought as he paused with his hand on the doorknob. He could feel Ramiel's eyes burning a hole into the back of his head.

"No, that's it. I need to get going. Thanks again," he lied, turning the handle and leaving the bookstore.

I just hope he hasn't learned to read minds outside of books as well.

Cleo needed to speak with one more person before continuing his search for his mother. It was his mother. Being incapable of locating the real thing immediately, he decided on the next best option, the version that he created himself.

He took the printed pages of the short version of *Terra Somniorum* that he wrote and stapled them together. He quickly found the mystical tree and entered in at the bottom of the hill where it stood. Cast off to the side of the tree, away from the setting sun, was a small shadow.

"Calliope," Cleo called out as he came within view of the shadow's source.

A young woman in her late 20's stood up from behind the tree. She looked almost exactly how Cleo remembered her. Her hair was a little shorter than he intended and her nose was slightly more pronounced than the real thing. Minor cosmetic changes aside, she could have been his mother's twin. She wore a yellow and blue sundress, her favorite one when he was younger.

"Hello young man, how can I help you?" she asked in the softest of tones.

> *Good, she doesn't recognize me. It will be easier this way. I don't need her to be my mother. I need her to be someone I can be completely honest with, before I lose my mind keeping it all in. She will be the confidant for all my dirty little secrets, not the woman to catch up the last six years with.*

"My name is Cleo. You don't know me. I'm not from around here. But I really need to talk with someone. If you're willing to listen."

Calliope did not look at him with a motherly concern. She was not created with the real Calliope's memories. Cleo designed her merely as a soundboard for his troubles. She played the part perfectly.

"Of course, what troubles you?" she said, smiling.

Cleo wasn't overly fond of conveying his feelings to strangers. He briefly saw a therapist when his mother "died" and hated going. It didn't get much better for his loved ones either. It was rare that he would open up.

This is different though. Essentially, she is just a robotic shell. This is my chance to let everything out. – He told himself.

"You know the saying 'The road to hell is paved with good intentions'? Well that's exactly how I've felt the last few months. Nothing that I do works out."

"That doesn't sound very pleasant. Tell me everything son," she said the word "son" with no attachment. Cleo may well have been a random boy she bumped into on the street.

"For starters…well, I don't actually know where to start."

Now that Cleo had a completely unbiased outlet for his admissions, he had no idea what to say.

"Start from the beginning," Calliope said.

"Alright, well it all started on my 16th birthday."

Cleo replayed the night he discovered his ability, the day he met Ramiel for the first time, and the exhausting search for the real life version of the woman standing before him. He referred to her only as "mother" and not her real name. He wanted to avoid having to explain to this other Calliope that she did not really exist.

"Do you wish you could go back to before all of this?" she asked.

"What kind of question is that? Of course not. That's ridiculous," he said, mildly annoyed by the insinuation. "Well…maybe a little. But even if I could, I never would." His immediate backtracking was a red flag to the Calliope copy.

"Do you really believe that, because I think if that were truly the case, then you would not be here talking to me right now. I sense you have many regrets over some of your decisions. Tell me what they are."

Hmm, maybe I went too far with the therapist idea. I should have made her more of a zombie that only looks and sounds like mom but not much more. She's becoming a little too intrusive. – He thought. I guess it shouldn't be that big of a deal. It's not as if she can tell any of this to anyone else.

"Well, I've made some poor decisions so far," he said, continuing to divulge more of himself to the woman. "Like I said, they've all come with good intentions. But their outcomes have been less than successful."

"How so?" she prodded deeper.

"For starters, I almost got my little brother, Linus killed. I then, did manage to get my best friend Penny killed, and even when I was able to bring her back from the dead, she may now be cursed for eternity."

She parted her lips slightly to respond, but Cleo continued talking before she could say a word.

"It's not important. That would be a much longer story," he said. "If that all wasn't bad enough, my ex-best friend tried to kill me. I went to patch things up with him and I ended up banishing him to an eternity of solitude on a deserted island."

"I'm confused, are you talking in metaphors?" Calliope asked.

"I wish I was."

"Alright, so assuming these events all happened."

"They did," Cleo said, cutting her off.

"You never know what the consequence of any action will be. No one does. You cannot shoulder all of the blame for what has happened."

Cleo appreciated her words of wisdom, but was frustrated that she would not understand what he was going through.

It is all my fault! Can't you see that! Mom, stop babying me!!
– He wanted to scream at her.

"It's not just the consequences of my actions that are wearing me down. The responsibility of finding her. I'm afraid it's too much for me to handle. I feel so weighed down by it. My whole family is counting on me and they don't even know it. I alone have the power to fix everything." Cleo's eyes were dark and saggy. His shoulders hung down and his back hunched over. He looked worn down, barely capable of holding himself up. "Sometimes I wish I could go inside a book and stay there forever. No more worries. No more responsibilities. Just peace."

The storybook Calliope looked at him not with pity, but understanding.

"You know that is not an option. You would never be able to forgive yourself. You can't run away from fate Cleo. Not forever."

This made Cleo think more about Bryce. He knew that he was not completely finished with him. He knew that one day, he would have to face the repercussions of his actions one way or another. A month, a year, a decade, it didn't matter how long. He had to see Bryce one more time.

> *Living for eternity alone in a world you don't belong, is a fate not even Bryce deserves.*

"What do you think I should do then?" he asked.

"You already know the answer to that."

Cleo looked up at the magical tree rising from beneath his feet. Like him, it was an anomaly created for a specific purpose.

> *What is our purpose?* – He reached out and placed his hand on its shimmering bark. He could feel a rush of energy flowing through its trunk and into his arm. *So is mine to find my mom? If it is, at what cost must it come? I don't know if I can do it alone, but can I truly justify endangering anyone else?*

He removed his hand from the tree, its essence still tingling through his palm.

"Thank you for listening," Cleo said to the woman.

"Any time."

I will find my purpose, and I will find you mom. I may not be able to control the consequences of my decisions, but I can sure as hell try. – He thought before vanishing from The Land of Dreams.

Remembering how Bryce found out the truth about him in the first place, Cleo made sure that the blinds in his bedroom were closed.

"Just in case," he said, smiling at Penny who was looking through his bookshelf. He invited her over to his house as soon as he returned from his trip inside *Terra Somniorum*.

"That's probably a good idea. Is this one mine?" she asked, removing *Island of the Blue Dolphins* from its shelf.

"Yeah sorry, I forgot I never gave it back to you," Cleo said, trying not to show the panic in his eyes.

How could I have left that out in the open? I can't let her read what happened between us. – He thought in a panic.

"When did you take it? I've been looking for it for like a month. I had to get a copy from the library for our paper."

"Um...I think it was that day on the bridge. When we were driving back I saw it in your bag." He decided to tell her the truth of when he took it.

Soon I'm going to lose track of what lies I'm telling. – He thought. *I need to tell the truth when I can.*

"Sorry I didn't ask, but do you mind if I keep it a little longer? I'm not finished reading it yet." He reached his hand out, hoping she would give it back.

"Yeah, that's fine. School's out, it's not like I have a use for it anymore."

The moment she handed it over, Cleo rushed to the bookshelf and crammed it between two of the thickest books he owned.

"The day on the bridge, huh? I have to ask you something. It has been really bugging me since that day. Cleo, have you told me the whole truth about Bryce? Did you really not see him in the forest that day?" Her question convinced Cleo that she suspected he was lying. He also assumed that she likely didn't have any proof and would not openly accuse him without any.

"I wouldn't lie to you Penny. I honestly do not know where he went that day. Maybe someday we'll find out," Cleo felt immensely guilty about continuing to keep what really happened from her.

It's still not time to tell her, but I can tell her something else.

"You know you saved me that night on the bridge," he said, changing the topic back to her.

"I know. He would have tossed you and that book into the river. I really don't think I would ever have seen you again," she said, proud of her actions.

"No, that's not what I mean." Cleo was looking down at the ground as he remembered the horror that he endured in the Homeric tale. "When I was trapped inside, I knew for sure that I was going to die. I didn't think there was any hope left. I fell to my knees, with this ruthless killing machine standing over me. He kept gloating about how he was going to finish me off."

Thinking of the nightmare he endured caused goose bumps to form all over his body. Penny was now standing at the end of his bed, twirling the hair behind her right ear with her fingers.

"I knew that it was over, and I accepted that fact. Then I started thinking of you. Not of Linus, my dad, or even of finding my mom. All I could think about was you. It broke my heart thinking that I would never be able to see you again. Then he swung his sword, or spear, or whatever it was, but it never touched me. Thinking of your face pulled me out of that story. I was scared, heartbroken, cut, bruised and bleeding when I appeared on that bridge, but when I saw you sitting next to me, it was one of the happiest moments of my life, Penny."

Cleo held his gaze into Penny's eyes.

Penny still had not said anything. She just sat there, unsure of how to respond. "Cleo...what are you trying to say?"

Before he could talk himself out of it, he answered her question by pulling her to him and pressing his lips against hers. It took Penny by complete surprise and the reserved look on her face instantly turned to a gleeful smile.

"I've wanted to do that for so long..." Cleo began to say.

This time Penny cut him off by kissing him back.

"You have no idea how long I've *wanted* you to do that."

Cleo laced his fingers with Penny's and brushed a strand of hair from her eyes.

"I guess I'm a bit of a slow learner," he said, again feeling the softness of Penny's mouth with his own.

Cleo wanted to stay in this moment forever. He wanted to abandon everything else. However, Calliope's warning of not escaping fate could not be suppressed. He moved back by only a few inches and looked deeply into her eyes.

"Penny, I have a favor to ask of you. A favor that I honestly have no right in asking."

"Anything," she responded, their faces still close enough that Cleo could feel the warmth from her breath.

"It all starts in *Alice's Adventures in Wonderland.* That's where I need to go to find my mother, but...I'm afraid. I'm afraid of what I may find. After what happened on that battlefield...I...I don't think I can do this alone. I need you to help me."

"You never need to ask me that. I will always be here to help you. Honestly, I'm shocked you waited this long," she said without hesitation.

"It's not going to be easy Penny. I'm so, so scared of you getting hurt." He almost said the word "again" but caught himself before it got out. "I'm more afraid of that, than I am of never finding my mother. At the same time, I know that I'm not capable of handling all of this by myself." It pained Cleo to admit weakness to anyone, especially Penny.

"You don't need to do it by yourself. I've been trying to tell you this whole time. You're not alone Cleo. I'm right here, and I'm not going anywhere," she said, running her delicate fingers along the back of Cleo's hand.

"You have no idea what we may be up against."

"Neither do you," she reasoned.

"You don't know just how much this means to me Penny."

"I think I have a pretty good idea. Now, enough talk. Your mother needs you." She let go of his hand and picked up the copy of *Alice's Adventures in Wonderland,* that was resting on his desk.

"Are you sure you're ready for this?" Cleo asked one more time, taking the book from her hands.

"I think the real question is, are *you* ready?"

> *Is it possible to have been ready for five years, and simultaneously know that I never will be?*

Cleo opened up the book.

"Only one way to find out."

> *The rabbit-hole went straight on like a tunnel for some way, and then dipped suddenly down, so suddenly, that Alice had not a moment to think about stopping herself before she found herself falling down a very deep well.*

Never before had Cleo been as anxious, nervous, or unsure of a decision in his life. He held Penny's hand and together they followed the same path that Carroll's adventurous teenage girl had through the dark, ominous hole. It mattered not to Cleo what unknown mysteries lay before them, for the journey to reunite his family had finally begun.

About The Author

Anthony Williams is an elementary school special education instructional assistant in the Seattle School District, pursuing a teaching degree in Special Education. Anthony found his calling after working for Americorps as a Washington Reading Corps Tutor. He is very active in the lives of the students he teaches. After school he coaches soccer for 3rd grade girls in the fall and spring, along with Kindergarten – 2nd grade in the winter, through the organization, America Scores. During the summer, when he is not writing, he works with Special Education students in the extended school year program.

The Cleo Bailey trilogy is Anthony's first published work. Prior to becoming a novelist he penned a successful movie review blog, as well as wrote multiple screenplays. One of which, Blink of an Eye, was a finalist in a nationwide screenwriting competition.

Anthony graduated from the University of Washington in 2007 with a Bachelor of Arts in History. He grew up in the small town of Yelm, Washington and has lived in Seattle for the past 10 years.

Special Thanks!

I would like to write a special thank you to the brilliant authors of the novels I used in this book. All of your work has shaped the course of literature and will stay with us forever. Without you, this book would never have existed. Thank you.

JULES VERNE.....................................*Journey to the Center of the Earth*

FRANK L. BAUM ....*Wonderful Wizard of Oz*

HOMER..*The Iliad*

HOMER..*The Odyssey*

J.M. BARRIE......................................*Peter and Wendy*

THE BROTHERS GRIMM ....*Hansel and Gretel*

SIR H. RIDER HAGGARD ....*King Solomon's Mines*

SCOTT O'DELL.................................*Island of the Blue Dolphins*

WILLIAM SHAKESPEARE...............*Romeo & Juliet*

Acknowledgements

★ Everyone at Brown Sparrow Publishing for giving me a chance.

★ Stephanie, you are one of the most wonderful and inspiring women I have ever had the privilege to meet.

★ Isaac, for creating the perfect book cover and art.

★ A special thanks to Drai Bearwomyn of Wild Redhead Design for her vision and creativity on layout and design.

★ Teva, your incessant criticism pushed me to become a better writer.

★ The staffs at Dubsea, Treehouse, Jewel Box and Café Ladro for the caffeine and a quiet place to focus.

★ Shannon and Barbara, you mean more to me than you'll ever know.

★ Abby, Amanda, Bobby, Davy, Rachel, Sarah and Sharleen for being my faithful readers long before there was even a book to read.

★ My kids, all 400 of you.

★ My family, for all your unwavering support.

★ Amy, I am so proud of the woman that you have become.

★ Aaran, you are so much more talented than I can ever dream to be.

★ Ashley, you will always be my little snicklefritz.

★ Mom and Dad, without you I would be nowhere. I love the both of you more than any words could possibly describe.

...and the journey continues

Book Two of the
Untold Tales of Cleo Bailey

will be released soon! To stay informed (and get cool updates and surprise advance tales) direct from the author, please visit www.brownsparrowpublishing.com\cleobaileyupdates.